VENGEANCE SQUAD

• DEVIANT MAGIC • BOOK FIVE

Scott Colby

DEVIANT MAGIC BOOK FIVE: VENGEANCE SQUAD
Copyright © 2022 Scott Colby. All rights reserved.

Published by Outland Entertainment LLC
3119 Gillham Road
Kansas City, MO 64109

Founder/Creative Director: Jeremy D. Mohler
Editor-in-Chief: Alana Joli Abbott

Paperback ISBN: 978-1-954255-41-8
Ebook ISBN: 978-1-954255-42-5
Worldwide Rights
Created in the United States of America

Editor: Alana Joli Abbott
Copy editor: Lorraine Savage
Cover Illustration: Ann Marie Cochran
Cover Design: Jeremy D. Mohler
Interior Layout: Mikael Brodu

Printed and bound in the United States of America.

Visit **outlandentertainment.com** to see more, or follow us on our Facebook Page **facebook.com/outlandentertainment/**

THE DEVIANT MAGIC
STORY SO FAR...

A Date with Death introduced Council of Intelligence Driff, an elven agent dispatched to investigate Harksburg, Illinois, a small town where no one can die. Driff discovered that the local reaper, having spiraled down into a deep depression due to a recent breakup, had been shirking his deathly duties. When our hero's attempt to solve this problem with the aid of a group of local losers blew up in all their faces, Driff learned that the strange events in Harksburg were just part of the devious Witch's plot to temporarily dispatch an elven hero and rob him of the Ether, a powerful magic he could only lose upon dying.

That magic became important in *Shotgun*, when failed family man Roger Brooks discovered it in his silverware drawer and it bonded to his old ten gauge. The elves returned him to their capital, Evitankari, and declared him their Pintiri—a warrior and figurehead with a position in their legislative body, the Combined Council. Roger eventually teamed up with Driff and the reunited Brooks family to fend off the Witch and put an end to the newly restored demon warlord Axzar long thought dead. The story you're about to enjoy begins mere hours after that final battle.

Diary of a Fairy Princess occurs parallel to *Shotgun,* revisiting certain events from a different point of view. Notably, it implies that the Witch may not be quite as malicious as she has seemed.

In *Stranger than Fiction,* Samantha Brooks—the Pintiri's daughter and Chief of Staff—unravels a plot against Evitankari by a secret society of shady immortals and discovers the truth behind the exploits of a group of former teen heroes. Remember that demon warlord from *Shotgun?* Roger learned that Axzar's spirit is now possessing his son, Ricky. To protect the boy while he finds a way to solve that problem, Roger dispatched a horde of shapeshifters who have assumed Ricky's form to all corners of the globe, hoping to confound any evildoers who want to claim the boy's dark cargo for themselves.

Which brings me to the matter at hand: *Vengeance Squad.* We're going back to Harksburg to check in on Ren Roberts and those pesky Tallisker towers that keep blowing up. Let's just say that's about to get personal for poor Ren.

— CHAPTER ONE —

Ren Roberts couldn't tear his eyes away from the television screen. He and his mother had watched the grainy cell phone video of Tallisker's Detroit headquarters exploding five, six, maybe seven times. *The curse of twenty-four-hour network news,* he thought morbidly. The outcome never changed, no matter how hard he willed it. One moment that stretch of midwestern skyline stood empty and blue; the next, one of Tallisker's infamous hidden towers exploded in a tremendous fireball that turned the surrounding block into a crater and sent debris raining down upon the city.

Ren wondered if his father had become a single piece of that debris or if he'd been blasted into several. The latter seemed more likely, but he supposed it didn't matter. Any recognizable parts would be scooped up and disposed of by Tallisker's fixers. Ed Roberts had always joked that there'd be nothing in his casket.

Ellen Roberts sat on the coffee table in front of Ren, beside his untouched afternoon scotch. She held her phone so tightly to her ear that Ren worried it might become permanently attached.

"Pick up, Eddie," she muttered every time she dialed. "Please pick up."

On screen, the billowing pillar of smoke was replaced with a shot of Twenty-four Hour Cable News Barbie sitting behind a curved desk in a slick studio trimmed with important looking computer generated bullshit. "Just who is this Tallisker Corporation?" she asked with perfect vaguely midwestern diction, her dark eyes wide with concern. "How does a multinational operation hide a skyscraper in plain sight?"

Well, you see, Ren's mental voice said with a heavy dose of parental knowhow, *when elves and demons decide they hate humanity very, very much, they put their heads together and use their magic to conceal all the important shit.*

"Why hasn't this story been squelched?" he mused to his highball, because he knew his mother wasn't listening. "Tallisker has armies of publicists, lawyers, and thugs whose only job is keeping the company's name out of the news."

Ellen pried her phone from her ear, punched a button on the touchscreen, and then reattached the device to her skull. "Pick up, Ed. Please."

Ren's mother had been on her way to her book club when the news hit. She was still dressed like a Patagonia model: designer jeans, brown puffer vest over a flannel shirt, her blonde hair up in a ponytail, just enough makeup to look good in a selfie with some friendly wildlife. Though he hadn't seen her face since they'd sat down, he knew her lip would be curled and her eyes bloodshot. The fingers of her free hand flicked back and forth across her wedding ring.

The wild corporate swinger parties just won't be the same, Ren thought evilly. A pang of something shot through his gut. Guilt? No, that couldn't have been it. Hunger, he decided. Or maybe just gas.

"Tallisker's complex web of holdings is nearly impossible to decipher," explained a middle-aged hipster in an off-putting corduroy jacket, live on location from what appeared to be his dining room. In the panel beside him, the anchor pursed her lips and shook her head. "Are they a financial services corporation? A secretive defense contractor? An experimental biomedical laboratory? Dangerous arms dealers? My research suggests they're all of the above, and more. The truth's somewhere down a dark rabbit hole I can't find the bottom of."

"Eddie," Ellen cooed, trying to spin her ring right through her finger. "Come on."

Ren knew how this particular story ended. His father had been drilling it into his head for as long as he could remember. The families of Tallisker executives allowed the demonic bastards to desperately clutch to a few shreds of their waning humanity, providing a safe harbor in the storm of madness threatening to break their grips on reality. Ed, true to form, had genuinely loved his wife and son—but that love had made Ren and Ellen significant targets even in the best of times. Removing or converting a rival's family was a great way to climb the corporate ladder or secure your position. A particularly vile piece of work named Demson had made it no secret that he wanted Ren as his protege, likely to slow or halt Ed's rise toward the board, or to ensure that he'd play along once he got there. Ren didn't want to turn into a beastly personification of evil. He'd always been content as a lay follower of the world's lesser vices. And so he had stayed in Harksburg, within his father's protective sphere, despite the opportunities offered by his family's wealth.

"Edwarrrrrrrrrrrrrd. Please."

The primary anchor appeared relieved to be alone on screen again. "Authorities are evacuating an area two square miles around the fallen skyscraper, lending credence to social media reports of chemical spills and clouds of strange gasses."

Ed Roberts's territory offered no security without the threat of the man himself enforcing it. That meant it was time for Ren to leave.

But where could he go? Life on the run or in hiding wouldn't inherently be any safer than staying put. A deceased Tallisker executive's family still held value as a grotesque display of power and influence, or even just as a means of satisfying an overactive ego. Demson or one of Ed's other rivals would find him eventually. Ren couldn't stand the thought of spending every waking hour looking over his shoulder for the pursuers he knew were just a step behind him.

"Pick up, pick up, pick up."

An interesting idea pierced the dark clouds hanging ominously in Ren's mind like a beam of morning sunshine. He considered it for a moment, and then took a hit of his forgotten scotch and considered it a moment more to make sure the idea held up. "This was an inside job, wasn't it?"

When she didn't respond, he leaned forward and spoke louder. "Ma. Conspiracy?"

His mother nodded, covering the mouthpiece as if worried someone on the other end might overhear. "Guaranteed. No one's dumb enough to take that kind of shot at Tallisker except Tallisker itself."

"My thoughts exactly," he replied with a tip of his glass and a triumphant swig.

It wasn't much to go on, but it was better than waiting around for the inevitable, and Ren possessed something he doubted the board's own investigators had: a sneaking suspicion that recent events in Harksburg, of which he'd been a key part, were somehow related to his father's summons to Detroit and that building's subsequent destruction.

Ren finished his drink. "I'm going out for a bit," he declared, rising slowly against a stiff pair of knees. "I need to have a chat with Death."

— CHAPTER TWO —

E ric Pepper," Ren said as he wrote the same with his brand-new mechanical pencil in a freshly procured Moleskine. "Assistant Manager for International Waste Relations. Dad reported multiple awkward interactions with this individual in the eleventh-floor bathroom to HR."

Ren surveyed the ring of dirt around his perch, wracking his memory. He'd already filled seven pages with the names and misdeeds of Tallisker employees who'd interacted even remotely negatively with Ed Roberts. Demson, of course, got the first page all to himself. Few of the others possessed the kind of stroke required to summon his father to Detroit—as far as Ren knew, at least—but he thought it wise to cast a wide net. Perhaps a few of them had worked together, or maybe one of the lesser middle managers who had nothing to do with Ed's death would recognize his vulnerable family as an opportunity.

He'd taken up residence in the driver's seat of the broken-down bulldozer, watching over the usual gathering place in the Works, the site of a long-abandoned attempt to stimulate Harksburg's economy with an injection of industry. In a way, he supposed, the amount of money spent on partying out there on the outskirts of town justified the aborted effort. The night was cool, crisp, and clear, though Ren worried the light breeze would become a frosty slap in the face as the evening progressed. The first few weeks of December hadn't been quite as frigid and snowy as normal, and he fully expected that to change abruptly and without warning. He'd left the firepit unlit, ostensibly so he could focus on buffing up his Tallisker notes but really because he'd never once been able to light the damn thing. Such tasks, he'd long ago decided, were best left to his blue-collar companions.

A stroke of inspiration set his pen into motion. "Brian Drew," he said as he wrote. "Reassigned to the Edmonton office because Ed hated his whistling."

Ren studied this one for a few moments, as he had several others, his pen wriggling in anticipation of angrily scratching out such a stupid incident. He turned the page, keeping it—for now. "This'd be a lot fucking easier if these fucking demons weren't such a bunch of petty fucking children," he said to the glass of scotch sitting beside him. That went for both his father and his numerous potential rivals.

He leaned back into the ratty couch cushions some enterprising drunk had recently duct taped to the broken-down bulldozer's rusty seat, picturing Ed Roberts at the dinner table as vividly as if he were once again a seven-year-old in his family's dining room instead of alone out in the Works. The man leaned his elbows heavily on the tablecloth, his scraggly chest hair puffing out from his unbuttoned dress shirt as if straining for a bite of roast beef. Cheap whiskey sloshed out of his highball and all over his fingers as he worked himself into a furor. "That motherfucker," his father snarled. Ellen shoveled a forkful of potatoes into her mouth without blinking, long ago having given up on maintaining any propriety at the dinner table when her husband came home all worked up. "That motherfucker Eric Pepper," Ed said again as little Ren watched on in awe, "had the *gall* to sneak up *right* behind me while I was *pissing* in the *urinal,* grab my hips, and say *errrrr hey there Eddie errrrrr need a hand with that*? And then he laughed. He *laughed.*" Ed brought his hand down on the table hard enough to make the silverware dance a little jig.

Ren flipped back a page and circled Eric Pepper's name in his notebook. No way that guy got off with just a stern talking to from HR. Ed would've lit his car on fire or at least ruined his credit score, or maybe tried to toss him out a window when no one was looking. That one would be carrying a grudge for sure.

His appointment emerged from the woods along the usual path just on time. Ren had always been able to set his watch to Kevin Felton. The man's awkward smile was right there in the dictionary beside words like "punctual," "conscientious," "scrupulous," and, frankly, "fussy," which was one of the main reasons they'd been best friends since the day they first met in kindergarten. Their individual neuroses meshed perfectly.

A tinge of disappointment shivered up Ren's spine when he noticed Nella at Kevin's side. He still wasn't quite sure what to make of his best friend's new girlfriend. She seemed nice enough, and she was certainly way too hot for a dork like Kevin Felton, but she'd also strung him along for years before only recently revealing that she was, in fact, a real person who'd been sneaking into his bedroom for midnight booty calls and not just some recurring wet dream with a strange blue skin tone. Ren couldn't fathom forgiving that kind of thing as quickly as Kevin had.

Then again, none of Ren's exes had dumped him to a pursue a career as a professional fuck toy for a bunch of Tallisker middle managers, like Kevin's former fiancée had, so he supposed some leeway had to be granted.

"I brought the good stuff," Kevin said, raising a bottle of twenty-year Glenlivet. He'd worn his favorite outfit—a black leather jacket, black T-shirt, and a pair of black jeans—and the wind had already mussed his unruly brown hair.

"We're gonna need it," Ren replied. He stashed the notebook in his peacoat's interior pocket and swung himself down from the bulldozer.

"Got some cheap swill too," Nella added with a glance down toward the dual six-packs she carried, "to distract the riff-raff." Her clothes matched her boyfriend's, though she'd worn higher heels and not a single strand of her long black hair had fallen out of place.

Ren bristled inwardly at the way she'd inserted herself into the group. Who the hell did she think she was, and why the fuck did she think she could ply Kevin's friends with cheap mass market booze? Her strategy was sound, of course, but she hadn't been employing it for a decade-plus like Ren and Kevin, and so her use of it was presumptuous at best. Ren deployed his brightest smile anyway. "As clever as she is beautiful. Remind me again why you're walking around with this troglodyte on your arm?"

"He doesn't litter and his mother's nice," Nella replied without hesitation. Ren remained impassive but mentally assigned her a few positive points on his scorecard.

The new arrivals stopped their approach a few feet away, right beside the old dozer's blade. Ren and Kevin stared at each other for a few moments. Things were about to change, and they both knew it. Ren flashed back to that day—fuck, almost ten years ago—when he'd wished Kevin the best of luck as he and Mrs. Felton packed up the car to move him off to college in the big city. He'd hated how stupidly emotional his best friend's departure had made him. Those same butterflies fluttered around Ren's chest again, lighting up every nerve they touched and setting him on fire. He still hated the sensation.

"I'm sorry about your father," Kevin finally said.

Ren's butterflies sprouted knives on the tips of their wings. "Ah," he grunted, buying time to find the words. "Thanks. We always figured a grisly end for Ed Roberts was only a matter of time. The man's taste in business associates was pretty terrible." A bright smile stretched his face. "Dad should've quit the moment he found out they hired your ex."

Nella's eyebrows leapt up toward her scalp. Despite her obvious efforts, she hadn't fully acclimated to the god-tier level of bullshitting their friend group lived and breathed. The really bad stuff still caught her off guard. Ren decided that was kind of cute.

Kevin, however, grinned like a madman. "No shit!" he replied merrily. "That one ruins everything she touches."

Ren flicked his eyes down to his friend's crotch. "Shame."

"That part made it through just fine," Nella interjected smoothly, "although he still cries himself to sleep a few times a week." Ren toasted her with a nod and a tip of his glass.

Kevin grunted just as he had every day in fourth grade when someone disparaged his off-brand Chicago Bears jacket. "We should probably get the complicated parts of this out of the way before the rest of the party gets here."

"I hadn't intended for this to turn into yet another high school reunion."

"I figured someone needed to plan your going away party. That's what you're about to tell me, right? That you're going on the run so Tallisker can't find you?"

That question burrowed into Ren's gut like a barely sharpened stick. In anticipation of Kevin's lack of insight into Tallisker's horrifying corporate culture, Ren had prepared a long-winded, thoroughly well-sourced explanation of why his father's death necessitated his flight from the only home he'd ever known. He had everything but PowerPoint slides and handouts, the latter only because his useless printer had run out of toner again. "How the hell did you know that?" he asked.

"My new job," Kevin replied, the guilt thick on his tongue. "Maeve Remini over in Bilton explained it all to me." When Kevin didn't elaborate further, Nella elbowed him in the kidney. "She'd been burned alive," he sputtered.

Ren emptied his glass with a long swig and set it down on the bulldozer's tread. Then he snatched the fresh bottle from his friend's hand and began working at the wrapper with his thumbnail. He'd met Maeve a couple years ago at the local Tallisker branch's family picnic. Nice person, albeit a bit naive about the company and her wife's role in it, and the beaded belts she made as a hobby sucked. "Anyone else?"

"Clint Pope in Hanton," Kevin said sadly. "Same cause of death. Whoever it was took the kids."

The map in Ren's head suddenly turned ominous. "They're headed this way."

"Sorry!" Kevin snapped as his body suddenly went rigid. "Gotta get to work."

And then he was gone. The little part of the Works Kevin Felton had filled mere moments ago now stood empty. Neither Ren nor Nella so much as blinked at his disappearance. They'd seen it before. The prospect of being left alone together, however, was jarring.

The water nymph recovered first. "Guess it's time for a beer," she said, setting the six-packs down on the ground and withdrawing a single bottle.

"And a scotch," Ren added, finally opening the expensive Glenlivet. He poured a couple fingers into his glass and studied the brown liquor as he swirled it around. A quick drink warmed his throat and settled his nerves. "You look better in blue."

She smiled. "Oh, I agree, but Kev worries what the neighbors might think." As Ren flinched at the disgusting nickname she'd bestowed upon his best friend, Nella reached back over her collarbone and released the clasp on her necklace. Her pale Caucasian skin turned a healthy shade of light blue as the necklace's enchantment dissipated. "For you, because you're leaving, but Rot, I fucking swear I will ruin every bottle of alcohol you own if Oscar or Doorknob or any of the others catch me like this." She punctuated her threat with an annoyed flutter of the gills in either side of her neck.

Another awkward silence settled upon them like the evening's mist rolling into a port town. "Take care of Felton for me," Ren blurted. His cheeks flushed. "Wanted to get that out while we had some privacy."

Nella nodded. "I will." The sharp *crack-hiss* as she twisted the cap on her beer seemed to second her. "Is Ellen leaving with you?"

Ren took another drink. "She's going to follow Dad's plan. He left us a list of safehouses and people he trusted." The statement reminded him of how his parents' swinger lifestyle had partly been a means of building out the family's options in the event of the unthinkable, and then he finished his glass to wash the thought away.

"Obviously you don't think that's a good idea."

"Of course not. It'd be naive to think one of these demon bastards hasn't put a similar level of preparation into hunting Ed Roberts's wife and son as he put into trying to protect them. Us."

"And she doesn't like whatever you're planning?"

"No," he said, his hands shaking as he poured himself a fresh beverage. "She laughed at me. Said I've got a death wish." *Like my father.*

Nella took a sip of her beer and then held the bottle out in front of her, underneath her free palm. "It would be my pleasure to offer your mother another option."

As Ren watched, droplets of water rose out of the bottle's mouth to collect in a growing sphere beneath the nymph's hand. The flow stopped a few seconds later when the sphere reached the size of a golf ball. It jiggled and then flattened into a shape like a hockey puck. Nella's eyes widened as she took a deep breath. When she exhaled, the moisture she collected flashed like a little strobe.

She quickly flipped her hand around to catch the falling wafer of bright blue crystal she'd created.

"This grants the bearer entry to Talvayne and an audience with the king," she said, holding the token out to Ren.

He plucked it from her palm and held it up where he could get a better look at it. The trio of fish-shaped runes carved into its face, their tails touching in the center, and their open mouths facing outward toward the edges, was unmistakable. "I didn't know you were royalty," Ren said with a deep bow. "M'lady."

Nella's cheeks flushed purple. "My family's a distant offshoot of the current king's line. We're not on the best of terms, but that token cannot be refused."

Ren pocketed the little tablet. "Your wisdom, like your beauty, knows no bounds, m'lady. Thank you."

She shook the beer bottle and grinned evilly. "Stop that right now, or by royal decree I will force you to drink the vile, partially dehydrated sludge remaining in this vessel."

"Anything but that, please." He raised a single finger to indicate the arrival of a brilliant idea. "Let's give it to Spuddner. Peel the label off and we'll tell him it's a hot new craft beer from the city."

"Don't tell Kev, but I like the way you think." She set to work on the corner of the label with her fingernail.

Ren took a moment to recompose himself from the violent, soul-twisting cringe Nella's nickname for his best friend had induced. "You're not going to at least *try* to talk me into going to Talvayne?"

"Would it work?"

"No."

"Then I'm going to take my boyfriend's advice and not waste my time." The flimsy label tore off in a single piece with a satisfying *slurp*. Nella flicked it onto the ground like a snot.

"Don't care so much about littering when it's not your home, huh?" Ren asked.

Her face flushed as she bent down, picked up the label, and slid it into her pocket.

Kevin Felton popped back into existence beside them. He'd obviously taken a moment to fix his hair before returning. "Heart attack in Green River. Nothing to worry about. What'd I miss?"

"I gave him the thing, he's going to give it to his mother, and we agreed on a plan to mess with Oscar," Nella replied.

"Don't explain about that last part," Kevin said gleefully. "I want to be surprised."

"I've got one more piece of business before I allow you to drink your faces off in my honor," Ren said, fighting the beginning of a slur. "Felton, what happened in the middle of everything last week that I don't know about?"

The reaper's eyes narrowed. "You don't honestly think I'm hiding something, do you?"

"Absolutely not. I've always admired and respected your candor. I wonder, however, if perhaps you experienced or heard anything you initially dismissed as unimportant or coincidental, or maybe that you didn't understand at the time. You are relatively new to all this secretive magic shit, after all."

"You're looking for a connection between your father's death and what went down with Billy," Nella said insightfully. Kevin's eyes widened, the gears in his mind obviously struggling to get up to speed.

"Bingo," Ren replied. "Driff stuck his nose in Billy's business at Tallisker's request. I'm thinking it may not be a coincidence that someone scheduled Harksburg's preeminent business demon for a week of meetings in a soon to be eradicated office not long after the conclusion of the elf's intervention." He looked to Kevin. "Who's Rotreego? Driff almost shat himself when you said that name."

Kevin blanched and plucked the bottle of dehydrated beer from his girlfriend's grasp. Nella pursed her lips but didn't protest.

"Another elf," he said. "We were prisoners together, in my neighbor's basement. He said he was the Pantari."

Ren groaned. "The Pintiri? Ffffffffffffffffffuck."

"You only elongate your f-bombs when something's really bad," Kevin said, considering the bottle in his hand.

"The Pintiri's their ringer, or maybe their enforcer," Nella explained. "He or she wields what's often considered the world's most powerful direct offensive magic. That magic resides in and flows through the Pintiri's weapon."

Kevin nodded dumbly, as if she'd just spoken a completely different language. "Rotreego said his magic sword didn't work anymore, and that my neighbor killed him several times. With Billy off the job...it didn't stick."

A pair of distant neurons flared to life and linked up in Ren's brain. "Nella, the Pintiri's magic is released from his weapon upon his death, right? Then the next in line has to go get it?"

"Supposedly," she said softly, her eyes wide. "But what happens if the last Pintiri doesn't stay dead?"

That question hung over the trio for several moments. Kevin frowned and scratched the back of his head, clearly struggling to work it all out. Ren's train of thought barreled down the same old track it had traveled countless times: toward the money. Somehow, some way, someone had set this Rotreego character up for his or her own benefit. Who stood to profit from the world's first living former Pintiri? The answer proved elusive, and yet Ren felt certain it tied into the attack on Tallisker's Detroit headquarters.

Kevin sighed and took a drink. Ren and Nella watched expectantly as he slowly raised the tainted bottle to his lips. The vile liquor exploded back out of his mouth as soon as it touched his tongue, spattering Ren right in the face.

"I assume that was intended for Oscar," Kevin sputtered, coughing as he wiped his face.

Ren pulled a handkerchief out of his coat's interior pocket and rubbed down his own mug, fighting the urge to retch. The overpowering malt smell of that sticky dehydrated beer set his head spinning.

"There's a witch, too," Kevin added, as if he'd just remembered. "A *fucking* witch, in Driff's words. I don't think they get along."

Ren tossed the wet handkerchief under the bulldozer's blade in disgust. "Never heard of any witches, but I'll keep that information in mind. Any idea where Rotreego is now?"

"The dude was so embarrassed that he threatened to geld me if I told anyone he needed my help with Mr. Gregson. He's probably long gone."

"Actually," Nella interjected, "he's hiding out at Donovan's. He went straight there after he escaped your neighbor."

Kevin frowned. "How'd you know that?"

"My book club meets there every Wednesday at lunchtime. He drunkenly tried to convince Barbara that JFK was killed by a werewolf who owed a major gambling debt to Hoover. Strange guy."

"That doesn't sound like the Rotreego I know. Did he say anything obnoxiously self-centered or that indicates a deep case of depression?"

She shook her head. "No, he just seemed a little...off, and sort of cheerful in a way, too."

Ren spotted movement in the forest on the other side of the clearing. The local talent was on its way. "I'll go to Donovan's tomorrow," he said. Although time was certainly of the essence, he figured it would be easier to deal with Rotreego when the fairy bar would be less busy—and he never would've admitted it, but he wanted nothing more than to get totally fucking shithoused with all of his oldest friends one last time.

"Hey there, assholes!" Oscar Spuddner squealed as he and Doorknob lurched out of the forest, each struggling with the weight of a cheap thirty rack and their broad, toothy smiles. "Party's not over yet, is it?"

With a gasp, Nella put her necklace back on, fumbling briefly with the clasp before it caught. Her blue skin turned a light shade of human pink once again.

"Gentlemen!" Kevin declared, spreading his arms magnanimously as he turned to face Oscar and Doorknob—and strategically positioning himself to block their view of his magical girlfriend in case she needed a moment to conceal the parts of herself they might find confusing. "I wholeheartedly assure you that we have *not...yet...begun...to drink!*"

"Could you possibly be more gauche?" Ren spat.

"Seems highly likely," Kevin replied. Nella giggled.

The two new arrivals set their precious beverages down gingerly in front of the bulldozer. "Kevin told us about your operation," Doorknob said sheepishly. "I'm sorry you have to go through that."

Ren noticed his best friend's smirk out of the corner of his eye and decided to play along. "I appreciate that, my good sir."

Oscar wiped a tendril of sweat from his brow with the brim of his old Cubs hat. "He told us everything. Me, I had no idea you had to go all the way to Boston to get your prosthetic testicles replaced every ten years!"

Kevin snorted. Nella elbowed him in the side.

As far as cover stories went, Ren supposed it would do—and that it was wholly appropriate, given the source. He refilled his highball and raised it to his friends as his devious mind, warped further by alcohol, fear, and something like grief for a father he couldn't really describe his feelings toward, generated what it considered to be the perfect toast for the entirety of his situation. "Well then: here's to good friends, and to my new pair of balls!"

— CHAPTER THREE —

T he strange blue asphalt leading to Donovan's didn't make a sound against the Jag's tires. Despite the early hour, Ren discovered several vehicles spaced out in the expansive parking lot. Local laws dictating closing time meant little to establishments that didn't officially exist. He wondered how many of the other cars and trucks had been there all night—or perhaps longer.

The night sky above him had also chosen to thwart the time. What had been a cloudy, gray morning had immediately become a clear, dark evening speckled with billions of twinkling stars as he'd pulled onto the secret access road. The sight was shocking, to be sure, and his foot had instinctively reached for the brake in brief surprise. He'd laughed at himself; in a world where demonic corporations could make entire skyscrapers invisible and water nymphs could show up looking just like the girl next door, an ancient being of unknown power fixing a beautiful view of the night sky above his domain didn't seem all that weird.

Ren parked halfway between the end of the access road and the wall of red vines that kept the riff-raff out of Donovan's, beside a towering orange pickup truck he hoped would hide the Jag from anyone chasing him out of the bar later on. For several moments he couldn't bring himself to cut the engine. It wasn't too late to turn around, drive back home, and link up with Ellen for the trip to Talvayne.

"Just think about it," she had said, desperately clutching Nella's token as if it might spontaneously decide to fly away. "Asylum, in the most beautiful, magical city on the planet! As guests of the royal family themselves! It'll be like a permanent vacation!"

Think about it, he had. All night. As he'd traded jokes with Kevin. Chatted with Nella. Won a round of hold 'em against Waltman, Tom Flanagan, and Junior Mullins, and then used his winnings to pay Oscar and Doorknob to strip to their skivvies for an impromptu sumo match beside the bulldozer. Whispered sweet nothings to Jess Darling, who he'd had a huge crush on in middle school, and then curled up in the bulldozer's blade and made out with until dawn.

He'd thought about it plenty.

"Have fun," he told Ellen. "I'm sure all your friends on the 'gram will love the pictures."

But in that parking lot, alone underneath an enchanted view of the cosmos that served as a reminder of the powers with which he'd have to compete, Ren thought about it again. He didn't have to stroll into a magical forest playland controlled by an eldritch creature in search of a disgraced elven hero to launch his foolhardy quest for retribution. Fuck, if that was just step one, what were steps four, five, and six going to look like, if he could even get that far? Turning tail and running was still on the table.

Gritting his teeth, he killed the engine and jerked the keys out of the ignition. "No more running from this shit," he said to the wheel as confidently as he could muster, "and no more hiding."

He left his father's Uzi in the glove box. Ellen had insisted he take it. "This thing won't help you much if you end up on the wrong side of some asshole who can throw lightning," she'd said, "but knowing you've got it will make me feel better." Having the little submachine gun made him feel better, too, but carrying it into Donovan's would send the proprietor the wrong message. He'd have to trust the King of the Forest to keep the peace if things turned dangerous.

Nella insisted the place was safe enough as long as I keep my nose clean, Ren reminded himself as he pocketed his keys and slid out of his beloved vehicle. The door locked automatically with an audible thunk a breath after he shut it. Ren flinched in surprise at the sound, even though he'd heard it hundreds, if not thousands, of times.

"Get your shit together, Roberts," he muttered to himself as he buttoned his peacoat against the chill. "These magic assholes can smell fear."

That wasn't entirely true, he knew, but it had been one of his father's favorite things to warn him about over the years, so much so that it had become a mantra. "The bastards all have the advantage over regular people, and they fucking know it," Ed slurred across the dinner table in Ren's mind. "Don't give them an opening. Make them think you know something they don't."

Hands in his pockets and a salesman's smile on his face, Ren stomped toward the wall of red vines marking the entrance to Donovan's. The bouncer—a hulking troll in a pinstriped suit and a matching hat—was even larger than Kevin had tried to drunkenly describe. "Dude, he's huuuuuuuuuge!" Felton had said, almost clocking Nella in the face as he spread his arms for emphasis. "And ugly. Like, the sort of ugly that makes you wonder why his mother didn't drop him off at the fire station. He's got a heavy brow, beady little eyes, and teeth like...like banged up headstones in a *really* old cemetery. Really nice guy, though!"

"Morning!" Ren called out cheerily, hoping the last bit of Kevin's description turned out to be as accurate as the rest. "Ulliver, right?"

The way the troll cocked his head reminded Ren of a mountain shifting. "Good morning, little human," he rumbled, not without a hint of suspicion. "Are you joining us for the brunch buffet?"

Ren shook his head. "I'm here on business, but perhaps I can make the time. I've been told there's a gentleman here by the name of Rotreego. I'm hoping he'll be kind enough to allow me to pick his brain."

Ulliver's chuckle reminded Ren of a gravel crushing machine he'd seen in a documentary. "Let's see some ID."

Ren fished his wallet out of his back pocket and withdrew his driver's license. He worried that the troll's sausage-like fingers would crush the tiny piece of plastic, but Ulliver plucked it away with a surprisingly gentle touch.

And then he raised it to his nose and sniffed it.

"Human, all right," he said as he spun Ren's license around to get a better look at it. "We don't get too many of those. Thought you might be a demon, or maybe something else in disguise. Anyway. Welcome to Donovan's, Mr. Roberts. The boss thought you might stop by." He produced a tiny pink drink ticket from his pocket and handed it and the license back to Ren. "Our condolences, on behalf of the entire Donovan's family."

Ren shoved both the license and the drink ticket roughly into his wallet. Leather slapped against leather as he snapped it shut. "I appreciate the sentiment, sir. In lieu of flowers, we're accepting donations to a fund that specializes in providing homes for those orphaned by acts of demonic corporate espionage. I'll leave a card with the bartender."

Halfway through that last sentence, Ren sidestepped the bouncer and continued onward along the strange blue pavement. A section of the wall of red vines retracted, forming a roughly circular opening. He wondered if the vegetation could detect the rage radiating out of his skull, and if it would clamp down tight on him in response. He hoped not; he hadn't noticed the toothy thorns studding the red vines until he'd taken several angry strides into the entrance.

"One drink ticket," he growled under his breath, running his fingers across the little slice of cheap paper in his pocket. "A recently deceased father is worth at least three drinks and a free fucking appetizer."

Later, when he finally realized how well his indignance masked the underlying sense of deep dread twisting his insides, he congratulated himself on a job well done. Donovan should not have been able to anticipate his arrival—unless, of course, the King of the Forest also believed that the death of Ed Roberts and the temporary passing of the Pintiri, Rotreego, were somehow two parts of a much bigger picture.

The other side of the tunnel of thorns turned out to be disappointing. As far as Ren could tell, he'd crossed onto just another lonely forest trail, surrounded on either side with densely packed local trees he'd never bothered to learn the names of. "The place is...is...is...fucking awesome!" Felton had said as he lay upon the Works dirt, closer to the fire than Nella approved of. "There are multiple rooms all named after the stars, and lots of bars, and games, and...and...stuff!" Kevin Felton had been very drunk at that point, however, so it was entirely possible he'd been embellishing or making things up altogether. Doorknob had assumed he'd been talking about a Dave & Buster's.

The crackling sound behind him, Ren knew, was the vines worming themselves back across the mouth of the tunnel to seal his exit. Despite the panic vibrating through his bones, he didn't bother looking back. Instead he glanced skyward, tracing the stars of the constellation labeling his position within Donovan's. He traced the stars for a couple minutes before he realized he had no clue what the hell he was looking at. Was that a kite? Maybe a foreleg? He shook his head and kept walking, anxious to take advantage of his free bereavement drink.

The trail ahead of him seemed to stretch on forever, slicing through the forest in a precise line too perfect to be natural. Ren *hated* being alone in the God damn outdoors, unless it was out in the areas of the Works he knew like the back of his hand. It made him feel like he'd made a mistake, like he'd forgotten to pay someone, or there'd been some kind of arrangement he'd failed to make. His skin crawled faster and faster with each step he took into Donovan's mysterious domain. The scenery didn't help matters. The view down that straight trail offered no hope of reaching anything even remotely resembling civilization. The only sounds were those of his own footsteps and his hammering heart. Shouldn't there have been birds or bugs or something?

To make matters worse, someone was watching him. He could feel it all along the back of his neck. It had to be Donovan, of course, but knowing the name of the watcher didn't make it any less creepy. He began to doubt the King of the Forest's intentions. Friendly bouncer or not, forcing a guest to walk such a strange path all alone wasn't exactly a warm welcome. Ren's mind paged through all the horrible possibilities. What if Rotreego had told Donovan something that had put the King of the Forest on the defensive? What if Donovan had something against Tallisker employees and their families?

Or...worst of all...what if he'd entered into a business arrangement with whoever'd been out to get Ed Roberts?

Something tapped Ren on his shoulder and he almost leapt out of his sneakers. He whirled to face whatever it was, fists clenched as tightly as his throat. The slender branch of a nearby tree watched him stoically. The tree's trunk had leaned nonsensically out into the path so it could reach him.

"Well," Ren said, straightening his lapels, "good morning to you too." *And I'm glad Donovan's finally done fucking with me.*

The tree's little red and orange leaves fluttered in what he took to be an equivalent greeting. The branch that had tapped him swung back the way he came, indicating a side trail he swore hadn't been there before.

"I thank you for the assist," Ren said with a little bow. "I'd appreciate it if you pass along to management that there are several easier ways to conduct this sort of business."

The leaves fluttered again, this time in a very different pattern that seemed to say "yeah, I thought we should've just put a sign over there, but the asshole who signs my paycheck insisted we do it like this." Its bark creaked as it eased itself back to its natural upright position beside its other tree friends, ending the conversation.

Ren backtracked and then turned a sharp right onto the trail. A sigh of relief streamed out of his nose. Just ahead, against the forest on the other side of a small clearing, a fully stocked bar awaited. Unimpeded by the nonexistent seating, a good twelve, maybe fifteen people could've comfortably sidled up to that granite top, and it only hosted a single bartender. She moved with an ethereal grace as she turned, selected a familiar green bottle from among the crystal shelves packed tight with liquor, returned to the granite, and deftly poured two fingers in a triangular highball.

As he approached, Ren held up his drink ticket like a police officer presenting his badge. "I've got a free one."

"Hold onto that for next time," the bartender said, sliding the freshly poured scotch across the mottled gray stone. "The Roberts family drinks for free wherever I'm working."

Ren let the highball slide into his hand and shut his fingers around it like a trap snapping down on some hapless animal. His parents had never mentioned befriending a local bartender. "You have me at a disadvantage, Miss…"

"Lil," she replied with a reserved smile. A surname, if one existed, remained a mystery.

"A pleasure to meet you."

Ren gave his drink a little jiggle and watched the caramel liquid swirl around the strange glass, considering the pointy ears peeking out through the bartender's thick blond mane. He knew that Tallisker and Evitankari worked together more often than either side liked to admit. The nature of that relationship had been one of Ed's favorite topics to ramble about after one too many drinks. "These assholes," he could hear his father say, "could make everything better for everybody if they were just a bit more aboveboard about all the shit they're up to!" Still, that didn't explain Lil. Was she more than she seemed? He supposed she could've been an undercover elven agent perhaps, or maybe a useful local information broker with shadowy connections to Evitankari's criminal underworld.

God damn, he hoped they didn't know her from the weird corporate sex parties.

He took a quick sip. She'd poured him the good stuff, the twenty-one-year. "I take it you knew my old man."

She chose that moment to finally turn away and put the bottle of Glenlivet back on the shelf. "I did. My condolences. I owe him a lot." Her voice cracked. Rather than turn back around, she grabbed a bar rag and set to work wiping down an obviously clean glass.

Ren couldn't imagine what his father could've done for this woman. Ed Roberts had never been a man of charity. "You work at a non-profit?" Ren remembered him gushing to Oscar Spuddner's dad at his tenth birthday party, in Uncton's bowling alley. "Christ, just throw your life away already." The man had even refused to give his pocket change to trick-or-treaters carrying UNICEF boxes. Ed Roberts was a bastard who wouldn't help anyone unless he knew it'd get him something worthwhile in return.

He risked a glance down at the slender woman's ass. *Yeah, it was the sex parties.*

"I needed to get out of Evitankari," Lil said, wrenching his attention up to the forest of curls on the back of her head. "Rotreego handled that part, but it was your father that found me a safe place to go."

Ren took another sip, processing. "There are few places safer than rural Illinois. What'd it cost you?"

Lil snorted and moved on to wiping another glass. "I know Rotreego chose to work with Ed because he felt like he'd have more influence over a standard issue middle manager than he would over Tallisker's upper tiers. And I know your father saw the whole thing as a way to curry favor with the Pintiri and improve his own standing within the organization." She turned around, the fire in her blue eyes threatening to scald anyone or anything that came too close. "I don't care about any of that. Rotreego and Ed Roberts saved my life."

He met her gaze as evenly as he could manage. "Help save mine, then, and maybe get some vengeance for Ed in the process. I need to speak with Rotreego."

Her eyes flashed. "I'd like to help you. I really would."

"But..." When she didn't answer, he filled in the depressing blank. "He's not here anymore is, he?"

"No, I didn't say that."

"Perhaps it's best we show the lad," a friendly voice suggested from Ren's left. "Assuming you believe he is who he says he is, of course."

Ren swung his head around to get a look at the speaker, but all he saw was a stretch of empty bar and the forest beyond. No one was there. He stifled his surprise. "The more powerful the magical bastard," his father had said more than once, "the more they enjoy making a dramatic entrance!"

A spindly old man in a garish purple suit stepped confidently out of a sturdy looking oak, seeming to melt into existence through the rough bark without distorting the underlying organism. He stood up straight, rolled back his shoulders, and jammed his ebony walking stick firmly into the ground between his feet. "I'm Donovan Pym, owner and operator of this fine establishment. Are you *really* Ren Roberts?"

"I believe so, yes."

The King of the Forest's mischievous eyes narrowed, and he leaned forward. "Mmmmm. Lil? What say you?"

The bartender set her rag down and crossed her arms, considering. "Where did Ellen and Ed meet?" she asked Ren.

"College," he replied nonchalantly, "when they both tried to walk into the same phonebooth at the exact same time. She dropped her books, he picked them up, and it was love at first collision."

"Favorite car?"

"A '67 Chevy. Baby blue."

"Who was his first boss at Tallisker?"

"Marafuji. The Director of Marketing. Guy's somewhere in the C-suite these days."

"What was his favorite color?"

"He didn't have one. My father was color blind."

Lil's lip twisted into a smirk. "Least. Favorite. Pizza topping."

Ren leaned forward on the bar, staring her down triumphantly. "Mushrooms."

Her eyebrows leapt up and she cocked her head. "Wrong," she said with a devious grin. "He always made a loud point against mushrooms because of how much Ellen hates them. It was their little inside joke. The correct answer is anchovies."

He finished his drink and sighed. "How is it that you know so much about my father, including things that I don't?"

"Ed liked to come check on me. Once a month, sometimes more. He'd get drunk and...start talking." She shrugged and looked to Donovan. "This guy's legit."

"Excellent!" the King of the Forest declared, spreading his arms wide. "I apologize for the interrogation, Mr. Roberts, but one simply cannot be too careful these days. There are so many untrustworthy characters *skulking* about!"

"So I've heard. Any in particular I should watch out for?"

"Mmmmm."

And this, Ren thought as he waited for elaboration that never came, *is why I didn't want to go to Talvayne: these fairy creatures never know when to stop putzing around and just give it to you straight.*

"If you're done with me, I'll head back to the main bar," Lil said. "Garganol's due for his usual digestif and he gets bitchy when Karen makes it."

The old man tapped one skeletal finger against the bulbous crystal topping his walking stick. "Why don't you accompany Mr. Roberts and me? Perhaps your familiarity with everyone involved can help us pull ol' Rotreego back from the abyss, eh?"

She sighed, clearly not looking forward to whatever that meant. "All right."

"Marvelous!" Donovan decreed. "Come along, then. There's no telling what mischief our addled friend has gotten into in my absence."

"You left him *alone*?" Lil protested as she stepped around the end of the bar.

"Not entirely, no, but it'd be best not to dally."

Ren took a deep breath and stared longingly at the bottle of Glenlivet 21, wondering what the fuck he'd gotten himself into. Every neuron in his skull—save the familiar, tiny cluster that often overrode the others whenever drunken shenanigans appeared on the horizon—screamed at him to politely say goodbye and pray to whatever god happened to be listening that the giant thorn bush would let him escape to the parking lot.

Fuck it, he thought, remembering Felton's words of warning from the night before, *this probably won't be any worse than being burned to death.*

He gave the bottle a respectful salute and then turned to follow Donovan and Lil into the forest.

— CHAPTER FOUR —

Donovan slipped through the densely packed trees like a wisp of smoke. Lil and Ren struggled to keep up, the former faring better than the latter.

"Had I known we'd be going for a hike I'd have packed a picnic," Ren said. He immediately stumbled over a thick root and received a leafy slap in the face from a slender branch strategically lying in wait. Up ahead, Donovan chuckled.

"Can't expect us to receive unfamiliar and possibly dangerous guests in one of the easily accessible public areas," Lil replied.

"Flattery will get you nowhere," Ren said as he ducked underneath another limb. "I would've expected more from the back room of the infamous Donovan's, however. A poker game played for a pot of magical runes, perhaps, or an illicit cockatrice fighting ring."

"Cockatrice fights are Wednesdays, under Aries," the King of the Forest replied nonchalantly. "Buffalo wings are half off."

Ren shivered at the implication. "But seriously, you couldn't have teleported us to Rotreego through the same tree you came in through?"

The old man clicked his tongue. "Most trees do not appreciate the passage of outsiders. Only a select few possess the required... restraint. The closest is not far now."

Ren stopped and eyed the thick oak to his left. "Please let me through. I'll pay you."

"The forest does not appreciate sass, Mr. Roberts. Hurry along now."

How anyone was supposed to "hurry along" through that tangled mess was beyond Ren's comprehension. Every inch of that forest was covered in vegetation. Where there wasn't a tree to gingerly sidestep, there was a patch of brambles to push through, or a fallen log covered with moss to carefully lunge over, or other random leafy green shit slowing his progress. He hadn't expected his journey in search of his father's killer to be easy, but he'd never pictured it becoming this obnoxious.

Frustrations aside, it was clear his decision to start with Donovan's had been the correct one. His father's secret history with the establishment and its mysterious bartender was an added bonus above and beyond what he'd expected to find with Rotreego—if anything about the Pintiri turned out to be useful at all. That seemed suspect given how Lil and Donovan had spoken of the elf as if he were the weird stepchild they'd hidden in the closet under the stairs.

Then again, whatever weird shit was going on with Rotreego had to be related to the attack on Tallisker's Detroit headquarters. Maybe Ren and the Pintiri had a common enemy, and that dastardly villain had done something to Rotreego to make an alliance between the two harder to create.

Ren Roberts, he scolded himself, shaking his head, *turning into a conspiracy theorist will get you nowhere.* The truth, he suspected, would turn out to somehow be both much simpler and much stranger. *But what if?*

The forest ended abruptly a few hundred yards later, right when Ren's capacity to stem his next round of complaints was about to explosively expire—and it did so suddenly, and with a firm boundary. Exiting those woods meant identifying a patch of moonlight between the tightly packed trunks wide enough for Ren to squeeze through. Donovan and Lil, of course, had no difficulty with this and offered no physical or verbal assistance, but Ren's chosen gap turned out to be a little too tight. Bark scratched against his peacoat, threatening to tear the sturdy wool, and then his back foot caught down low where his planned exit narrowed, leaving him hopping on his front foot as he tried to extricate himself. A mighty leap sent him tumbling forward, head over heels.

He rolled once along his spine into a reasonably comfortable sitting position, breathing deeply to catch his breath and soothe his wounded pride. He ran his hand through the intensely green, impossibly soft grass beneath him. Would lying back into it and taking a quick nap be so bad? It had already been an exhausting day, with the promise of worse to come.

Donovan stopped and turned around. "Don't let the lawn tempt you into anything foolish. It gets pushy when it's hungry."

Ren frowned, unable to immediately process the concept. Then the lightbulb in his mind lit up like a supernova. *You're in a magic forest, dipshit, and that ain't normal grass.* He jerked his hands up over his head to put as much distance between his exposed skin and whatever abomination he'd just been absentmindedly caressing, then tucked his legs underneath himself and stood.

"Thank you," Ren said, "but perhaps a 'Keep off the Grass' sign is in order?"

"Mmmmm."

The perfectly square clearing they'd entered felt wrong somehow. Despite Donovan's warning about the grass, nothing within the area seemed dangerous or exuded ill will. Lil and the King of the Forest waited impatiently beside a lonely little apple tree in the clearing's center, the glittering night sky above them as beautiful as ever.

And then it hit him: the surrounding forest *hated* this place. The densely packed trees along the border had grown in a way that resembled a wall or a fence. Not a single branch reached out over the grass. Those thick trunks were a barrier designed to keep something contained. Angry, ugly whorls twisted their jagged bark. They were watchful, and they were not fucking happy about it.

Ren chewed on his bottom lip. Had he been led to a prison? Had Donovan's promise to introduce him to Rotreego been a trick? Did Lil know Ed as well as she did because she was working with his worst enemies? He couldn't find the gap he'd fallen through, and the others he spotted certainly weren't large enough to facilitate an escape. Fuck, he wished he'd brought that Uzi.

"This little dude's friends don't seem to like him," Ren said, nodding to the apple tree as he tried to saunter confidently toward the others.

"*She* does not mind outsiders, which makes her a pariah among her peers," Donovan explained. "There are others like her, of course, but they are few and far between. They are no longer a part of this forest, but thankfully they remain loyal to its king."

"Can't escape politics anywhere I go," Ren said with a smile.

"Mmmmm."

As he got closer, Ren questioned whether the apple tree was real wood, bark, and leaves, or if it was an apparition. He could sort of see right through it. Was it a hologram, or a projection? He dismissed the thought immediately. The strange not-tree in the middle of a magical forest could only be that way for one reason. He'd need to shift his thinking going forward, he knew, if he wanted to keep up.

"One quick turn around this beauty here and we'll reach our destination," Donovan said. Lil fell into line behind him. "It's been years since I've lost a guest, but I'd advise sticking close just in case."

Ren did as he instructed, becoming the caboose in their little train. His hyperactive and terrified imagination spun into motion as they proceeded around the tree. Could this half-assed parade be another trick? Was the point to run him in circles around that tree until vertigo knocked him back down into the hungry grass? Was it purely a distraction meant to stall for the arrival of his father's enemies? There was no way to know for sure. Lil followed Donovan without hesitation. Ren supposed he had no choice but to do the same.

Half a turn around that tree, the landscape changed. He stumbled up the sudden slope beneath his feet. Gone was the meadow and its imposing guardians, replaced instead with a gentle rise sparsely populated with wary trees. Ren glanced over his shoulder and found a different apple tree, its branches drooping under the weight of ripe fruit.

"Still got all your fingers, Mr. Roberts?" Donovan asked as he led the pair to a dirt path winding uphill.

"I had three thumbs when I got here, right?"

"The forest *still* does not appreciate sass."

"How does it feel about gentle ribbing?"

"Mmmmm."

Up the hill they went. Ren looked skyward again, begging the twinkling heavens to show him something familiar—for whatever good that would do. He couldn't even find the kite-thing he'd noticed above that previous bar. If shit went sideways, any direction in which he chose to run would be instinct at best. There was no telling how far into Donovan's domain those magic apple trees had transported him.

No more following eldritch creatures to second locations, he promised himself. *Dad wouldn't approve.*

Or would he have? Though Ren's epic quest was barely a couple hours old, it had already presented enough new information about his father that he'd begun to question just how well he knew Ed Roberts. For all Ren knew, traipsing through the wilds with absurdly powerful avatars of Nature's will had been one of Ed's favorite hobbies. Maybe he even moderated several online forums on the practice or had published a couple of how-to guides. Ren didn't fucking know. Perhaps that part scared him the most.

Donovan waited for the other two to catch up at the top of the hill. The view on the other side took Ren's breath away, primarily because it wasn't at all what he'd expected. Winding terraces carved into the slope supported the largest collection of arcade machines he'd ever seen—everything from old-fashioned pinball machines to simple cabinets with a pair of joysticks and some buttons to shooters with plastic pistols or shotguns to car racing games with plush leather seats and comfort grip steering wheels. The lights and sounds wafting upward belonged in his mental picture of a touristy beach town's boardwalk, not the middle of the woods right outside his NIMBY hometown.

Honestly, he'd expected something much weirder.

"There," Donovan said, pointing toward a pair of figures sitting beside each other at a picnic table about a quarter of the way down.

Lil's superior elven eyesight could make out detail Ren's couldn't. "You left Rotreego with fucking *Muffintop*?"

Donovan shrugged. "Muffintop has been one of our best and most loyal patrons."

Lil gaped at her boss as if he'd just told her elves weren't real. "The last time you left those two alone together..." She shook her head.

"Hence why I suggested it would be best not to dally."

Lil stomped down the hill. "Let's fucking go, then."

Ren paused beside Donovan. "I've heard horrible things about this Muffintop character. His scrapbooking hobby, for one."

"Mmmmm," the King of the Forest said, thoughtfully for once. "We are entering delicate territory, Mr. Roberts. This is a mess. Truth be told, I'd hoped to acquire your father's assistance with it. My communiqué, unfortunately, was too late."

"Dad knew them well?"

Donovan smiled. "Surely you've already surmised as much, but yes. Moving Lil out of Evitankari was your father's first project with Rotreego, but from what I understand, the partnership didn't end there. Lil certainly knows more about both men than she'll admit, even to me."

Ren decided to ignore how uncomfortable that statement made him feel. "And Muffintop?"

"A reliable regular, as I've said, albeit one with a unique collection of idiosyncrasies. I would not want to find myself on that one's bad side."

That didn't jibe at all with Felton's description of the little troll. "He's a weird, crooked fucking thing," Kevin had said. "Remember Doorknob before all the therapy? That's Muffintop." Words like *clingy, uncomfortable,* and *ultimately harmless but if he told me not to go to school tomorrow I'd sure stay the hell home* came to mind. Yet here was Donovan Pym, the King of the Forest, all-powerful within his domain, stating matter-of-factly that he wouldn't cross the guy. What the heck did that mean?

"Muffintop commands an army of termites, doesn't he?"

The king smiled. "I've no doubt he could, if he set his mind to it."

Lil, thanks to her head start, reached the picnic table first, and then hovered behind the strange pair like a suburban mother worried a little role-playing game might convince her precious children that devil worship maybe wasn't such a bad idea after all. Neither Rotreego nor Muffintop seemed to notice her, engrossed as they were in the latter's tome-like scrapbook.

"This!" the bent little troll squealed gleefully. "My fourteenth year at Burning Man. This nice man offered me some really tasty mushrooms! I don't remember much after that!"

"God damn commies," Rotreego growled. Even next to the much smaller Muffintop, he somehow looked small and shriveled, as if he'd been starving for weeks and what was left of him wanted nothing more than to retreat into the folds of his bright blue bathrobe. The hand he'd laid atop the picnic table shook almost as violently as his eyes.

"Drugs?" Ren whispered to Donovan.

"Worse," the king replied. "The man responsible tells it best. Muffintop, how goes it?"

The troll's bulging left eye swiveled upward to examine them, leaving its comically small companion staring down at the table. Ren couldn't help staring at the bony growth jutting off the side of his skull that looked just like the breakfast pastry for which he'd been named. "We're great, thanks for asking! Did you bring us a new friend?"

The way Muffintop said "friend" made Ren want to make a run for it. The word dripped with desperation. He flashed back to first grade, when Doorknob begged him to go play with the dead beaver he'd found by the river.

"I sure did bring you two a new friend!" Donovan said mischievously. Ren wanted to slap him. "This is Ren Roberts."

Rotreego went suddenly still. "Roberts," he croaked. "A good, American name for a good, hardworking American family. You come from strong stock, kid, regardless of what the damned liberal media says. Ed Roberts is a true patriot, a real man among men."

"Ed's dead," Ren replied flatly, mostly to see what would happen.

"Then this is a dark day in our country's history. Without Ed Roberts, the lizard people will surely win," Rotreego replied, shaking even worse than before. Behind him, Lil chewed on her lip in dismay, watching him as if he were a bomb about to explode.

Ren looked to Donovan. "I take it this is new behavior."

"Muffintop," the king said warmly, "would you be so kind as to tell us about how you met your friend Rotreego?"

The troll lit up like a Christmas tree. "I sure would!" He cleared his throat dramatically, a sound Ren could only compare to a frog dying in a blender. "It was 50-cent wing night! I never miss it. I get boneless with barbecue sauce, because tendies are better than wings! The bones are gross!

"Anyway, when I come in there's this new guy sitting alone at the bar! He's dressed kinda funny, but I can tell he needs a friend. So I sit right down next to him and I say 'Hello! Would you like to be my friend?' And he looks at me like maybe he's thinking about hurting me. But then he says 'Depends. Can you help me scramble up everything I know so the a-holes and c-words that want it can't use me anymore?' I think he was doing that thing people do when they don't really want an answer, but I say 'Sure!'"

Muffintop's shoulders sank like a pair of deflating basketballs. "I was lying. I wasn't really *sure*. I mean, I had an idea, but I thought it might kill him! I tell him we'll need something else to fill his head with, and that he'll need to sit reeeeeeeeally still for a really long time. 'What the h-e-double-hockey-sticks,' he says, 'like I've got anything better to do.' I think he'd been drinking a lot!

"Ulliver was nice enough to let us borrow his radio! We go station by station, searching for just the right stuff. Finally, we hear a very angry man saying the Omaha shootings were a false flag set up to hide evidence of an underground pedophile ring behind the drive-in movie theater! I still don't understand most of those words, but I sure have never seen Rotreego smile so brightly!

"So he lies down on the ground and closes his eyes and I put my hand on his forehead, and we listen to the radio. I concentrate as hard as I can on moving the words and sounds coming through the speaker right into my friend's head! His skin gets really warm and I think maybe I fried something, but he insists I keep going.

Three hours later, the show's over! Rotreego sits right up and says 'The New World Order's gonna be P-O'ed. You've done a great service for America, Muffintop.' And now we're friends forever!"

Ren gaped at the ugly little troll for a few moments, then released the sort of delayed sigh that catches in your throat, as if it can't believe its own existence is necessary. He knew exactly the radio show Muffintop had somehow jammed into Rotreego's mind. A few years ago, he'd briefly dated a girl who thought everything the host said was true—emphasis on briefly. "Okay," he finally said, "but why did Rotreego want to go through all that when he could've just asked someone to dust him?"

"The transdimensional psychic vampires have horrible, horrible ways of making people talk!" Rotreego shouted.

"It isn't easy, but the dust can be undone," Lil translated, "and Evitankari has ways of retrieving a corpse's memories."

"So he turned his brain into a total mess," Ren mused. "That's brilliant. Like he encrypted it all underneath a layer of pure bullshit."

"The Illuminati think they're so smart, with their standardized testing, and their fluoride, and their vaccines," Rotreego gloated. "I'll show them! America will never fall into their grimy socialist clutches!"

Ren shook his head. "As fun as all this has been, it doesn't really help me. Do we know if there was something in particular Rotreego wanted to hide?"

"He was the Pintiri," Lil said. "There's no telling."

"I may have discovered one scant clue," Donovan offered. "On his way in, Rotreego told Ulliver...and I quote: 'If that fucking witch tries to follow me, punch her in the face and toss her ass in the river.'"

Ren stiffened. He wasn't sure if sharing his information was wise, but the others had certainly noticed his reaction. He decided to take a chance. "'Fucking witch' was the last thing Driff said to Kevin Felton."

"Mmmmm," Donovan said. "The plot thickens, though I must admit I am unfamiliar with any such person. Lil?"

"No," she said slowly, "Rotreego never mentioned anyone like that before."

Ren sat down on the bench opposite Rotreego and Muffintop. The troll pushed his scrapbook forward hesitantly, then pulled it back when he found Ren studying the former Pintiri instead. "Rotreego, who's the witch?"

His eyes flicked up to Ren, down to the scrapbook, up to the stars, then back down to the table beside his quivering hand. "She's a commie bitch who wants to take your guns and make it illegal for you to homeschool your children."

Ren stifled a laugh. "Did my father know her?"

"You'd have to ask the pencil neck geeks at DARPA recording all of our phone calls and text messages."

"Okay, so you don't know." He drummed his fingers on the picnic table's rough wood, thinking through how to phrase his next inquiry. "Ed was set up—probably by someone within Tallisker. He was ordered to a meeting at the Detroit headquarters. That tower was destroyed yesterday. Do you know who would've wanted him dead?"

Rotreego seemed to gather himself, clenching his fist, sitting up straighter, and taking a deep breath before unleashing the torrent swirling around in his cracked mind. "Let me tell ya, Ed Roberts was no friend to the neoliberal scumbags manipulating the markets to oppress everyday American citizens who just want to do their jobs and support their families. We're talking the Bildebergers, the Rothschilds, all the ass grabbers prancing around in the Bohemian Grove, the psychic crustacean humanoids running drugs and guns out of the Hollow Earth, all of 'em. Every scumbag on the planet. If you hate freedom, you hated Ed Roberts, God rest his soul!"

"Yeah, I was worried about that."

Across the table, the elf's head vibrated in a way Ren took as a nod. His bony fist spasmed back open and he slouched down into himself. That semi-lucid explanation had clearly taken a lot out of him.

"This is the clearest he's been since the...mmmm...procedure," Donovan said softly. "Keep it up."

Behind Rotreego, Lil winced at the king's suggestion. She leaned forward as if to object, then rocked back onto her heels without a word—but clearly poised to pounce if Rotreego needed the assistance. Ren thought she'd made a good point: he'd come here for information, and he wouldn't get it if his line of questioning put the former Pintiri into a coma.

But what else could he really hope to get out of the poor guy? Rotreego and Ed obviously knew each other, though maybe not well. The elf's former position had certainly made him privy to a wide variety of important secrets, but what kind of insight into Tallisker's operations did Evitankari really have?

His gaze drifted sideways to Muffintop's scrapbook.

A knuckle rapping on the table drew Ren's attention back to Rotreego. "Let me tell ya something, kid," the elf drawled, every word clearly a monumental effort. "Ed Roberts was about to blow the lid off a conspiracy that'd make George Soros crap his pants." Then he slumped backward, clearly exhausted. Lil lunged forward and caught him before he could fall off the back of the bench. She half-glared at Ren, clearly blaming him for Rotreego's near collapse but maybe not willing to admit how much she cared.

"So Dad knew something and he was about to act on it," Ren said thoughtfully, his mind whirling. "Thanks, Rotreego."

"You're on fire!" Muffintop squealed.

"Yes," Ren mused, "I suppose I am doing a good job translating."

"I believe Muffintop meant me," Donovan said sadly.

Ren turned to look over his shoulder. The left side of the king's wispy mustache burned like a birthday candle. As everyone watched, a second tiny flame burst to life from his right elbow.

Lil gasped. "Where is it?"

"Far enough away that we are not in any immediate danger," the king replied calmly. Before he could continue, a squirrel darted out of the darkness and clambered up his side to sit on his shoulder. He listened intently as it chittered in his ear. "It seems you were followed, Mr. Roberts, by a...*walking conflagration*? That can't be right." Donovan frowned at the little rodent, which rebuked him angrily and then leapt away.

Ren swallowed in a dry throat. According to Kevin Felton, Maeve Remini and Clint Hope had been burned alive. Whoever was targeting the family members of recently deceased Tallisker employees had made it to Harksburg sooner than expected. Any chance of getting a head start on the bastard was long gone.

"I should probably go," Ren said, rising. He'd hoped that maybe he'd have another chance to get something useful out of Rotreego, but overstaying his welcome sounded like a great way to end up barbecued. "I imagine I've attracted one of the few things the forest enjoys less than sass."

"Mmmmm."

He waved to the others as he climbed over the back of the bench. "Thank you all for your gracious hospitality. I'll leave a five-star review online." Then he saluted Rotreego, who leaned heavily against Lil's chest, as if all his muscles had seized. "And thank you especially. I know that wasn't easy. Magic sword or not, you're still the Pintiri on the inside."

The elf's lower lip quaked. He slowly leaned forward, his mouth twisting into a snarl, and he jabbed a slender finger toward Ren, as if impaling an enemy. "One lone patriot, no matter how courageous, does not stand a snowball's chance in hell against the penetrating tentacles of the globalist elite and the hordes of sheeple who mindlessly do their bidding—but there isn't a force in the universe that can stop Americans when they rise up, together, in the pursuit of freedom."

Rotreego gritted his teeth and tried to stand. He mostly made it, though he leaned heavily on the table. His breath sputtered like a busted muffler.

Lil swooped in behind him and took hold of his arm. "Oh, no you don't. You are in no shape to run off and fight the Illuminati, buster."

He jerked his arm free and wormed his fingers into hers. "*Together*," he hissed.

"You cannot be fucking serious," she replied.

Muffintop slammed his scrapbook shut, leapt up onto the bench, and launched a clenched fist toward the sky. "Together!"

"You cannot be fucking serious," Ren said.

"Mmmmm," Donovan interjected. "I think that's a marvelous idea."

"What?" Lil and Ren shouted in eerie unison.

"Mr. Roberts and the former Pintiri appear to have a common enemy, one that might be best understood by further investigating the shared history in which Lil plays an integral part."

Ren jerked his thumb over his shoulder. "What about Doughnut Hole over here?"

The king's left toe caught on fire. "If I were you, I'd take all the help I could get."

— CHAPTER FIVE —

T heir next conga line through the maybe-holographic apple tree network dropped the group beside a lazy stream winding through the forest.

"The parking lot's ten minutes that way," Donovan explained, pointing down a narrow path through the rugged old oaks. Flames danced along his right eyebrow and a tendril of smoke steamed out of his back pocket. "Alas, this is where our paths diverge. I've other guests to see to, and a walking conflagration to confront."

Guilt spurred Ren's tongue into motion. "I'm sorry I brought this trouble to your forest. Will you be all right?"

"Mmmmm." The king looked off into the distance as he brushed ashy flakes from the cuff of his sleeve. "My domain is large and has proven resilient, but fire is one threat I cannot afford to take lightly. With any luck, whatever it is will leave as soon as I tell them you've departed."

In this case, Ren didn't mind being bait to draw the bad guy away. The thought of Donovan's entire forest and all he'd built within it burning just because he'd been kind enough to help made Ren want to crawl into a hole somewhere and cry himself to sleep.

"Thank you," Lil croaked, "for everything you've done for me." Rotreego, who clung to her side like a baby koala clutching its mother, nodded weakly.

Donovan bowed. Another flame lit up above his kidneys. "It's been a pleasure, my dear, and I do hope that this is not our final goodbye. But if it is, then I'd ask simply that you take my kindness and pay it forward to those in greater need."

The elf nodded. Her eyes darted from Ren to Muffintop to Rotreego, clearly unenthused with her boss's request. "I'll do my best."

"Then you will do more than enough." Donovan straightened. "Farewell, friends. May each of you find what you're looking for."

"Bye-bye!" Muffintop said with a Muppet-like wave as the King of the Forest walked around the apple tree and disappeared.

Donovan's departure left Ren feeling deflated. This, then, was the end of the first leg of his epic quest to avenge his fallen father. Though he would've been hard-pressed to describe what he'd expected to gain from this initial effort, he knew that this sure as shit wasn't it.

"We should get a move on," Lil said. She nodded toward Ren. "Take Rotreego. I'm going to scout ahead."

Ren stepped forward and ducked underneath the former Pintiri's crooked arm. "You're expecting trouble?"

"You're not?" Lil said as if he'd just questioned the color of the sky.

He wasn't, but her comment made him think about it for a second. "Sure, the walking conflagration could be a distraction designed to flush us out so someone in the parking lot can pick us up."

"And *they* want *you* to believe the world is round," Rotreego said, rolling his eyes. His breath was uncomfortably close and fetid on Ren's cheek.

"My thoughts exactly," Ren replied. "We'll guard the rear."

Lil ignored him and darted forward, leaving Ren with Rotreego leaning heavily on his side and Muffintop looking up at him expectantly. Babysitting was *definitely* not what he'd expected.

"Onward, ho!" he declared.

"Yaaaaaaaaay!" Muffintop added, pumping his fist like he'd just scored a game-winning goal.

Rotreego elbowed Ren in the ribs and raised one wavering finger to his lips to shush them both.

The former Pintiri, it turned out, was a lot heavier than he looked. His steps were short and jerky, and his unsteady legs clearly couldn't hold the rest of him up anymore. Dragging him across that uneven forest floor, through grasping brush and around fallen logs and under low-hanging branches, was like dragging a sack of rocks uphill, in the snow, in sandals. There was definitely some solid muscle hiding underneath that fluffy bathrobe. Ren didn't understand how Muffintop's mental meddling had caused Rotreego's physical deterioration, or if it would be permanent. He made a mental note to ask later.

Assuming there'd be a later. He doubted the four of them would stand much chance against anyone waiting for them in the parking lot. What was Lil going to do if she found a gang of goons up ahead, make them a drink? Or maybe she could ask them to hold really still while Muffintop pushed some crackpot YouTuber's personality into their skulls.

Or...what if he got himself killed on purpose? Felton would do him a solid and let him stick around as an incorporeal soul until the smoke cleared—and maybe, angered by an attack on his lifelong best pal, the local reaper would turn his considerable fury upon those responsible. The problem with that idea, however, was that there was no guarantee he'd be killed immediately—and it was entirely possible that anyone waiting in ambush knew that murdering him in Harksburg would be really dumb. Kevin couldn't save him if they kidnapped him and moved him out of the reaper's territory. Plus, he knew from experience that dying fucking sucked and being a disembodied soul sucked even worse. He shivered just thinking about the time he'd spent in Billy's to-go cup.

A stupid plan began to coalesce in his mind as he dragged Rotreego along: *if I can get to the Jag, I can get to the Uzi.* Maybe that was a big *if*, but he did have three convenient distractions tagging along with him.

Would he be able to pull the trigger, though? He thought so, especially if the hypothetical goons were ugly, twisted demons from the deepest pits of Tallisker's seedy underbelly. He'd never actually fired an Uzi, though, which felt like a pretty big flaw in his plan. Was it an automatic, or a semi-auto, or some other technical term that meant there was no way he'd be able to figure it out on the fly? Shit, was it even *loaded*?

Change of plans: *if I can get to the Jag, I'm fucking out of here.* Donovan probably wasn't wrong to imply that Ren needed help— but what good were a bartender, a withered conspiracy theorist, and a stunted troll against even mid-level Tallisker demons? Living to fight another day wouldn't be possible without the living part.

He glanced down at Muffintop toddling along beside him and felt a momentary pang of guilt. Not a big one, nor a particularly sharp one—just a little tap from his conscience, reminding him it was still there. He told it to shut the hell up.

Ren's breath caught in his throat as Lil melted out of the woods to his right. "We have a problem," she whispered, her eyes hard. "Leave Rotreego and come with me."

Together, they lowered the former Pintiri into a sitting position against a sturdy oak. Rotreego thanked them with a shaky thumbs up and waved them onward.

They moved forward at a crouch, using the scraggly brush and the densely packed trees as cover. Lil led the way. Ren did his best to match his footsteps to hers as closely as he could, trusting her obvious skill at moving quietly through the woods. He bit back the occasional curse at the wispy branches of unnamed vegetation that clawed at his skin and clothing. Perhaps, he wondered, these little annoyances were the forest's revenge for his prior sass.

The pair stopped a few yards back from the tree line. Lil lay flat on her stomach and directed Ren to do the same beside her, giving them both a decent view of the parking lot underneath the branches of a leafy green bush. They had a problem, all right: a pair of figures in all black waited for them in the center of the parking lot, one flanking either side of a white Corvette. They looked normal—human—but Ren knew that didn't mean much.

"I need you to distract them," Lil hissed, her voice barely audible. "Get them both on this side of the Corvette, so they're between you and the trunk."

Ren hated her plan immediately. "*You* distract them. I've got a weapon in the green Jaguar over there." *And a one-way ticket out of here.*

She rolled her eyes and shook her head. "I know you can't tell with your shitty human eyes, but those are *demons.* Running at them with a gun will only get you laughed at, and then dismembered. Let me take them out."

Ren saw his chance of escape dwindling. There was no way he could reach the car unless one of the others drew the thugs' attention away from him. He believed Lil could drop two demons like he believed Rotreego could run a marathon. "Trust me," he said, slapping on the smile he'd used on so many women, so many nights at the Burg, "I got this. I'll get to the car and—"

"Hi guys!" Muffintop squealed from up ahead. Somehow he'd snuck past them both while they argued. "Want to see my scrapbook?"

The two figures turned to appraise the little troll as he toddled across the parking lot, right into the position Lil had described. A few more steps toward Muffintop and the goons would be right where she'd said she wanted them.

And in a position where Ren would never be able to dart around them and reach the Jag.

"What did you say?" the smaller of the goons asked through the black scarf wrapped around her face. She'd buzzed all the hair off her head and replaced it with what looked like light blue tattoos.

"My scrapbook! I like to show people!" Muffintop said happily, producing the thick tome seemingly from out of nowhere. "Nothing's better than making new friends!"

The other goon took a step forward, cocking his head in interest underneath a dark hood that hid all of his features except a bushy red beard. His black leather jacket strained against a chest that seemed far too big for his body, like an old-timey strongman jacked up on anabolic steroids. "I can think of a few better things."

"No way! Like what?"

"Watching the sun set from your front porch next to someone you love," the woman mused, taking another step forward.

"A cold beer after a satisfying day of hard work," the man said, matching her stride.

"The season's newborn calves frolicking in the field."

"The hometown team's first win of the year."

"Oh man!" Muffintop squealed with a strange waggle of his butt. "Those are great! Keep going!"

The woman smiled, showing her fangs. "Dining upon the flesh of your enemies while their children watch."

The man unzipped the front of his jacket. A pair of twisted, heavily muscled arms unfurled from his chest. "Beating an innocent to death with nothing but your own four fists."

"I'm not sure those things count," Muffintop replied sadly.

In the forest, Ren looked to Lil. "That gun'd be kind of useful right now."

The elf reached over and took his hand. Did she think he'd try to run? Would his touch make her feel better about Muffintop's impending doom?

The goons took another step forward, putting themselves directly between the troll and the back of the Corvette. Lil smiled. Every nerve in Ren's hand caught on fire. Hot, paralyzing pain streamed up his arm and into his core, making his body go stiff and his jaw clench. He wanted to scream, but the necessary muscles wouldn't react.

Lil reached out with her free hand and swatted the air, swinging her fingers right to left.

On the other side of the bushes, a small brown hatchback tipped on its left side, sliced through the air between Muffintop and the Corvette and plowed through the two demons with the force of a freight train.

The pain subsided, but only briefly. Once again in control, Ren tried to wrench his hand away. Lil's grip was iron. She rolled on her back and lit him up again, paralyzing him once more. This time she angled her index finger back the way it came and beckoned something toward them. Rotreego zipped over their hiding place and into the parking lot, coming to rest gently against the Corvette's bumper. He waved weakly.

Lil finally let go. "That is why I wanted you to be the distraction," she snapped. "Muffintop barely would've felt that."

"Shut the fuck up and let's get out of here," Ren snarled, clutching his red, inflamed hand to his chest as he staggered to his feet. Pins and needles raced up and down his arm.

Worse, though, was the pain burning in his ego.

— CHAPTER SIX —

So," Ren said as he sat down on the edge of his bed, "what's your deal?"

On the other bed, Muffintop sat up and swung himself around. "What do you mean?" The miniature troll's legs dangled off the side of the bed, his clean white socks pulled up to his knobby knees.

For that night, the mismatched pair were roommates. Lil thought it best to split the team up to make it harder for their enemies to create an ambush. She'd assigned Ren and Muffintop to room 301 on the top floor of the Happy Valley Motor Inn. Lil and Rotreego were in 152. The Jag, much to Ren's chagrin, was parked out back by the Dumpster where it couldn't be seen from the adjacent highway.

As far as lodging went, room 301 was certainly a motel room. Two twin-sized beds, a tiny flat-screen TV perched atop a massive dresser, a bathroom so tight you could barely fit a matchbook between the tub and the side of the toilet. The interior decorator's style could best be described as mid-century "let's slap pictures of Illinois everywhere because fuck it, the only people staying here are drug addicts and hookers."

Ren took a moment and really studied the little troll. Though he'd previously dismissed Muffintop as an afterthought, further consideration of the sort of magic he assumed was required to rewrite someone's brain had him second-guessing that assessment. There were so many questions Ren wanted to ask him, all of them varying degrees of inappropriate. What the fuck had happened to his face? Did he see differently when he switched his focus from the big eye to the little eye? Could he read? Had he ever gotten laid? How the hell did he balance his crooked, bulbous ass on a toilet seat without keeling over the side? Had anyone introduced him to the concept of deodorant, because that tiny room was starting to smell way too much like a ham sandwich? And why the fuck had he grabbed the remote and flipped to the financial news channel as soon as they'd walked in?

He finally settled on something simple. "Tell me about yourself."

"What would you like to know?"

Damn it. "Ahhhhhh...where are you from?"

"All over! I travel a lot! I can show you in my scrapbook!"

"Is there anywhere in particular you think of as home?"

"Well, there was Donovan's!" Muffintop frowned. "I hope he's all right."

"Me too." Ren paused for a second to make clear that he meant it. "What about before that?"

"I lived in a different forest! That king wasn't as nice as Donovan, but he made better food." Muffintop's gaze drifted to the stock ticker streaming across the television screen.

"I take it you're an investor?"

Muffintop shrugged, a gesture like a mountain range rolling from left to right. "The king...four forests ago taught me."

Ren leaned forward, rubbing his chin. Here was something they had in common. Ren had been diversifying his own portfolio since before he could walk. "Any hot tips?"

"Yeah: don't play the market."

Ren chuckled. "Fair."

Muffintop looked down at his swinging toes. "I get it. You want to ask about the bad parts of my life, but not directly."

Given the obvious cue, Ren hesitated before following up. "I like to know the people I'm working with."

Muffintop swung his legs back up onto the bed and leaned hard into the pillows. "I don't. Not like that. I save that stuff for my *real* friends."

That, Ren realized, made a certain amount of sense. Though Muffintop was clearly desperate for companionship, what he really wanted was something even deeper. "All right," Ren said, slapping his knees and then standing up. "Well, for the record, I look forward to working with you. Thanks for what you did in the parking lot today."

"You're welcome!"

Just because he *understood* Muffintop didn't mean he was *satisfied* with the lack of answers. Ren suspected Lil would be able to fill in at least some of the blanks, and he needed to have a conversation with her anyway. "I'm going to make sure the others aren't causing trouble. Need anything while I'm out?"

Muffintop's gnarled face lit up. "Do they have chocolate milkshakes in the vending machine?"

Ren couldn't help smiling in response. "I doubt it, but I'll check."

"Thank you! Your dad used to buy me milkshakes, sometimes! He was a nice guy!"

Somehow, out of all the new things Ren had learned about his father that day, this latest revelation was the strangest—and somehow the most touching. "Thanks, Muffintop," he replied, a blush rising into his cheeks.

Putting on his shoes one handed was a struggle, but after much cursing under his breath he managed a pair of misshapen knots. Outside, a shadowy and unseasonably warm nowhere-Indiana evening greeted him. They'd driven south-southeast all day, doubling back and changing highways before settling on the Happy Valley Motor Inn as their refuge for the night. Putting some distance between them and their pursuers was paramount, even though Lil had emptied the Uzi's entire—and only—magazine into the white Corvette before they left.

The cheap decking creaked under his weight. Below, the parking lot remained mostly empty, save for a few beat-up old sedans and a panel van that belonged to either a drug dealer, a pedophile, a terrorist, or perhaps one of each taking a road trip as a trio. The cracked two-lane road running parallel to the building barely counted as a highway, and Ren couldn't remember its assigned route number. Another forest loomed across the street, dense and somehow foreboding.

Here be dragons, Ren thought as a jacked-up truck roared past, the stars and bars rippling from a pole jutting from its bed, *and probably a lot of meth.* He was surprised to spot Lil sitting in one of the Adirondack chairs beside the metal firepit. A little privacy would be nice, given the circumstances.

He stuck close to the side of the building as he headed for the stairwell, keeping his distance from the rickety railing that appeared to have been built with the cheapest two-by-fours available. One section a few doors down twisted almost like a piece of licorice. The heads of thick nails jutted here and there from the woodwork like mushrooms from a log. Rather than pound them in, maintenance had slathered right over them with the same white paint that covered everything else. Tetanus, Ren decided, should've been listed on the Happy Valley Motor Inn's welcome pamphlet beside free Wi-Fi and complimentary breakfast.

A flat echo chased his steps down the stairwell. Between the first and second floor, an aspiring local artist had spraypainted the biggest set of boobs Ren had ever seen. Thanks to his association with Oscar and Doorknob, he'd encountered more than his share of cartoon genitalia in his time, and he had to say—this work couldn't have been more impressive. His hand reflexively reached for the smartphone in his pocket. Under normal circumstances, this would be a definite snap 'n share. The boys would love it.

He'd left his personal phone at home, on his desk. The device in his pocket was just one of several burners he'd brought along. Its address book was purposefully empty. He let his hand go slack at his side. *So this is life on the run,* he thought sadly. Preparing himself to face mortal danger was one thing; dealing with an intense feeling of disconnection had turned out to be a whole other ballgame. God, he needed a drink.

Lil nodded at him from within her little cloud of cigarette smoke as he sat down beside her. The lit Marlboro in her left hand and the trio of fresh butts in the nearby ashtray suggested she'd been steadily working her way through the pack. "Accommodations to your liking?" she grunted.

"I've stayed in nicer places, but not many," he replied, which was actually true. He hadn't traveled much.

"I bet." She took a long drag and exhaled slowly, letting the smoke streaming out through her lips extend the silence between them. "We got some things to discuss."

Ren's inflamed hand tingled. "We certainly do."

She turned her head so they could look each other in the eyes. "I was elven intelligence for twenty-three years. I wasn't the exact tip of the spear, but I was pretty close to it."

When she didn't elaborate further, Ren took the hint. "All right. I'll follow your instructions next time."

"You'd damn well better." Lil shook her head and ran her free hand backward through her blond curls. "I'm sorry about your hand. Without an external energy source, I can barely levitate a coin."

That explained a lot. "It's all right. A hatchback's a lot heavier than a quarter. Thanks for wiping out those two demons, by the way."

She nodded. "For a second there, I thought you were going to run. Just take off right for your precious car, hanging me and Muffintop out to dry." Her face hardened. "If I catch that vibe again, I will drag the other two the fuck out of this shit and leave your ass to rot. Got it?"

He decided not to waste time with denials. "Got it."

"Good." She flicked a hunk of ash onto the used butts. "Now, all that said—I need your help."

"It would be my pleasure, madam," he said with a little bow, flinching as the motion scraped his bony ass across the head of an exposed nail.

"No," Lil replied, shaking her cigarette at him, "not like that. I don't need the arrogant, entitled prick that sauntered into Donovan's like everyone in there owed him an explanation. I need the smart, attentive, hardworking son Ed Roberts always told me about."

That demand landed like a slap to the face. Ren's father had never been the type to throw around compliments. That's not to say he was unsupportive—just that he rarely used blunt language to show it, which had often left a much younger Ren unsure of himself and the things he felt proud of. As Ren grew, he learned to interpret Ed's brusque nods and suggestions for how he could take his successes *just one step further* as all the signs of approval his father felt necessary. Learning that the words Ren had often yearned to hear coming from his father's mouth had instead been saved for his secret bar friends was a strange combination of unsettling and uplifting.

"All right. Obviously, we can't stay here forever. We need a plan."

"Yes, we do. I take it you weren't planning to head home after your stop at Donovan's. What's in the car?"

Ren closed his eyes and ran through his mental inventory. "Two changes of clothes, six burner phones, $10,000 in cash, one bottle of Glenlivet, and enough nariidisone to keep me lucid for a month.

Which is a problem, because now there are three of us who need it."

Tallisker families and elves living or traveling outside of Evitankari relied on daily doses of nariidisone to stave off the small amount of narii compound circulating in the water supply. Ren had been taking it every day since he'd turned twelve. The stuff wasn't powerful enough to stop a face full of narii dust, but it did the job against the trace amounts used to prepare the populace for the subliminal messaging Tallisker deployed through the media to defend its secrets. It wasn't like you could pick it up at the local drugstore. Nariidisone was only legally sold through authorized dealers licensed by Tallisker. Needless to say, that was a risk the group couldn't take.

Lil clicked her tongue. "That's ten days' worth, twenty-ish, if we stagger it. One of us can skip a dose every day, but yes, we'll need to get more. We'll also need weapons, new identities, and ideally defensive wards or masking enchantments."

"Ed left us with a disaster plan, including the locations of several safehouses. If my geography's right, the closest is two hours south of here. I'd planned to avoid them all because I'm not sure how secret they really are."

"Smart—but if you've got a more likely source of the things we'd need, I'd love to hear it."

Ren looked across the highway. "Think the king of that forest can help?"

She shook her head. "I love Donovan like family, but one of the first things they taught me in spy school was to be damn careful around the Pyms."

He couldn't argue with that logic. "Then I guess we're going to Ed's safehouse."

"Tomorrow," Lil said. "Rotreego needs his rest."

"Tomorrow, then."

"Good. I'm glad that's settled. What about after that?"

"Well, I've never been to Detroit."

Lil took a long moment to commune with her cigarette. "Might as well head straight for the scene of the crime."

Ren leaned back in the uncomfortable chair, feeling like he and Lil had found some common ground. He hadn't realized how desperately he'd wanted that. Even his hand felt a bit better.

And it filled him with confidence. "What do you know about Muffintop?"

Lil pulled another cigarette out of her pack. "You'd better get comfortable, 'cuz you're not going to believe this…"

— CHAPTER SEVEN —

When he wasn't watching the road, Ren watched Muffintop in the rearview mirror. The stunted troll spent most of the ride with his big eye glued to the window, watching the sparse scenery and the rare passing traffic. Occasionally he'd call out an out-of-state license plate or point out a sign promising roadside ice cream.

Was Muffintop really the latest reincarnation of an insanely powerful troll shaman or was Lil just fucking with him? It was a wild story, and her amused smile at the end of their conversation the night before hadn't made any of it clearer.

He could see it either way. On the one hand, Muffintop had overwritten an elven hero's entire personality based on some crap he'd heard on the radio. On the other, well, Lil had surely learned a thing or two about manipulating assets while working in elven intelligence. Supposedly the idea had originated with Donovan and the kings of other forests that had hosted the strange troll.

God, Ren needed a drink.

They'd left the Happy Valley Motor Inn at nine in the morning, after they'd swapped the Jag's plates with a pair stolen off a banged-up black sedan. His protests that no one in fucking South Dakota owned a car as magnificent as his beloved Jaguar had been ignored. The week-old onion bagels at complimentary breakfast hadn't improved his mood. At least his hand didn't hurt anymore.

Silence filled most of the drive. He'd considered turning the radio on to try to get some news, but he didn't want to risk spinning Rotreego into an extended tirade. In the passenger seat, Lil browsed the web on one of his spare burners. Rotreego, shaking and clutching his robe tightly, leaned forward from the backseat to read over her shoulder. Beside the elf, Muffintop smiled as he swung his legs and stared out the window.

This is like a family vacation on some of the local meth, Ren thought to himself.

Which further made him wonder—what was this, really? *Family* didn't fit, and he doubted any of the involved parties wanted it to. Were they a team? A squad? A fellowship on an epic adventure? Or just a gaggle of fucked-up degenerates sticking together momentarily because they had no one else?

The lack of a definitive word for their little group bothered him, he realized, because this was the farthest he'd traveled sans parental supervision. He'd never once left his father's territory without Ed at his side. Someday, when he told people about his first big adventure, he wanted to be able to describe the people with him as something more than "uh...them." He realized this was silly, and that he had more important things to think about, and that the chances he'd ever get to tell anyone about any of this probably weren't great...but he couldn't help himself. For someone used to being surrounded by a familiar group of longtime friends, traveling with a trio of randos he'd known for just over a day could not have felt more wrong.

Lil nudged his elbow, shocking him back to the real world. "That's our exit."

"Right," he muttered, heat rising in his cheeks. "Thanks."

"Yay!" Muffintop crowed. "I really have to go!"

"Number one or number two?" Ren asked, subconsciously channeling his father.

"Number three!"

Ren cut the wheel a little too much leaning into the exit. "Number...what?"

"Trolls go number one, number two, and number three!"

He quickly glanced over to Lil for confirmation. She smirked in response. "Certain species of nymphs go number two and number four."

"Okay, I feel a bit behind. Is there a wiki or docuseries I can watch to get myself up to date on all you strange magic people?" He pulled the Jag to a stop at the upcoming red light and tapped his finger on the steering wheel. "Rotreego, are these two fucking with me?"

"A 2013 investigation into the chemicals in our wastewater processing plants revealed the existence of organic compounds previously unknown to science. Researchers believe they're extraterrestrial in origin."

And then, he did the strangest thing: he laughed. Ren hadn't seen him do that before and had thought that maybe he'd been rendered incapable of doing so. Rotreego's laugh was like a thunderclap, sudden and loud, and his face twisted into a ragged grin as his whole body shook at once.

Muffintop laughed next. Then Lil covered her mouth and stifled a few. Then Ren leaned back, shook his head, and chuckled under his breath.

Was this a moment? Had they just had a moment? It sure felt like it.

Behind the Jag, the driver of a big red semi honked his horn in annoyance. Ren hadn't seen the light change. He flipped the truck off in his mirror and powered the Jag through the intersection.

The car bounced and jostled along a narrow two-lane road pocked with potholes that belonged on the surface of the moon.

The surrounding land was flat, featureless, and exceedingly brown, even for early winter. Callously discarded garbage, occasionally captured in poorly maintained snow fences, lined the sides of the road like fans watching a race. The farmhouses they passed were tall and bland, ancient guardians watching over wide tracts of cheap land that might once have been small family farms but were now mostly used to store grimy children's toys and broken-down vehicles that hadn't run in years. Ren supposed this was an improvement over the depressing strip malls they'd passed closer to the bigger highway.

"Nice of Ed to pick such a scenic location," he muttered.

"This is real America," Rotreego boomed from the backseat, "the kind of place the coastal elites pretend doesn't exist! Of course, that doesn't stop 'em from dispatching their brainwashed corporate lickspittles out here to take over the agriculture industry. As if a bunch of pencil neck accountants know anything about farming!"

"Exactly," Lil added. "It's a great place to hide people and materiel, and the idea of stashing your yuppie ass out here damn sure put a big smile on Ed's face."

"I don't know if I want to go number three in a place like this," Muffintop whined.

Even though he didn't understand what number three entailed, Ren couldn't argue with that. "I'm sure the safehouse Ed picked out is very nice."

It wasn't, at least from the outside. The address belonged to an ancient brown Victorian that looked like it might give up on life and collapse in a giant cloud of musty dust at any moment. Plywood covered all the windows on the first floor, and a few two-by-fours nailed to the front porch's two main pillars blocked off access to the front door. Tall brown grass surrounded the building like angry villagers demanding to be let inside so they could immolate the monster hiding in the basement. Oddly, the lot on which it sat forced the road to make a broad curve around it, almost as if the asphalt was afraid to get too close. The gray sky only added to the eerie effect.

"Bet they don't get many trick-or-treaters," Ren muttered as he pulled into the gravel drive. The Jag shuddered as its right wheels slammed across a deep divot.

Lil tensed and leaned forward in her seat, her eyes scanning the dismal, depressing landscape for threats. "Roll forward a few more feet and then stop. I don't want to get too close to that garage."

Ren did as instructed, although he had a hard time describing the outbuilding ahead as a garage. A shack, perhaps, or maybe a crooked fucking death trap. A shed, at best. Still, it'd be a great place from which to launch an ambush on an unsuspecting vehicle.

"Is someone else here?" he asked softly.

Lil nodded but did not elaborate. "The entrance is in the back, correct?"

"Yeah," Ren replied. "The actual facility is in the basement."

"That's the only way into it? Not through a bulkhead, or a tunnel somewhere behind the house?"

"Not that I know of."

She drummed her fingers on the dashboard, thinking through their options. Ren had one he particularly liked.

"Let's get the fuck out of here."

Lil sighed. "You know of another place we can get everything we need?"

"Yeah, my father's other safehouses."

"How far is the closest that doesn't take us back toward Harksburg and the walking conflagration?"

He looked up at the ceiling as he worked through the list in his head. "Uh…it's in Oklahoma."

"That is not on the way to Detroit."

He wiped his eyes with his hands. Lil was right and he knew it. The longer it took them to reach the scene of the crime, the less likely they'd be able to find anything useful—and the more time the walking conflagration would have to catch up with them. They needed to grab the weapons and supplies in that safehouse and then they needed to get their asses moving northeast.

"You're right," he said hesitantly.

"Okay. Ren, I need you to go first. We have to hope that whoever's here is expecting you to come alone."

A lump formed in Ren's gut. His suspicion that anyone after him would want him alive—at least for a little while—didn't make him any braver. "All right."

"Good. Muffintop, you and I will follow. We have to be quiet, and I need you to hold my hand the whole way, even if it hurts."

"Okay!" Muffintop chirped merrily. Ren wondered if the little guy understood what Lil was really asking for, and how he might react if it turned out he didn't.

"Thank you. Rotreego...lie down in the backseat and don't let anyone see you."

The elf's upper lip twisted as if Lil had just asked him to drink Muffintop's number three. "The voice of the voiceless does not cower in fear of degenerate commie scum!"

"Stop it," Lil snapped. "You're the backup plan. If nobody comes back for you in fifteen, get inside and give those commies what for."

Rotreego grunted like a cow in heat, seemingly mollified.

Lil nodded. "After you, Ren."

Outside, a chill whipped across that open plain and viciously destroyed Ren's poor, productless attempt at a hairstyle. He zipped his coat up and hesitated before closing the car door, scanning the area for signs of whatever had tipped off Lil. Nothing jumped out at him. Fuck, he felt so out of his element. Though he never would've admitted it, he was damn glad he wasn't doing this alone.

The only sound out there was the gravel driveway crunching under his feet. Had the lack of any bird or animal sounds tipped

Lil off to danger, or was that just normal for the area? He stopped in front of the garage, daring anyone who might be hiding inside to show themselves. He stood up on his tiptoes to get a look through the grimy windows running atop the door. From what little he could see, the interior was full of random construction detritus: old wood, broken doors, some metal hunks that might've belonged to a water heater or an oil tank. It reminded him of Doorknob's front yard.

With a deep breath, he continued onto the narrow path between the house and the garage. This, he realized with a spike of cold dread, would be an even better place to lay a trap. Avoiding an attack from above, coming down from either roof, would be impossible. He resisted the urge to look upward and quickened his pace.

The path took a sharp left toward a set of rickety steps leading up to the back deck. The thin, cracked treads creaked ominously as he ascended, and he didn't dare touch the ragged handrail. At the top, he turned to take in the scenery. A hundred yards farther behind the house, a gentle hill rose to hide the horizon. It would've been a great spot to sit and read or to take in the sunrise over a morning coffee, or gather for a few drinks with friends—if only the deck itself didn't feel like it might collapse at any moment.

A flap of screen hung from the storm door like a pair of half-unbuttoned overalls. The heavy fiberglass door behind it was windowless and locked up tight. Ren stopped to count the cedar shakes covering the back of the house as his father had taught him. Sixteen shingles up from the decking, then seven over to the right. He grabbed his target and roughly pulled it away from the wall, exposing a numeric keypad beneath. With a shaking finger, he punched in the secret code he'd given to his father: Kevin Felton's birthdate. The panel responded with a cheerful beep. Ren slipped inside, careful to prop the door open behind him using the deadbolt.

The door, however, wasn't having any of that. It beeped once in displeasure, then retracted the bolt and slammed shut. "God damn it, Ed," Ren muttered. He'd need to be there to let Lil and Muffintop inside.

In the meantime, he took a step forward into the surprisingly nice kitchen. The recessed lighting bloomed to life at the instructions of a hidden motion sensor. Stainless steel appliances glistened at him from nooks within the dark cabinetry. On the wall to Ren's left, an abstract painting that looked like someone had knocked over a few cans of black, gray, and silver proved beyond a shadow of a doubt that Ed Roberts had designed this kitchen. Ren knew he'd find salad forks and a special spoon for every occasion in the drawer to the right of the sink. His attention was drawn to the island in the center, however, and the care package set upon the attached breakfast bar: a bottle of California red, a bottle of Glenlivet, and a pretentiously textured envelope sealed with the family crest in black wax.

"Dad really did think of everything," Ren murmured as he strode toward his beloved liquor.

Across the kitchen, the double doors in the cabinet above the refrigerator burst open. Harsh blue light streamed out, bringing with it a feeling of intense, all-consuming cold. The arctic blast caught Ren square in the face before he could raise his arms in defense. He flinched backward and then collapsed onto his side, his arms reflexively wrapping around himself for warmth. He'd spent extra on a warm coat, God damn it, but whatever magical bullshit streaming out of the cabinet didn't care. His teeth chattered, and then everything became so cold that even his jaw refused to vibrate.

Behind him, someone knocked on the door. *Fuck,* his brain stammered as he curled into the fetal position. *Lil.*

"Oh!" said a friendly voice from down the hallway beside the refrigerator. "Hello there!"

The asshole that walked into the kitchen looked like he'd just stepped off of the kind of golf course that had only recently started admitting minorities after losing a long legal battle. A bleached smile stretched ear-to-ear across his plastic block of a face. A blue polo shirt and starched khakis told the world he had the money to dress well but not the time, because he had people to meet and things to do.

"It's Ren!" the asshole declared, spreading his arms and rocking on his heels like he was trying to show off for an impatient four-year-old. "Well, it sure is nice to finally meet you!"

All Ren could do in return was grunt. Fuck, it was so fucking cold. Lil banged on the door again, more insistent this time.

"My name's Brian Drew!" the asshole continued, punctuating the announcement with a quick whistle. "And now you know how fucking cold it gets in fucking Edmonton!"

— CHAPTER EIGHT —

I t took a few moments for his frostbitten brain to work things out, but Ren couldn't fucking believe he'd just been fucking ambushed by the guy his father had fucking banished to the ass end of fucking Canada for fucking whistling.

"I sold your father this place!" Brian said happily as he pulled Ren down the hallway toward the living room. "Or, more accurately, a subsidiary of a subsidiary of my shell company sold it to him! Gosh, I sure hated that prick!"

Ren's teeth chattered in response. He felt lucky that reflex had decided to start working again. None of his other muscles wanted to budge. The only parts of his body that felt any warmth were his ankles, where Brian's sweaty hands gripped them.

Brian, who was operating with quite the beer gut, stopped pulling and stood up straight for a moment to catch his breath. "You know, your father always knew I was better than him. Those first few years we were on the same team, I won all the big accounts. I sold soooooo many guns in Serbia! Provided samples of HIV for DARPA experiments! Hell, I even helped the Reinsehoffers set up their slave ring in the Hamptons! Ed...well, Ed was really good at going to get the rest of us coffee!"

"Mmmmnnnnmmmmmnnnmmm!" Ren responded, trying to simultaneously shout to the guy to fuck off and tell him that he sounded like a certain ruined former Pintiri.

Brian grabbed Ren's foot and started pulling again. "But your old man was a charmer, let me tell you! Really knew how to play the game!"

The hardwood under Ren's back gave way to a plush white carpet that grasped and clawed at his frosty coat. Brian leaned hard around the corner and heaved Ren into the living room proper with a gasp, grunt, and then a stiffening of his spine. For a moment, Ren thought maybe he'd caught a break, and the asshole had thrown out his back. No such luck. Another jerk slammed the side of Ren's shoulder into the thick leg of a metal coffee table.

Brian whistled again, a sound like a songbird in a blender. "One by one he turned the rest of our team against me. I'm still not really sure how he did it! I had no idea what was going on until the day the executive VP above our team handed me my transfer papers. Boy, was I surprised!" His demeanor suddenly shifted. "As I walked out of the office with a box of my things, no one even said goodbye. No one but Ed. And that was how *I knew.*"

He threw Ren's ankle down at the floor. The thick carpet and Ren's frigid nerves cushioned the impact, but it still fucking hurt. The sound of Lil's insistent knocking barely carried into the living room. Ren tried to straighten so he could claw his way back to the kitchen, but his arms refused to do anything other than shiver against his sides.

His worst nightmare had come to pass. He'd feared this moment for the last fifteen-ish years of his life, ever since he'd first learned the truth about his father's work. Finally outside of Ed's protection, one his rivals had leapt at the chance to claim Ren as his own.

I can't believe it's the whistler, Ren thought. *I really expected bathroom harassment guy.*

Brian touched something on the fireplace. The entire wall, beige paint and red brick and all, shimmered and disappeared, revealing a small holding cell with concrete walls and a drain in the far corner. Someone in jeans and a gray sweatshirt was already in there, sitting against the back wall with her legs pulled up against her chest and her head hanging between them. Strands of long black hair dangled out of the hood that obscured her face.

Somehow, of everything he'd encountered today, discovering a woman in his father's safehouse's holding cell struck him as the strangest. Why in the hell was she there? Had Brian brought her along as a hostage or slave or—he shivered—afternoon snack? Had he abducted her because she'd been snooping around the place? It didn't make sense.

The asshole knelt close to Ren's face. His black tongue snaked out of his mouth, and, with a row of crooked fangs in its tip, smiled at him, then extended out several feet to lick Ren's forehead. "Oh, I suppose the two of you haven't met!" Brian managed to say around that vile appendage, which Ren swore was staring him right in the eyes. "Isabel! Hello in there! This is Ren Roberts! Ren, meet Isabel Salinas Hernandez…your adopted sister!"

Before Ren's frigid lips could mangle an attempt to say "Oh what the fuck," Brian grabbed him by both ankles and whipped him into the holding cell. His skin tingled as he passed through the invisible magic barrier separating the two spaces.

Back in the living room, Brian leaned forward and put his hands on his knees. His horrible tongue shot back up into his mouth. "I know it *looks* like there's nothing keeping you in there, but I wouldn't advise getting too close to this ward. Ed Roberts really did pay for the best of the best in his safehouses." The knocking on the backdoor filled his momentary pause. "Please, get to know each other while I deal with whoever's trying to rescue you. We'll talk later!"

Something warm and reassuring wrapped itself around Ren's torso. Isabel. She'd swaddled him in her sweatshirt. "Come on," she said, "let's get you warmed up." She pulled him in between her legs, pressed his back to her chest, and wrapped her arms around him.

Ren's brain said, "Thank you." His mouth managed, "Th-th-th-th-th-th-ooooo." He decided that was a sign of improvement.

And then he thought *who the fuck is this woman, and why does she smell so damn nice?*

Brian left the faux wall open so they could see. He sat down in the middle of the big suede couch, fished a remote out from in between the cushions, and activated the big screen TV mounted on the wall opposite the holding cell. Another button press kicked the display over to a grid of security cameras arrayed both inside and outside the safehouse. Brian selected the camera overlooking the backdoor. Lil's angry face filled the screen. Beside her, Muffintop did a ragged version of the pee-pee dance.

"Well now," he mused to the microphone in the remote, "who's this knocking on my door?"

Lil froze mid-knock, her eyes suddenly searching for something—the speaker emitting Brian's voice, Ren realized after a dumb moment. "Elven special forces detachment 7A," she said smoothly, slipping into an official tone Ren hadn't heard before. "We're accompanying Mr. Roberts at the request of the Combined Council. You will allow us to enter, or we will do so by force."

"Elven special forces detachments work in groups of six," Brian said, like the kid in the front row of class who was too proud of his own ability to name the state capitals. "I see one of you, and...half of something else."

"Please let me in!" Muffintop wailed. "I really have to go!"

"Sorry son, but this establishment's restrooms are for paying customers only. Move along now."

"Awwwwww, nuggets!"

"Force it is, then," Lil replied. Her grip on Muffintop's hand tightened.

Brian chuckled. "Unless you're hiding a nuclear bomb somewhere in those tight jeans, you're not getting in here. Every exterior wall is built with eight inches of overlapping armor of various materials. There are no windows underneath that carefully positioned plywood. Any breach of the house's external shell will trigger the immediate deployment of internal security doors, each of which is also eight inches thick. This place is impregnable."

Lil replied with a confident smirk. Outside, metal shrieked as something heavy and dense was torn apart. Ren really hoped that was the garage door and not part of his car. A tremendous bang rattled the house as Lil's projectile slammed into its side. Ren perked up, hoping for something, *anything* to happen. He would've settled for another crash, or an alarm going off, or Brian getting his dad bod off the couch to investigate the damage.

Instead, Lil's smirk simply turned into a frown.

"There's plenty of junk in the garage if you want to throw it around," Brian said, "but all that'll accomplish is attracting the local law enforcement. Probably not something you want to deal with right about now."

The elf rolled her eyes. "Fine," she growled. "You can have the mouthy bastard. He's all yours."

Ren's heart sank as Lil spun on her heel and dragged a clearly distressed Muffintop away from the door. He couldn't believe it. Were they really going to just abandon him here like that, after Lil had the *nerve* to scold him for almost abandoning them?

Well, a dark corner of his brain said, *you were dumb enough to give her the spare key to your car and show her the secret compartment where you hid all your cash. That entire Ren Goes First plan was probably a set up. Idiot.*

Brian switched the active view onscreen to a camera above and slightly in front of the Jag. Lil stomped into the scene, opened the backdoor, and waved Muffintop inside. Rotreego's head popped up inside the vehicle, looking dazed and a bit annoyed. Lil opened the driver side door, slithered inside, and slammed it closed. The car purred to life as she fired up the ignition.

Ren closed his eyes, unable to watch them back down the driveway and leave him a prisoner.

— CHAPTER NINE —

We've got a lot to do, the three of us," Brian said, looming just outside the cell like a divorced father on an enforced visit. "I need to prepare a few things. Spend the time getting to know each other, won't you? It's not every day you meet a secret family member! Gosh, I just can't understand what Ed was thinking, keeping you apart!" He tapped a button on the remote, and a concrete wall replaced the view into the living room.

Ren let himself be manipulated. Yeah, just what *the fuck* had Ed been thinking? Why hadn't he told Ren about Isabel? Why the hell did he need an adoptive daughter anyway? What, was his biological son not good enough? Was the whole thing an outlet for his demonic side's desperate need to be a total piece of shit?

He wanted to swear, and to pound his fists on the ground, and maybe even cry, but he was still so fucking cold.

And then it clicked: Isabel Salinas Hernandez was a victim of the exact Tallisker bullshit he himself had been attempting to flee. If the other demonic assholes were stealing each other's family members just to fuck with their rivals, well, it stood to reason that Ed was doing that too. That motherfucker.

As his mind stormed down dark corridors, Isabel's finger traced repetitive shapes on his forearm. It took him a few angry minutes to realize those shapes were repeating—and that they formed capital letters.

HE CAN HEAR US

Clever, Ren thought. He swung his right hand down toward the floor and reached his fingers up into the bottom of her pant leg, finding the warm skin inside. He tapped her ankle twice, hoping that'd be taken as confirmation. His digits wouldn't move reliably enough to form coherent letters.

WE MUST TALK THO

"My name is Isabel Salinas Hernandez," she said, hitting all the accents in a way that proved she was a native Spanish speaker. "I am twenty-four years old. I'm the daughter of illegal Mexican immigrants who fled the cartels. I was born in the back of a coyote's van a mile into the United States. My mother did not survive childbirth."

CAN U GET US OUT?

Ren double tapped Isabel's ankle again. A few months ago, Ed had installed a smart home system in the safehouses that responded to voice commands following a set codeword. Getting out of the cell wasn't a problem; dealing with Brian, especially while battling hypothermia, was a different matter altogether. And they'd get one shot at this; if they failed, and Brian didn't kill them outright, stopping them from triggering the voice controls a second time wouldn't be particularly difficult.

But how the hell was he supposed to communicate all that? He double tapped Isabel anyway. Then he followed up with a quick single tap, another quick double tap, and a final single tap.

"We went to live with my great aunt's family in El Paso," Isabel continued. "My father, my older brother, and I all slept on old mattresses on the floor of their garage. The cousins obviously didn't want us there at all, but it was my aunt's property, so she was in charge."

SO MAYBE?

Close enough. Double tap. He stretched his legs and rolled his shoulders, testing his body. Though a chill remained, his range of motion was returning. If he could get back on his feet before Brian returned, maybe there was a chance. Then again, what hope did the two of them really have fighting hand-to-hand against a Tallisker demon? Brian's lamprey-like tongue was likely only the tip of his magic shitbag iceberg.

"Papa and my brother built houses with the cousins. Tia watched me during the day, raising me like I was her own. We didn't have much, but I was happy. I used to decorate my corner of the garage with flowers. Tia always hung my finger paintings on her big old refrigerator. The family taught me to read and write. Papa worried that if he sent me to school, we'd all get caught and sent back. There was no proof that I'd been born in the United States."

2NITE THEN

Tap tap. Their best shot at escape would be to avoid Brian entirely.

"Two days after my seventh birthday, someone lit Tia's house on fire. Everyone escaped, but the structure was a total loss. Papa and my brother and I moved into a shelter. I didn't understand why we couldn't stay in the garage, which hadn't been touched by the flames." Her voice turned sad and soft. "Sometimes I still wake up at night and think I smell smoke."

"S-s-s-s-s-sorry," Ren stammered, proud that he'd managed that much.

Isabel squeezed his arm gently. "It's okay. We think it was one of the local gangs. My cousins liked to bet on the soccer games. They weren't very good at it.

"The shelter is where immigration finally found us. I remember the little room they put us in, how it smelled like disinfectant. We had bunk beds and a table with chairs and a TV in the corner. To my seven-year-old self, this wasn't any worse than the garage— except we couldn't leave, and it needed more flowers. We were there for three days. Papa cried himself to sleep every night. My brother watched television and didn't say a word. Even I knew what was going to happen next: we would have to go back.

"When the lawyer arrived, Papa couldn't believe it. At first I thought he was going to refuse to go with the man. I couldn't blame him. I'd only ever seen people dressed like that on TV. I didn't believe she was real. I remember she caught me staring at the ring on her finger, this big hunk of perfectly smooth jade. She bent down beside me and let me touch it. I think that's when Papa decided to trust her."

Ren thought he knew that particular ring, and the tough as nails lawyer it belonged to: Joanie Lawrence, his father's favorite fixer. She'd visited the house a few times.

"We were released that afternoon. The lawyer took us with her in her limousine. I'd never been in such a fancy car. The ride wasn't long. Papa looked at me just once, then crossed himself and closed his eyes. When we arrived at the hotel, Papa and my brother got out. The lawyer made me stay. I watched out the rear window, bawling my eyes out, as the limousine pulled away and the men of my family walked into that hotel.

"I met Ed Roberts for the first time two days later. The lawyer's people bathed me, tied bows in my hair, put me in a pretty pink dress, and left me sitting alone in a comfortable room overlooking a lake. You know the first thing your father ever said to me? 'Christ, who put her in those stupid bows.'"

Ren laughed, a sound like gargling with gravel. "That's Ed," he muttered.

"Ha. Yeah. But then he knelt beside me and he smiled. 'Stick with me, kid, and you'll never want for anything ever again,' he said. I told him that if he didn't give me back my family, I was going to punch him in the nose. He told me I was about to meet more family than I'd ever imagined." She hesitated. "Turns out I wasn't the only child your father bought."

Ren's brain turned itself inside out trying to comprehend all of this. He'd always known that his father was into some shadowy things, but this...this was something else. He had so many questions, none of which he had the facilities to ask at the moment.

"Ed knew he was in trouble," Isabel continued, "but he did not tell me why. His last instructions were that if anything happened to him, I should find you and make sure that you were safe. I came here yesterday after discovering your home in Harksburg empty. I've always wanted to meet you. This is not how I'd hoped it would happen."

Just as Isabel inhaled in preparation to continue her story, the illusive wall separating their cell from the living room disappeared.

— CHAPTER TEN —

Me again!" Brian announced with a reptilian smile. In his left hand, he held a stubby automatic weapon with a giant banana clip. In his right...he carried a cheese grater.

Isabel tensed and pulled Ren closer. "I missed you," Ren croaked.

"I knew you would! Glad your tongue is defrosting." He wiggled the barrel of his gun. "I trust you can roll, crawl, or otherwise make your way into that corner, away from your sister?"

Ren hesitated. "Do it," Isabel whispered, gently pushing him forward. "We'll get through whatever this is."

He rolled sideways and onto his hands and knees. The awkward crawl to the corner made him feel like a beached fish flopping toward water, but he made it. Rather than prop himself up, he lay on his side with his back against the wall. Moving gave him his first good look at Isabel's face. He recoiled in surprise at the leather patch covering her right eye. Dark black veins radiated out from underneath as if a corruption was spreading to the rest of her face from that diseased socket. Without the baggy sweatshirt concealing her body, Ren realized she was totally jacked. Isabel would've looked right at home in an MMA ring.

She caught him staring and seemed to cringe inward on herself, enough so that a strand of her long black hair swung protectively over the unhealthy eye. "Nice to put a face to the n-n-n-name," he said. The side of her mouth ticked upward in response.

"So here's what's going to happen," Brian said slowly, like he didn't think Ren and Isabel could understand him. "I'm going to take Ed Roberts's beloved firstborn under my wing and escort him into the life of decadent villainy Ed worked so hard to shield him from, and I am going to enjoy every second of it. Consider today... your orientation!"

Across the cell, Isabel sighed dramatically.

"This weapon is loaded with crowd suppression rounds. One burst *probably* won't kill you, but these rubber bullets sting like a *bastard*. One of them might even break a bone or put out an eye." He glanced viciously at Isabel, then back to Ren. "And if I have to use them, I will be *very* unhappy. I might even come back with live ammo the next time!"

Ren had seen videos online of what those rounds could do to someone. At such a close range, in an enclosed space conducive to ricochets...he didn't want to think about it.

"Isabel, I'm going to need you to lie face down in the center of the cell."

She glared hot daggers at him until he motioned with the barrel of his gun, then she uncurled forward into a prone position, her arms wrapped underneath her face. Ren hadn't realized just how tall she was.

"Thank you," Brian replied. "Please maintain that position until instructed otherwise."

Then he underhanded the cheese grater toward Ren. It bounced of the wall and then landed near his knees with a pair of metallic clanks.

"This isn't an official Tallisker orientation center, so we'll have to get a little creative," Brian mused. "Ahhh, I still remember my orientation like it was yesterday! I'd slogged away in the mail room for *six years* before finally landing a sales position upstairs. Me and all that month's other new hires were taken on a retreat to a Tallisker camp in the Catskills. Nice place, if you like it rustic. I'll take you sometime. *Anyway,* after a morning of ice breakers and grab ass, each of us met solo with HR for our official onboarding. There was some paperwork, of course, tax forms and proof of citizenship and all that, but then…then there was our first real test.

"How bad did I want to work for Tallisker? More than anything in the world, I said. I'd spent plenty of time around the muckymucks working up on the thirtieth floor. I'd seen the suits they wore, the watches on their wrists, the cars they drove, the smokin' wives on their arms. I wanted it more than anything.

"So they trotted in this orphan from some godforsaken third world country, and the HR lady pulled a hammer out of her desk drawer. And when she told me to break one of his fingers…I didn't hesitate. God, I still remember that *crunch,* and the way he shrieked and recoiled in pain, looking up at me like I was the worst monster in the world." He nodded and grinned, clearly pleased with the deep fatherly wisdom he was about to impart. "You never forget your first, you know!"

Ren's gaze darted from the cheese grater to his sister. *Oh fuck.*

"It escalated quickly from there, of course. In our next session, I pulled out all of his toenails with a pair of pliers. I sliced up the soles of his feet with a scalpel. They gave me a custom-made brand so I could burn my name into his cheek. Twice a day, every day, for the two weeks of orientation, I learned how *awesome* it is to have that kind of power over another human being." His snakelike tongue darted out of his mouth as if to say hello. "Started sprouting this baby four days in. HR was impressed. Usually the physical changes don't happen until a month or two after!"

"I could've taken my orphan home with me. I broke his legs and left him in the woods." He shook his head and rolled his eyes skyward. "Gosh, I wonder whatever happened to him!"

Bile rose in Ren's throat. He fought it back down, unwilling to give Brian the satisfaction.

"Hey! Did your old man ever talk about his orientation? Hmmm, judging by that pasty tone you've taken on, I'd guess not. Oh! You should ask your sister about hers! I mean, how the hell do you *think* her face got like that? Maybe ask her how many people she killed for your father while you're at it!"

What. The. Fuck. Ren pinched the skin above his elbow, desperately praying that doing so would cause him to wake up in his bed back home. He'd always known his father was no angel, but he couldn't force his mind to picture Ed participating in the sort of acts Brian was describing. His father must've hurt people at some point, though, or he never would've become a powerful enough demon to rise through the ranks at Tallisker. And Isabel...well, shit, Ren had just started to like her, and even to feel bad for her. Now he wasn't sure what to think, and he felt kind of dumb for not realizing what her appearance implied.

"I don't know *what* kind of safehouse *doesn't* have a *toolbox*, so we'll have to get creative with the kitchen implements!" Brian declared. "We'll start simple. Let's see what that cheese grater does to the skin on Isabel's back."

Again Ren's gaze traced the foot of space between the kitchen implement and his sister. "F-f-fuck you," he replied.

Brian extended his free hand as if offering a lifeline. "Ren. Buddy. Come on. You just met this woman twenty minutes ago! Hell, your father *bought her* when she was a little girl! She's nothing! What's the harm in giving her a little flesh wound?"

The harm, he knew, was Brian's attempt to make him normalize violence. Ed had warned him about that more than once. "Humans don't turn demonic without putting in the work," he remembered his father saying. "It takes some momentum, but once you get going..."

"No," Ren said. "I won't."

"There are twenty-four rounds in this clip," Brian said with another shake of the gun. "I've got four more if I need them. One swipe across her back and I leave you in peace for the rest of the day. I promise."

Ren knew what that promise was worth, and he didn't doubt that Brian would follow through on his threats. Still, he had never intentionally hurt anyone before, and he didn't want to start now.

"Do it," Isabel said. "Please." She reached out with her right hand and nudged the grater toward Ren.

Realization dawned. *She has a plan. She wants me to make it look like I'm playing along, and then she's going to tell me to drop the containment field so she can surprise the bastard.* A demon's physical deformities often came with magic abilities. Isabel had just been waiting for the right moment to spring, and she'd found it.

He pretended to mull it over some more, and then he reached out and snatched up the cheese grater by its handle. The ease with which he lifted it surprised him, both because he didn't entirely trust his muscles yet and because he expected anything used as a torture device to have more weight to it. The grating slots along each of its four sides looked sharp and unused.

"See?" Brian said. "There's nothing to it!"

Ren crawled toward Isabel slowly, dragging the grater with him. If she had a plan, she wasn't yet ready to show him her hand. He tried willing her into motion, silently pleading through whatever fragile step-sibling connection they might have for her to *do something*. She didn't. Maybe the time wasn't right? Maybe she needed him to be closer? Perhaps her magic worked like Lil's, by channeling energy from another person—but if that was the case, she could've done something earlier when they were pressed up close together.

Isabel finally moved when Ren arrived at her side. She reached back, collected her long hair, and pulled it over her shoulder, exposing the brown skin of her neck and upper back that her tank top didn't cover. "It's okay," she whispered. "We'll get through this."

Maybe she's really trying to lull Brian into a false sense of security, Ren thought. *Maybe touching the grater to her back will charge it up somehow so I can throw it like a grenade. Maybe her skin's actually made of diamond. Maybe her flesh will absorb the metal and reforge it into a bullet she can launch through her bad eye. Maybe her blood has been replaced with a hive of ravenous insects that'll spill out and eat Brian alive.*

He positioned the grater on Isabel's back, just to the right of her spine. Nothing happened.

"Uh-uh!" Brian chirped. "Flip it over and use the rougher side. I'm going easy on you for now, but not *that* easy!"

Ren did as instructed. The grater suddenly felt heavy in his hand, like a brick. For a moment he hoped that was Isabel's demon powers kicking in, but when he lifted it a little to test it, all that emotional weight melted away. Damn it.

"Attaboy," Brian said. "Just one swipe. Two inches, maybe three. No big deal."

Terror gripped Ren's throat. This was so, so fucked up.

Brian swung his gun forward and gripped the front of the stock with his previously free hand, steadying his aim.

"It's okay," Isabel whispered. "I'll live."

Did that make it right? Was doing something harmful to someone who'd given their explicit approval really evil? Was it the effect on the victim, the basic action itself, or the intent of the attacker that mattered? Ren didn't know. Brian's silence seemed to suggest that Isabel's consent didn't directly contradict his plans.

"These bullets are going to really hurt," Brian said, his voice oozing. "If I have to pull the trigger, she gets the next turn with that grater—and she won't hesitate, no matter which part of your body I tell her to use it on."

"Damn right, I won't," Isabel replied immediately.

Fine. Ren dragged the grater sideways across his adopted sister's right shoulder blade. Isabel stiffened and hissed in pain. Blood welled up through the gashes in her shredded skin, pooling underneath the metal grater. Ren lifted it away and chucked it forward, his stomach roiling at the sight of the meat the device had exposed. That *he'd* exposed. The grater bounced across the floor and into the containment field. Sparks flew as the magic sent a burst of electricity coursing through it. The grater bounced back toward them, blackened and broken.

"Oh, you did so *well!*" Brian crowed. "Ed would be proud. Really, he would."

Isabel turned back toward him briefly, her teeth gritted and tears running down her cheek. The pain etched on her face struck Ren like a slap. The act had been vile enough; the repercussions were something else entirely, even though she'd encouraged him to do it.

Unable to look at what he'd done, Ren fell backward and scrabbled into the back corner. Tears streamed down his face as he curled into a ball and shook. Was the threat of violence really enough to make him violent himself? Was that okay? He'd never faced anything like this in his easy life, and he couldn't process it.

A warm presence wrapped itself around him. Isabel again. "It's for the best," she whispered. "You protected us from worse—just as I would have." He couldn't process that either, so he gave up trying and lost himself in bawling his eyes out.

— CHAPTER ELEVEN —

Brian left the cell wall open this time.

"Maybe tomorrow we'll try a potato peeler," he mused as he took a bite of leftover pizza from the box on the coffee table and washed it down with a swig of Glenlivet straight from the bottle that had been left in the welcome basket. He'd kicked off his boat shoes and planted his fat ass on the couch, the gun propped up beside him. "Back of her leg, I think. We'll get you looking her in the eye next week. Not quite sure you're ready for that kind of pressure yet."

Ren wasn't sure how long it had been, but at least he'd stopped crying and shaking. His muscles felt more useful, too, although his right leg had fallen asleep underneath his left. He couldn't make himself care, and he really didn't want to open his eyes.

Isabel hadn't let go. She'd been right there beside him the whole time, her arm wrapped around him protectively. She hadn't said a word. He still couldn't understand it.

"Let me go," he whispered.

"No way," she replied.

Her sweatshirt still smelled nice, he noticed, although he couldn't believe *that* was what his stupid subconscious had chosen to key in on.

"I think we'll save the corkscrew for week three," Brian said in between mouthfuls. "That one takes some effort, but trust me when I say it's worth it!"

The television beeped and came to life. "Well, shit," their captor growled. "Look who's back!"

Isabel rubbed his shoulder. "You'll want to see this."

Ren tentatively opened his eyes into a squint, then they burst open when he realized what he was seeing. On screen, Ren's Jaguar rumbled into the driveway, sporting a broken left headlight, a dinged-up grill, and a trio of scratches down the side panel that made it look like it'd lost a fight with a wolverine. Somehow, the sight of his beloved vehicle in that condition pissed him off more than anything else that had happened that day.

The driver side door opened and Rotreego tumbled out onto the gravel. He lurched to his knees, dusted off his bathrobe, and then leaned back heavily against the car. "Attention enemies of America!" the elf said with his trademark snarl. "I know you're here! I know who you are! I know what you want! And I will... not...stand for it!"

"Jesus Christ," Brian said with a chuckle. "What the hell is up with this poor bastard?"

"United we shall stand!" Rotreego continued. "Dividing is for pussies and communists! It doesn't matter how much birth control you sneak into the water supply, or how many psychotropic chemicals your jets unleash in the skies above our beautiful land! We—"

Brian picked up the remote and pressed the mute button. "You've got some *weird* friends, kid." On screen, Rotreego continued to ramble silently, occasionally accenting his words with a pair of middle fingers pumping up and down like stuttering pistons.

There was no sign of Lil or Muffintop. Rotreego returning alone seemed unlikely—which meant his little show was a distraction, and one that Brian had unfortunately dismissed. Isabel squeezed

Ren's arm as if to say *do something*. "That's the Pintiri," Ren croaked. "Well, former."

Their captor froze just as he was about to take another bite. His tongue oozed out into the room and curled around as if it wanted to get a look at the screen. "No shit?" Brian mumbled around the appendage, slowly lowering what was left of his slice and placing it back in the box. "What's his name, then?"

"Rotreego. He used to have a flaming sword." Ren had no idea why Brian seemed so interested in this, but he wasn't going to pass up what seemed like an opportunity.

Brian cocked his head. "That he did. That he did."

"Harksburg's reaper was...out of commission for a bit. That's when it happened. Rotreego was murdered. His magic went away...and he came back from the dead."

He turned to study the screen, stroking his chin. "You don't say."

"The troll did something to his brain," Ren continued. "Rotreego's trying to hide something, I think. I'm surprised he came on his own. He's...not really in great shape right now."

Brian's chin stroking stopped and became a vise grip on his jaw. "I know this is a trick," he said. Ren's heart sank. "But I also know a lot of people who would *love* to get their hands on a former Pintiri. Looks like you two are getting a new roommate."

As the asshole stood, the air in the room changed. A noxious smell streamed out of the safehouse's HVAC system. Brian hesitated, his eyes narrowing as he took a few sniffs and tried to identify the aroma. It reminded Ren of rancid eggs that had been left out in the sun for three days, mixed with a pile of garbage, and then finished with a dash of fresh manure.

And then an overpowering wave of the stench rushed in through the vents. Brian doubled over, gagging and coughing. Ren covered his nose and mouth with his hand, but human flesh was no match for that horrible smell. His stomach twisted and bile rose in his throat. He tried to push Isabel away so he wouldn't vomit all over her if it came to that, but she held fast and leaned in even closer.

"Now," she whispered.

Now what? he wondered momentarily. Then he noticed that the stench didn't seem to be affecting her, and he knew exactly what she wanted.

"T-t-t-talora," he gasped, the rest of his command to the smart home system cut off with a gagging cough as his lungs fought back against whatever bullshit he'd just inhaled.

Isabel frowned in confusion. "*Talora?* There's a Talora here?" Ren had no clue what the hell she was talking about. Had Ed also given her the codeword for the safehouse's systems? He must have. But then why hadn't she used it earlier?

Out in the living room, Brian collapsed to one knee and puked all over the floor.

"Talora," Isabel said, pushing herself to her feet like a predator preparing to strike, "open the holding cell."

"Acknowledged," a hidden speaker in the living room replied.

Isabel darted forward, scooping up the blackened cheese grater and whipping it into the living room. It passed cleanly across the threshold—proving the invisible ward had been deactivated—and clanged off the side of Brian's square head. She was on top of him before he could look up, pinning him to the carpet with her hands around his throat. She reached up to her face and slid the leather patch away from her eye. Ren could barely see what was underneath; he swore he saw dark tendrils of ghostly energy snapping and writhing from the side of her face, reaching out for Brian.

"Oh," the asshole said, "oh fuck."

Brian's body went rigid, and then began to quiver, like he'd just been shocked. Isabel stared intently down at him; the energy emanating from her ruined eye strained hungrily toward her victim's face. An animalistic wail tore up and outward from Brian's lungs. It was the most terrifying sound Ren had ever heard.

He knew, beyond a shadow of a doubt, that Brian was in soul crushing pain.

The wail suddenly died. So did Brian. His skull popped, spattering the living room with brains, blood, and bone. Ren wanted to look away but just retched all over the floor instead.

Isabel, stained crimson with Brian's insides, slid her eyepatch back into place before she turned to Ren. "I'm sorry you had to see that."

"I-i-i-it's okay," he managed, scared as shit and still unable to breathe. "Can we go outside now?"

— CHAPTER TWELVE —

L et me get this straight," Ren said, leaning heavily on the breakfast bar. "You drove to the nearest gas station and offered people ten grand to come back here with you until some delivery driver accepted. Then you gave Rotreego my fucking car and told him to create a distraction. While he did his thing, you siphoned energy from the delivery driver to telekinetically lift Muffintop up onto the safehouse's roof, where he went number three in the air intake of the HVAC system."

Lil finished the last bite of her slice of Brian's leftover pizza and then wiped a speck of sauce off her chin. "Yup."

Ren blinked and shifted away. "And how do you think your former colleagues in elven intelligence would grade this plan?"

"B-plus," she replied. "Would've been an A, but I didn't have any dust for wiping the delivery driver's memory."

From the corner of the kitchen, Rotreego snorted. Rather than sit at the breakfast bar and eat his pizza like a normal person, he'd plopped down on the floor in the corner and proceeded to slowly lick the cheese and sauce off the dough. His face was covered in muck, but he seemed to be enjoying himself. He wore an empty roll of duct tape on his wrist like a bracelet. Lil had used all the tape to seal up the cabinet containing the frost ward, just in case.

"I almost couldn't hold it!" Muffintop crowed from his seat to Ren's left. He'd inhaled his own slice in one gulp without bothering to chew.

"Well, Isabel and I are glad you did, and I must personally thank you for not letting whatever that was go in my car." He turned his attention back to Lil. "Seriously though, next time you have to choose between my life and not dinging up my ride, please prioritize the Jag."

"Noted. You're sure this woman is your sister?"

After a round of brief introductions and a few minutes to let the safehouse air out, Isabel had disappeared to the upstairs bathroom to wash the Brian out of her hair. Ren still wore her sweatshirt, and it still smelled amazing. "No, but she seems to know at least as much about Ed as you do."

He still hadn't fully come to terms with all the new things he'd learned about his father's affairs. Part of him was glad Ed had shielded him from the stranger parts of his life. Part of him felt betrayed and wished he'd just gone to Talvayne with his mother. Yet another part of him hoped whatever was left to be discovered would knock on the safehouse door right then and there to get the big reveal over and done with.

"If you ever get to see the shit I've seen," he remembered Ed telling him one night, "you'll start to wonder just how in the hell any of this works."

At the time, Ren had taken that in in broader terms, as an indictment of society and all the horrible systems competing to get as big a bite of it as they possibly could. But maybe, he thought there in the safehouse kitchen, staring down at the bubbles in his glass of soda, maybe Ed had been referring to their posh, safe, comfortable family situation. How could Ren's easy, pleasant existence have been built on the back of so much horror? In a way, he felt like the whole thing had been a big, blatant lie.

"You look like you need to go number three!" Muffintop said, snapping him out of it.

"Nah, just thinking. Hey, anybody know what a Talora is?"

Lil and the troll both shook their heads. In the corner, Rotreego perked up. "Talora's a state-of-the-art artificial intelligence designed and deployed by the Bildebergers to monitor and control the population."

Ren frowned. "That...sounds oddly plausible."

"It's close, although I am not sure about that last part," Isabel said as she stepped into the kitchen. Her wet hair hung heavily down onto her shoulders, and she wore a fuzzy blue robe that wasn't all that different from the former Pintiri's. "Talora is a Tallisker project focused on building a type of smart assistant. Ed seemed to think it was important. He asked me to start keeping an ear out for any mention of it around this time last year, and he mentioned it again during our last communication."

"Do you think it's important enough that someone might've killed him over it?" Lil asked. Ren was glad she had; his mind had spun off in the same direction, but he couldn't make his mouth form the right words.

Isabel pursed her lips. "I cannot say for sure. I got the impression that it is not a widely known project within the organization. He warned me never to mention or ask about it directly, only to listen and report back. I never heard that word from any lips but his."

"And you think there's one controlling this safehouse?"

She nodded. "I do. Talora, dim the lights in the kitchen."

"Acknowledged," a hidden speaker replied as the ceiling lights dropped in intensity.

"Ed could've made that the codeword in any old smart home system, but that'd be a heck of a coincidence," Ren said.

"Talora!" Muffintop chirped. "Bring me chicken tenders with honey mustard!"

"I'm sorry, that is not within my functions."

"Awwww, cockroaches!"

"Where do you think..." Ren caught his question to Isabel, realizing there was an easier way to get an answer. "Talora, where did Ed connect you to the rest of the house?"

"There is a control room in the basement."

"Then that's our next stop," he said, "but first—Isabel, let Lil look at your back." He tapped his finger on the plastic shell of the first aid kit they'd found under the kitchen sink.

"I'm fine," Isabel replied, pulling the robe around herself even tighter. "Really."

"None of that," Lil snapped as she pushed her stool back and slid to her feet. "Turn around and let me have a look at whatever it is Ren's been so worried about."

Isabel blinked a few times as if she didn't understand, then acquiesced. She turned away from the others and loosened the sash of her robe. Lil pulled it down to get a look at her injury.

"How the fuck did that happen?"

"I did it," Ren said sadly, his eyes glued to the granite countertop between his elbows. "Brian wanted to turn me."

Lil stomped back across the kitchen and slammed the first aid kit open, looming over Ren in judgment. "*You* did that?"

He tried to make himself small. "She said it was okay."

Lil slapped him in the back of the head so hard even Rotreego flinched. "Don't hurt your sister, asshole."

"I'm sorry!" Ren shouted desperately. "I didn't mean it!" He looked to Muffintop for relief, but the little troll just shook his head.

"You've betrayed everything good about this great nation," Rotreego grumbled.

"Oh, don't you start!"

Although Ren hadn't thought he could possibly feel any worse about what he'd done, the judgment of these three people who'd been strangers to him less than forty-eight hours ago somehow kicked his guilt into overdrive. He really hadn't meant it. He'd been caught up in the moment, weakened by the frost spell and Brian's manipulation, and deathly petrified of what a hail of rubber bullets might've done to both of them in that cramped space—and the knowledge that Isabel was prepared to act if he hadn't. Why had that been the thing that had spurred him into action? Had it been the prospect of serious injury, or the fear of what it would be like to experience such a thing at his sister's willing hands?

The simplest answer was that he'd been a coward. The other possibilities would require further thought of the sort he tended to delay as long as possible.

They sat in silence as Lil patched Isabel up. She covered the wound with an antiseptic salve, then secured a strip of gauze over the top with a few strips of medical tape. Isabel stood like a statue through it all, oblivious to both the others in the room and her own existence. Rotreego somehow managed to get even more pizza on his face. Muffintop had produced his scrapbook from God knew where and slowly paged through it. Ren watched over his shoulder, curious but hoping not to draw attention to himself. The beat-up tome was overflowing with ticket stubs and photos of a smiling Muffintop at all the country's biggest music festivals.

Exhaustion quickly set Ren to leaning back on his stool with his eyes closed. *What in the fuck is going on here?*

"There," Lil finally said, hoisting the back of Isabel's robe up over her shoulders. "That'll do it."

"Thank you," Isabel replied, clearly embarrassed.

"Yeah," Ren added, "thanks."

The elf rolled her eyes. "Rot, let's find this fucking Talora thing and everything else we need and get a fucking move on."

Nobody wanted to argue with that.

Access to the basement was through a door in the front mudroom, which meant crossing through the living room first. What was left of Brian remained right there on the floor where his head had exploded. Crimson stains streaked the walls, curtains, and furniture, and the carpet underneath him looked like someone had dumped a whole gallon of red paint. The bottle of Glenlivet stood forlornly on the coffee table, barely used but ruined forever by Brian's vile mouth and a coating of ichor. As they entered the room, a little strand of brains that had been clinging to the television lost its grip and plopped to the floor.

Muffintop licked his lips. "Can I—"

"No," Lil snapped. "Whatever you were about to ask, you can't, and you need to keep it to yourself."

"Oh. Okay."

"The enemies of America get what they deserve," Rotreego muttered as he stepped over the corpse.

Beside Ren, Isabel shivered. He felt his arm swinging up toward her reflexively and jerked it back down. They weren't there yet, and he wasn't sure if they ever would be.

The basement door waited, sturdy and solid, beside an empty shoe rack and a row of empty coat hooks screwed into the drywall. The knob stuck a bit, but the door gave easily after Lil fiddled with it. Beyond, the stairway was steep and narrow, the creaking treads covered with cheap pink carpet. Ren brought up the rear, watching the others descend. The thin handrail wouldn't have been much help if someone took a tumble.

"Looks like a basement," Lil said as they gathered at the bottom. She wasn't wrong; the concrete floor, roughly plastered walls, and occasional red support post definitely denoted a basement. Ren found it a bit eerie. There was so much room for stuff down there, and yet it was empty. He swore he could hear their breathing echo.

"This is boring!" Muffintop said, his words bouncing around in that void.

"Talora, can you direct us toward the…uh…control center?" Ren asked.

"Acknowledged."

A section of the wall far to their right shimmered and disappeared, exposing a dark hallway. Ren didn't know much about construction, but that should've been a part of the safehouse's foundation. A mechanism somewhere in the corridor clicked and activated a soft light somewhere deeper in.

Though the group moved forward mostly as one, Lil stood in place and raised her hand to indicate a stop. "Talora, are you going to kill us?"

"If I were, I wouldn't tell you."

Not missing a beat, Ren strode past the others. "At least it's honest," he muttered.

"That's what you think," the hidden speakers said

Ren somehow managed not to stumble.

The corridor replicated the basement space with less elbow room. Above, a wire cable rack hanging from the ceiling carried a thick bundle of data cables connecting the house with whatever command center they were approaching. Lighting came from narrow tubes embedded in the concrete walls. They proceeded single-file, leaving—Ren noticed when he looked back over his shoulder—enough space between them to create the illusion that at least some of them could escape if the artificial intelligence in charge decided to cause a scene. He swallowed down his fear and continued on.

Ed built this, he thought. *At the very least, I should be safe.* That guilt he'd recently come to hate welled up in his throat, hot and acidic. Not worrying about the safety of people he considered companions and potentially friends felt like an exotic luxury. Like seriously, he'd never worried that turrets would suddenly descend from the ceiling to vaporize Kevin Felton.

Ren tapped Rotreego on the shoulder. "Obviously we're walking into a secret DARPA installation for harnessing signals in the magnetosphere that can trigger earthquakes and redirect hurricanes."

The elf glanced back with a lopsided smile. "Or a nuke-proof bunker in which the super-rich can weather the apocalypse while securing their wealth and propagating their bloodlines."

That one hit a little close to home. The family's finances had always been a bit of a mystery. Ren knew they were fucking loaded, but he'd never really thought about what it meant to be the kind of fucking loaded that could afford to purchase and supply half a dozen safehouses. He sure didn't feel like a member of the global elite. No one had ever given him a certificate or a membership card or anything.

Thick steel doors at the far end of the corridor swung open as they approached, granting access to the cavernous room beyond. "Welcome, Ren Roberts," Talora said as they stepped through. "I've been expecting you."

"Pleasure to be here," he mumbled as he took it all in.

Several dozen high-definition screens covered the wall across from the entrance, each displaying a live feed from a different camera inside or outside of the house. To their left, a semi-circular sofa surrounded a coffee table and an entertainment center to form a makeshift living room. To their right, a series of eight open doors led to bedrooms, a bathroom, and what appeared to be a storage area. A kitchenette with a range, microwave, and full-size refrigerator filled the back corner.

"Talora," Lil said as she drifted toward the back of the couch, "why were you expecting Ren?"

"Ed said I should. He left a message. Would you like to hear it?"

"Yes," Lil replied instantly.

"I'm sorry, I can only play the message with Ren's permission."

Which made sense for security reasons, he supposed, but also suggested that Ed may have left behind something personal. He hated personal shit, especially when it was done in front of other people—but in this case, he supposed he owed the others a chance to listen in. Each of them had worked to save his life in his or her own way.

"Talora, please play my father's message."

"Acknowledged."

The wall of screens went dramatically dark and then flared back to life, combining to form a giant display of Ed's face. He'd been blessed with the bright eyes, straight nose, and rosy cheeks of a beloved local newscaster, but from that angle his hairline didn't appear to be receding so much as it was beating a desperate retreat. The salt and pepper at his temples betrayed a lapse in his color treatments. The collar of his favorite pink polo shirt barely poked up from the bottom of the screen. Ren wasn't sure he could precisely identify the off-white wall behind his father, but he was pretty sure it belonged to the study at their home in Harksburg.

"Ellen, Ren...if you're watching this, I'm dead," Ed said flatly. "If you're watching this and I'm not dead, cut the shit and go home."

Lil and Isabel snorted in eerie synchronicity. Ren already regretted doing this with an audience.

Ed's nostrils flared as he inhaled and steadied himself. "You know I don't want you anywhere near my work and its bullshit. Unfortunately, I think it likely my enemies will assume you know what I know and take action above and beyond the usual. It's unlikely that my safehouses will remain secure for long. If you stay in one place, they will find you. If you run for it, they will catch you. Your only chance is to take the fight to them."

"Thanks, Dad," Ren said melodramatically. "Never would've figured that out on my own."

Ed's message continued. "This is all about the device replaying my message: Talora. I managed to scrounge up enough of the devices to put one in the three safehouses closest to home. You will only need a single Talora. Attempting to recover the other two would be a stupid risk.

"Tallisker—as I have told you many times but will repeat again because I know Ren can be a little thickheaded sometimes—is not the monolith it presents itself to be. The company is subject to the same politics, infighting, and bullshit social gamesmanship as any other major American corporation, with that extra special something that comes from employing several thousand evil demons constantly attempting to satisfy their base urges while simultaneously battling each other for position within the corporate hierarchy. Tallisker consists of many groups, official and unofficial, and those groups always have their own secret projects they're working on for their own gain.

"Three years ago, my boss, Marafuji, instructed me to infiltrate and report on one of those projects. I'm sure by now you can guess which one. Talora is a state-of-the-art artificial intelligence powered by some old magic crap nobody really seems to understand. You can hook it up to Wi-Fi to keep up appearances, but each Talora is linked to every other Talora through a network not unlike the one that links the transport stones Evitankari and others use to teleport all over the damn place. This allows for instantaneous, unstoppable transmission of information to and from each unit. The eggheads also rigged it up so it functions as a smart assistant through which its owners can play music, buy groceries, call Grandma, the whole nine yards—which makes it marketable, and makes it something every idiot human will want to put in their kitchen.

"The utility of this thing is absurd. Picture a world where there's a Talora in every home, and remember that the information flows both ways. Tallisker now knows everything about everyone, and there's no stopping its propaganda from reaching the public. You think the subliminal messaging on the TV is bad, just wait 'til they're using this fucking thing." Ed then paused for dramatic effect.

All the usual Orwellian fears bubbled up through Ren's mind. Regular humans, he knew, would abuse the shit out of such a system; how far would beings driven by insatiable evil be willing to take it?

"They're looking to minimize their reliance on Evitankari," Lil mused. Ren suspected she was right. If Tallisker could control the entire narrative, and use the things it learned through Talora as blackmail, well…why bother with the dust?

Ed continued. "Some of us within Tallisker believe that's going too far. We've survived as long as we have by being pragmatic and by not over-extending our reach. It is in our very nature to want more than our fair share, but the entire damn organization was founded as a check on those impulses. We've got a good thing going here, and it's in everyone's best interest that we don't fuck with it. The system we have works just fine."

This was not the first time Ren had heard his father express such sentiments. He'd always described Tallisker as a necessary evil, a dam holding back a flood. Ren himself wasn't sure how accurate that really was.

"The really fucked up thing is that these devices are intended for use by Tallisker employees as well as the general public. The company typically communicates confidential information with its staff and network of agents using a series of numbers stations. Listen to this."

Ed fiddled with something off-screen, and then a woman's monotone voice began reading a series of numbers in an eerily even cadence. "Twenty-seven. Nineteen. Five. Thirty-three. Twenty-seven. Two. Twelve. Ninety-sev—" Relief washed over Ren when his father silenced the voice. Something about it just gave him the creeps.

"Numbers stations!" Rotreego crowed, like he'd suddenly been proven right about something and needed to lord it over the others. "Haaaaaaaaa!"

"These strings of seemingly random numbers are broadcast over known radio frequencies and can be decoded using one-time use cyphers. The team behind Talora is embedding the usual feeds into the device as an additional selling point for upper management. Broadcasting through our own magical network rather than over traditional radio technology makes the whole thing even more secure than it already is. Thing is…there are new codes using a cypher I don't have, prefaced with a different introductory header. Like this."

Ed fiddled again. This time, the voice belonged to a squeaky man instead of a woman. "Attention. Attention. The bodies in the lake cannot hide their secrets from grasping roots. Attention. Attention. Eighteen. Seven. Fifteen. Fifteen. Eight-f—"

"I believe the conspirators are using these streams to pass their own messages through the Talora network. I never found a way to crack it. If you can…well, now you've got a bargain to make with Marafuji. Bring that bastard something important to trade, and he will see to it that you are taken care of.

"Sounds hard, right? Yeah, it's gonna be. Can't say I envy you. There's plenty in the safehouses you can use for protection, but don't forget what you're up against. If a Tallisker demon wants you, it will get you. Two pieces of advice.

"One: find Isabel. She knows to look for you in the event of my death. I've also left her burner phone numbers and email addresses with the Taloras. She's a badass and I trust her with your lives.

"Two: find a demon named Crim, or someone close to him. He's Tallisker's Executive Vice President for Special Projects and Outreach, and far as I can tell he's the main man behind the Talora project. His home office is the Detroit tower. Don't fuck with him, just steal as many of his cyphers as you can.

"And I guess that's that. Ellen, baby, I love you. Ren…don't be a pussy."

The screens faded to black and then returned to their original views of the security cameras. For a few moments it seemed like no one breathed. Ren wanted to hide under the couch but didn't have the guts to move.

Lil was the first to speak. "The header for those unidentified number strings is an elven code phrase."

Well, Ren thought, *that sure as shit doesn't make this any easier.*

"It's sort of a joke among the old timers," Lil explained. "They work it into conversation when they want to fuck around and talk shit about their operations, or if they want to haze some new guys." She turned her voice deep and dramatic. "Yeah, go see Sully the troll up in Helsinki. Tell her 'The bodies in the lake cannot hide their secrets from grasping roots' and she'll give you the package." She cleared her throat. "It's ridiculous, but it'd be weird if it were a coincidence."

As could be said about so much of my life right now, Ren thought. "That doesn't help you translate the numbers though, right?"

She shook her head. "No, we need the cyphers. They're a key or a map, linking the numbers to letters, words, or phrases, depending. Typically each cypher is only good for a single message, and the correct cypher to use is defined by the header statement and the first few numbers in the string."

"Like a dubstep song!" Muffintop said happily.

"Ah, sure," Lil replied.

"Speaking of things that can't be a coincidence...Dad said this Crim guy is based out of Detroit."

"I caught that too," Isabel said, "but what I can't figure out is why the leader of the Talora project would attack his own home office."

"It's a false flag," Rotreego growled, oddly on topic.

Lil nodded. "Could be. Maybe Ed decided to bring the fight to Crim and took the whole place down in the process. Could also be one of the other factions within the company standing up for itself, or something else entirely. I don't think we can draw a conclusion on that one yet."

Corporate intrigue, elven codewords, numbers stations, secretly magical smart home doohickeys...Ren suddenly hoped the bottle of Glenlivet in the welcome basket wasn't the only one in the safehouse, and that his father had possessed the foresight to leave a solid supply in the storage room as well.

"We should spend the night," Isabel suggested. "It's been a long day, and we'll need a little time to take stock of what's useful here."

"Agreed," Lil said, though not without a hint of concern. "Talora, seal the doors. I don't want any more surprises today."

"Acknowledged."

The bunker's doors swung slowly shut, then the locking mechanism engaged with a heavy thunk. "Talora, there's another way out of here, right?" Ren asked. Though he couldn't have been gladder for the extra security, his paranoia reminded him to make sure they had a means of running away.

"There is an emergency exit through the storage room. It is a tunnel connected to a garage about a mile away on another property."

Convenient, Ren thought. *Dad really did think of everything.* He wouldn't have been surprised if Ed had attended multiple corporate seminars on how to build a proper safehouse.

Muffintop toddled over to the living area, plopped himself on the couch, and used the remote to activate the TV and tune it to the afternoon's financial news. Markets were up. Rotreego shrugged and wandered over to lie on the other end of the couch.

Isabel looked to Lil and Ren and then nodded toward the storage room. "Shall we?"

— CHAPTER THIRTEEN —

T he safehouse's storage room reminded Ren of his parents' walk-in closet back in Harksburg: long, narrow, and impeccably organized. Rather than pack the shelves tightly with goods, Ed had given every item its own home and a precise amount of space best described as "plenty of room to breathe." A laminated sheet of paper taped to each shelf described its contents: 100 cans of kidney beans, 50 cans of beef stew, 1,000 doses of nari-idisone. There were various outfits sized to fit the three members of the Roberts family, falsified identification and passports, stacks of cash in various denominations, a couple of automatic pistols and corresponding ammo clips, enough first aid gear to outfit a suburban hospital, camping equipment packed and ready to go, and other things that weren't going to fit in the Jag's trunk.

Ren's stomach rumbled, reminding him he'd only eaten a single slice of pizza since breakfast. He grabbed a can of peaches and popped the top open with the pull tab. "I was expecting more magic shit," he said idly.

"Back here," Isabel replied.

Ren found her intently studying a set of metal shelves beside the clearly labeled emergency exit. He leaned around her to get a closer look at the inventory sheet. "Okay, I know what 'five doses of narii dust' means, but what the heck is the rest of it?"

Isabel smiled, and Ren swore her leather patch glittered just as mischievously as her good eye. "Ed left a manual, but…a little demonstration would be more instructive."

They returned to the main room with one of each of Ed's magical toys. There were three things in all: a little blue bouncy ball, something that looked like a bright pink glow stick, and a plastic windup car suspiciously shaped like Ren's beloved Jaguar.

"Looks like a bunch of random crap," he said around a mouthful of peaches.

"It's very difficult and expensive to enchant items in such a way that humans can trigger them—even more so when you need the power of those enchantments to survive an unknown amount of time in a closet," Lil said.

He wiggled his little can of fruit. "Can't just add some preservatives?"

"Sort of, but not really." Behind her, Muffintop peeked up over the top of the couch like a puppet entering the scene. Ren half expected the little guy to impart a life lesson or try to teach them all the alphabet song.

Standing near the doors that led to the bedrooms, Isabel held up one of the blue bouncy balls. "This is a Bant ward," she said. "Break it against a hard surface and it creates a short-lived anti-gravity force." She reached out with her right arm and whipped the ball down at the floor. It splattered against the concrete in a gooey mess a few steps from her toes. "Throw one of those peaches at me, over the ward."

"Starving children in third world countries where they don't have peaches would not approve."

Lil sighed. "You heard the part about this thing being short-lived, right?"

"Fine," Ren replied melodramatically. He plucked a peach out of the can, shifted his fingers around it to get a better grip, and then underhanded it toward his sister. When it crossed over the blue spatter it leapt upward, slammed into the metal ceiling high above them, and stuck there.

"Neat-o!" Muffintop squealed.

Isabel took a step to her left. "The effect lasts ten seconds max, but it is highly recommended that you *never* step over a broken Bant ward."

"Always treat a reptilian humanoid like it's about to bite your head off and regurgitate your brains to feed its young!" Rotreego roared from his couch.

"Got it," Ren said. "What's the deal with the car?"

She held the little toy up in the palm of her hand like it was the prize on some cheap gameshow. "This is a distract-o-gram. Pop the trunk, turn the key inside clockwise five times, then put it down and let it go."

Isabel followed her own instructions, mouthing the count silently as she wound the toy up, then she carefully set it down on the floor and let it go. The car zipped forward as expected...except a life-size vision of Isabel hovered above it, walking forward in the same direction the toy moved. The hologram passed clean through Ren as the car moved between his feet.

"I assume the cranking transfers energy from the user to generate the hologram?"

"Exactly."

"One of those got me out of a rough spot in Romania," Lil added. "Mine was a Corvette."

Isabel brandished the pink glowstick, then took one side of it in each hand and snapped it. The plastic tube stayed intact, but the air around it seemed to briefly vibrate. She cast it aside. "Shake my hand."

"No!"

"Ren," Lil chided, "shake your sister's hand."

"I don't wanna! It's gonna hurt!"

"Only for a few seconds," Isabel said. "That one's called a heater. The magic dissipates on its own in two to three minutes. Water extinguishes it immediately." She strode over to the kitchenette and rinsed her hands under the faucet.

Ren finished his last peach. "I find myself...disappointed."

"It's not a bad little kit," Lil said. "Most importantly, none of those things will blow your stupid human fingers off if you use them wrong."

"Won't blow anyone else's fingers off either," Ren grumbled.

Isabel dried her hands and then stepped over to stand beside him. "Don't worry, big bro. Lil and I will protect you."

She took his hand. He flinched away immediately as if he'd just pressed his palm to a hot stove. "Ow!"

"I lied about the water," she said with a triumphant but friendly smirk. "Figured I owed you one."

— CHAPTER FOURTEEN —

Despite his exhaustion, Ren couldn't find a way to make himself fall asleep. He counted sheep. He mentally alphabetized the contents of his liquor cabinet back home. He even pictured that time in third grade when Oscar Spuddner somehow gave a forty-five-minute book report on some shit about caterpillars. None of it could bring him the blissful repose he so desperately craved.

Fall the fuck asleep like you should have the instant your head hit the pillow, he tried commanding himself. No luck.

He tried lying on his left side, and then his right, and then on his left again with his knees tucked against his chest in the fetal position. His back protested as it always did after a few minutes of trying that angle. Lying prone had never worked, so he didn't even entertain the idea.

Which meant it was time to get up. A snack and some TV might help. Normally he would've gone for a hit of the Glenlivet, but the only nearby bottle he knew of was still upstairs, ruined forever. For some godforsaken reason Ed had neglected to stock the secret bunker with even a single bottle of his son's favorite libation. As far as Ren was concerned, that one missing detail had rendered his father's attempt at preparation an abject failure.

He pulled his pants on, decided against the shirt, and shuffled out of his room. His eyes struggled to get their act together in the face of the bright fluorescents hanging from the ceiling. A monotone voice steadily reading off numbers somehow made him feel unsteady.

"Can't sleep?" Isabel asked. His vision cleared, and he found her sitting on the couch, carefully writing on a legal pad balanced on her knees.

"No, but a few minutes more of that voice might do the job. Same for you, I assume?"

"I haven't slept in five years."

You're not wearing a shirt! a back corner of his mind shrieked in embarrassment. *Whatever,* a different part replied. *She's family.*

He fell heavily onto the opposite side of the couch to watch. Isabel listened intently to the numbers station, comparing each set of digits to a confusing metal decoder she'd propped up on the coffee table at her side. When Ren had first seen the thing, he'd joked that it looked like the menu from some pretentious steakhouse in a renovated mill that served French fries on top of old machine parts. Isabel's backpack sat open on the floor. Lil had watched the cameras like a hawk when they'd let her return upstairs to retrieve it after dinner.

"You trust her?" the elf had asked.

"As much as I trust you."

Lil's snort had sounded oddly approving.

"Getting anything useful?" Ren asked Isabel.

"Useful, no. Interesting...yes. The company's towers in Los Angeles and Moscow have also fallen. They're evacuating the remainder and enforcing a strict work-from-home policy."

Ren's eyes narrowed as his sleep-starved brain cells worked through the implications. "Sounds like Ed's enemies didn't drop an entire tower just to kill him."

"Likely not," Isabel said as she translated a number. "I suspect the perpetrators saw Ed's death as a bonus."

"Tower's going down anyway, might as well fill it with people we don't like."

"Yes."

"Do we know how many fatalities, or who they were?"

"No."

"And no one's claimed responsibility?"

"Not yet, although that station we don't have the cyphers for has been very busy."

Though he appreciated—and was impressed as fuck with— her patience with his questions while she was so focused on decrypting a demonic corporation's communications, he wasn't sure how to express it. He settled on giving her a few minutes of silence. In the meantime, he watched her, thinking about nothing and passing no judgments. The whole process was strangely freeing.

Now I know what it's like to be Doorknob, he thought wistfully.

"What did you want to be when you grew up?" he blurted out, unable to stand the silence any longer.

Isabel tapped her pen against the top of her pad where the previously used pages puffed out over the cardboard backing. "I wanted to be my tia. I wanted to take care of the people I cared about."

Ren chewed on his lower lip. He'd always wanted to be the CEO of a Fortune 500 company, or maybe the kept man of a woman in that same position. "I have a friend who always wanted to be a racecar."

Isabel's pen slipped as she giggled. "I would like to meet this friend."

Oh, that set the gears in motion. He tried to picture Isabel in the Works. She'd get along really well with Kevin Felton, he knew, but what about the others? Try as he might, he couldn't quite picture

Isabel bullshitting with Jim Jimeson, or listening to Doorknob ramble about the raccoons trying to steal the change from his truck's cupholders, or cheering on Oscar during a keg stand, or even just sitting on the bulldozer to watch all the mayhem. She seemed far too grown up for all of that.

A cascade of tangential questions flooded his thoughts. *Does she even drink? What would she wear? Was she the type to arrive early, or late, or right on time? How far into the night would she stay? How does she feel about toasted marshmallows, hot dogs, and other fine cuisine skewered upon a stick and cooked over an open flame?*

"I'm sorry I hurt you," he said suddenly.

The pen came to a stop, and she looked over at him. "It is all right. Please don't let what happened earlier today keep you awake."

She reached down into her open backpack, rummaged around for a moment, and retrieved a small green bottle of Glenlivet. "Ed told me I should bring a bottle. You've earned it."

— CHAPTER FIFTEEN —

They reconvened over breakfast in the living area the next morning. Isabel made pancakes using a box of mix from the storage room.

"So," Ren said in between bites, "anyone ever been to Detroit?"

Everyone shook their head, frowned, or both—except for Muffintop. "I've been!"

Someday, Ren thought, *I'm going to use this whole cracked-out adventure to prove the axiom that when magic and magic people are involved, the strangest thing that could happen is also the most likely.* "You know your way around?"

"Not really. I mostly took cabs or got rides from other people." The troll balled up a syrup covered pancake and tossed it down his throat.

Ren tapped his fork on the edge of his plate, debating whether to stifle his next question. He decided he was too damn curious to care about the possibility of being offensive. "Muffintop, my friend, I have to ask: how is it that you can go to music festivals around the country, take a billion pictures with people who don't know what the hell a troll is, and not freak everybody out?"

The little guy smiled so big there would've been room to land a fighter jet on his teeth. "I can make it so people only see what I want them to see!"

"Show me."

Muffintop set his plate down on the coffee table, slid off the couch, and took a few steps toward the television. He spread his arms wide and slowly turned in place, rotating 360 degrees. Suddenly, the awkwardly stunted troll was gone. In his place stood a blue-haired raver girl in cut-off jean shorts and suspenders, a black and red band t-shirt, and knee-high socks sprouting out of a pair of pink Chuck Taylors.

"Hi there," Muffintop said through supple red lips in a feminine tone that spiked Ren's blood pressure.

He tried to blink the illusion away, but Muffintop's disguise persisted. "What...in the fuck?"

The girl batted her heavily mascaraed lashes, drawing him into the depthless black wells of her anime-character eyes. "My name's Missy! Nice to meet you, senpai!"

Ren looked around the room at the others. "You guys seeing this shit?"

"Seen it," Lil said in between bites.

"God damn chemtrails," Rotreego said, and then drank from a glass of maple syrup.

"Isabel?"

She leaned forward and squinted. "I don't think it's working on me."

Missy put a hand on her hip and shoved her narrow ass out sideways, lips pursed in a pout. "Some of you demons are just too smart for me."

"Okay," Ren snapped, freaked out by the stirring in his loins. "That's enough, thank you. Turn it off."

And then Muffintop was himself again, and Ren felt every muscle in his body loosen. He didn't want to think about the troll's unsettlingly attractive alter ego, but he had to admit there was a certain clever art to the whole thing. What drunk, stoned, horny festival goer *wouldn't* want to be friends with Missy?

All the weird shit's starting to make too much sense, he realized. *That's probably not a good sign.*

"Attention," Talora's voice interrupted. "There is a vehicle pulling into the driveway."

They all turned to watch as the individual camera feeds on the video wall combined once again into a single large screen displaying a view of the driveway. A familiar white Corvette rumbled up behind the Jaguar and came to a jerky stop.

"Shit," Lil said.

"You know that car?" Isabel asked.

"It belongs to a couple of hoodlums who tried to jump us in Donovan's parking lot," Ren explained.

Isabel snorted. "The hoodlums are just accessories. That's Ash's vehicle."

The pieces clicked together in Ren's mind. "Don't tell me the fucking walking conflagration is fucking named fucking *Ash*."

"Ashley, technically," Isabel said, "but she *hates* when people use her full name."

The driver's door swung open. A short woman with frizzy black hair wafted out into the driveway. She looked for all the world like a humanoid piece of used charcoal; her face and hands were singed a whitish gray, and her jeans and vest were burned black and seemingly fused into her flesh. When she looked up at the camera, flames flickered in her dark eyes.

"No way those are her real teeth," Ren said. "You don't get choppers that white without some serious treatment."

"She's always been a vain one, in her own way," Isabel confirmed.

"Hello in the house," Ash said to the camera, her voice crackling. Her black tongue darted out to lick her parched lips. "You have two minutes to turn over the former Pintiri."

"Fucking globalist scumbag," Rotreego replied. He forgot to finish swallowing before speaking and pushed a mouthful of maple syrup back out through his mouth and all over his face and robe, where it joined the remnants of yesterday's pizza and a few specks of the can of gravy he'd had for dinner.

"Talora, take a note," Ren said. "We need to hose down Rotreego tomorrow."

"Acknowledged."

"Talora, all the doors are locked, correct?" Lil said nervously. She brought her hand up to her face and started chewing on the nail of her index finger.

"Yes."

"Any activity at the garage?"

A feed of the empty gravel lot outside the emergency exit appeared in the bottom left corner of the huge display, looking empty and boring. "None," Talora said, "but I will continue monitoring that area."

"Thank you."

"Talora," Ren said, "can we speak with the asshole in the driveway from here?"

"If you like, yes."

He smiled evilly. "Rotreego, anything to say? Talora, begin... uh...broadcast."

The elf froze, his tongue mid-lick against a spatter of syrup on the back of his right hand. He leaned back into the couch, straightened his robe's lapels, and unleashed holy hell.

"I bet you and all your bootlicking friends think you're hot shit, don't ya? Real movers and shakers among the global elite. Ya got people who got people who got people who do the dirty work for all you useless traitor assholes. You think that makes you special? You think that makes you better than the hardworking Americans who make this the greatest country to grace God's green earth? I'm about to let you in on a little secret—"

On screen, Ash took a deep breath, held it for a moment, and then belched a steady stream of bright red fire all over Ren's Jaguar. The headlights cracked and shattered, followed by the windshield and side panels. Flames danced across the upholstery. The car sagged as the back tires melted. Black spots blossomed on the side panels, slowly devouring the forest green paint. The horn honked once and then went silent as the alarm struggled to life and then failed. Seconds later, the whole thing was engulfed in flames.

Isabel clapped Ren on the back—hard—to get him breathing again. That next breath felt like the first breath of the rest of his life. Regardless of how dangerous, strange, or obnoxious life became, he'd always assumed his beloved Jag would be there to face it with him. To see it destroyed with such callous disregard for fine automotive engineering was like watching someone pull off one of his own fingers.

No, scratch that; he would've rather lost a digit than lost his car.

"I know this is a bad time," Isabel said hesitantly, "but that's your other sister. She and I are estranged. I suggest you adopt a similar attitude toward your relationship with her."

Ren's jaw went slack as every neuron in his skull simply stopped working. "Oh, what in the fuck?"

And then the flames punctured the gas tank and the Jag exploded. The camera fizzled and then went black. Talora shifted the view to a different device mounted on top of the garage. The frame of Ren's once beautiful car stood out like a skeleton in the raging inferno. For a split second, he allowed himself to hope the blast had taken out Ash too. There was a certain romance, he thought, in the idea that his loyal vehicle had gone down swinging.

And then she stepped right through the flames, seemingly untouched by the heat, and smiled up at the camera. "Want to see what's left of Donovan's?" she hissed. Her hand darted into her pants pocket and then tossed a few chips of burnt wood onto the ground by her feet.

"We're leaving," Lil snapped. "*Now.*"

— CHAPTER SIXTEEN —

T he Talora turned out to be a neon green hockey puck attached to the back of one of the video screens. A single network cable connected it to the rest of the safehouse and provided power. Talora assured them her internal battery would last six hours. Once they unplugged her, however, she lost access to all the safehouse's command and control functions. Ed had never bothered setting up Wi-Fi.

They took the money, the guns, and the magic shit from the storeroom and got the hell out of there. Lil slapped a can of beans out of Rotreego's hand and ordered them all out into the long, narrow tunnel on the other side of the emergency exit.

Ren glared hard at Isabel's backpack as they hustled single file down the tunnel, the Talora device bouncing against his thigh in his front pocket. He was downright exhausted by the constant revelations about his father's life, so much so that he would've curled up in a corner and cried himself to sleep if the current situation had called for anything other than a desperate retreat to safety. When they got to wherever the hell they were going, he would insist that he and his sister have a very long, very detailed discussion. No more fucking surprises.

"I stashed my RV in the lot behind the shopping center," Isabel said. "If we can reach it, I have things inside that might make Ashley think twice."

"Might?" Lil grunted. Rotreego leaned heavily against her side, his arm draped around her shoulders, and she'd done an admirable job of keeping pace with the others as she dragged him along.

"She is in a more...persistent mood than usual."

"Does she know where the garage is?"

"Doubtful. Ed knew better than to trust her, and often reminded me to take the same precautions. She did not know the location of his safehouses."

"How the hell did she find us, then?" Ren asked.

"Probably bugged the car back at Donovan's," Lil said.

"I'm sick of this bitch messing with my ride," Ren growled. He was glad none of the others felt the need to remind him that wasn't going to be a problem anymore.

The tunnel ended several tense minutes later with a spiral staircase in front of a concrete wall. A wooden door in the ceiling a few feet above the highest tread concealed whatever was above. They paused for a moment, each staring up in trepidation. Ash *probably* hadn't beaten them there, but no one wanted to be the first to find out for sure.

Ren puffed up his chest and forced himself forward. He still felt like he had something to prove to both Lil and Isabel. "I don't know about the rest of you, but I could sure use some fresh air," he said with false bravado as he stepped onto the first thin tread.

The ceiling door gave easily with a light push. A sensor of some kind reacted by sending power to the fluorescents dangling precariously from the metal ceiling. Ren reached up and unfurled a rope ladder attached to the garage floor, then scrambled up a few rungs and into their destination. Cobwebs so thick they resembled webbing from a party supply store covered the cinderblock walls.

To Ren's right, a bright blue tarp covered what looked like a little sports car.

"Oh fuck," he called back down into the tunnel, "the place is full of gnomes!"

"Don't fucking joke about that," Lil said as she pulled herself up beside him. "That's the last thing we fucking need."

"Gnomes are bad news!" Muffintop's squeal echoed down in the tunnel.

"Gnomes are a shining example of American ingenuity," Rotreego added meekly.

As the others emerged through the hole one-by-one, Ren turned his attention to their vehicle. There was something oddly familiar about the shape underneath the tarp. His brain refused to go there, but his heart decided it was all right to pound a mile a minute. He took firm hold of the blue plastic, steadied himself, and then dramatically ripped it away.

"Oh my fucking shit."

It was a Jaguar. Forest green. Cream interior. A few years newer than his own, but almost a carbon copy.

He fell to his knees, flicked his eyes skyward, and mouthed Ed a heartfelt thank you.

"That is not going to fool Ashley," Isabel said.

"Don't ruin the moment," Ren replied.

"I'm driving."

He leapt to his feet. "No you are fucking not."

"Do you know the way to the shopping center where I parked my RV?"

"No, but you can direct me."

She opened the door, but Ren darted into the driver's seat before she could. Her smirk as she gave in and walked around the front of the car to take shotgun filled him with confidence.

Lil lifted the garage door open and then piled into the back beside Rotreego and Muffintop. It took two turns of the key, but the engine flared to life with a familiar purr that stirred Ren's loins in a way that would've made Missy slink off in defeat. He gave the engine a rev just for fun, and then did it again, and then pushed his new car down the gravel driveway and out onto the empty street.

The seat wasn't broken in right. The gas pedal didn't fight him. The buttons on the steering wheel that controlled the sound system were a little different. But it was close enough. He wiggled around to build up an appropriate butt groove and pushed the accelerator to the floor.

"Yeah, that won't fool Ashley either," Lil said from the backseat.

"Take a right at this intersection," Isabel interjected before Ren could get fresh.

The new Jag powered through that turn like a sharp knife through warm butter. Ahead, the long, straight road sliced through an empty pasture. That late in the year, the ground looked brown and dead, abandoned to the ravages of the Indiana winter. The bleak landscape combined with the conspicuous lack of traffic to give the view through the windshield a melancholy, haunted quality. A gentle hill obscured the horizon and whatever civilization they might be approaching. In the back of his mind, Ren wondered if they'd reach the top and just launch off into the sky.

"That's her," Lil said, her sharp elven eyes glued to the rearview mirror. "She's way behind us, but she's gaining. Drive normal for now and let's see what she does."

Ren talked his foot out of slamming down on the accelerator and took a look at the mirror to his left. There was definitely a white car well in the distance. He couldn't tell if it was Ashley's Corvette or not. It hadn't yet reached the road to the garage, but at the rate it was traveling it wouldn't take long. If they were lucky, it'd take that turn and they'd all breathe a heavy sigh of relief. If they weren't... well, then, Ren thought he might end up regretting not letting Isabel drive.

"The shopping center's another five minutes away," she said. "It is unlikely that Ashley won't notice us turning into the parking lot."

"Give it a few seconds," Lil insisted.

It seemed like even the Jaguar held its breath as the Corvette approached the turn off. Ren tapped the wheel as if to tell his new car that he believed in it, that he knew it could blow the doors off any Chevy on the market, and that if it got them through all this, he'd buy it a detail and a nice wax.

The Corvette blew right past the turn.

"Aww, French fries!" Muffintop said.

"Faster," Lil snarled. "Now."

Ren's foot heeded the elf's command before his brain could consciously process it. The Jag leapt forward as if shot out of a cannon. Ren's knuckles went white around the wheel and his eyes flicked back and forth between the road and the speedometer.

"She's gaining," Isabel said.

The Jag was doing a hundred and five. "How the fuck is that possible?" Ren asked. "And what the fuck do we do about it?"

"Your job is to watch the road," Lil snapped. "Leave the cursing and the clever countermeasures to the professionals. Isabel, pass one of those Bant wards back here."

She reached down to the backpack between her feet, unzipped a side pocket, and extended a handful of the little blue wards toward the backseat. "One's good, but three or four would be even better."

"Rotreego," Lil said, "would you do the honors?"

"For God and country!"

Wind roared through the vehicle as Rotreego rolled down his window. Ren risked a glance in the rearview mirror to see him toss one of the Bant wards over and behind the trunk. The elf tossed another every few seconds.

"Yeah!" Ren shouted. "No way she gets through that shit!"

"Eyes forward," Lil replied.

"Yes, ma'am."

They reached the base of the hill and began to ascend. Ren couldn't believe how smooth the ride was at that speed. There hadn't been much call for doing a hundred plus back home. Not like the Burg was going to run out of beer if he didn't get there fast enough.

He glanced out at his mirror just in time to see the white Corvette reach the first Bant ward. The little enchantment flung the sportscar skyward like something out of a video game.

"Whooooooaaaaaa!" Muffintop cooed, leaning over the back of his seat to watch through the rear windshield.

The car arced through the sky like it'd launched itself off the top of a ramp. An intense sensation of awe rose in Ren's core, relaxing his jaw muscles. That gently soaring car brought to mind a vision of an orca leaping up out of the ocean. But whereas that majestic mental cetacean sliced easily back into the blue sea, the Corvette slammed down hard into the gray asphalt and bottomed out, squealing and sparking and skidding to a sideways stop.

"Well done, Pintiri," Lil said with a smile. Beside her, Rotreego beamed and spasmed.

"Well done, Ed," Isabel said with a wink at Ren.

"Well done steak tips!" Muffintop added. Everyone laughed.

Concerned that the peak of the hill would exert a similar influence on the Jag, Ren eased off the accelerator just a bit. Their heroics would be all for nothing if he wrecked their own ride. Still, seeing their pursuer thwarted—and knowing that it had taken a team effort to make it work—warmed parts of his face and torso he hadn't realized cared about such camaraderie. His spleen had always been an excellent employee, but it'd never done anything to imply it was hanging around for more than a paycheck, you know?

He took a quick peek at each of the others, all of whom appeared content. *Maybe I've got the right crew for this adventure after all.*

The Corvette remained motionless until they crested the hill, and then began to stir. It accelerated first toward the side of the road, then banked quickly into the opposite lane—where Rotreego hadn't thrown any of the other Bant wards.

"Shit," Lil snarled.

"We're close," Isabel said, her voice instantly soothing Ren's blood pressure. "We'll get there first."

"After what we just did, is she going to give two shits about whatever you've got in your RV?" Ren asked.

"Probably not. Ashley is known for her temper. But we can at least switch vehicles."

The thought of abandoning his new Jaguar so soon made Ren's heart skip a beat. Still, he couldn't deny the logic. He caressed the steering wheel, looking for some poignant, heartfelt shit to telepathically beam into the Jag. *Thank you* was the best he could do.

The shopping center sprawled across the top of that hill like a spider guarding its nest. Newer offshoots from the older main building devoured chunks of the expansive parking lot: an all-glass garden center, a liquor store inexplicably trimmed with faded clapboard, an automotive unit painted a blinding shade of orange, a sterile grocery store attached to a tiny health clinic, and a really unhealthy-looking fast food hut. It was, Ren realized with some disappointment as he pulled into the half-empty lot, everything the locals needed.

"There," Isabel said, pointing at the rear end of a huge white RV parked by the clinic. "That's my ride."

"That's an elven Mark Eight Mobile Espionage Unit," Lil said, her voice walking the line between awe and confusion. "Where the fuck did you get that?"

"Ed gave it to me."

"Check my website for all the goods, services, and armaments a noble American patriot needs to defend his home and his family," Rotreego said happily.

Ren swore he could hear the puzzle pieces clicking together in Lil's brain. "You *sold* a Mark Eight Mobile Espionage Unit to Ed Roberts?"

"Do reptilian humanoids control the United States government?"

"No, but I get your gist."

The Jag slid easily into a spot where the RV hid it from the road. As the others disembarked, Ren lingered. He'd barely been in that driver's seat for fifteen minutes and he wasn't quite ready to depart, even temporarily. They still had so much to learn about each other and so many places to explore. The supple leather of the driver's seat had only just begun melding itself to the shape of his ass. As far as he was concerned, that first ride had ended far too soon. He hoped the car felt the same way.

"I'll be right back," he whispered lovingly after the others had gotten out and shut the doors behind them. "I promise."

The seat seemed to cling to him as he slid out. He had trouble tearing himself away. "Shhhh," he muttered. "It'll be okay."

"Stop talking to the fucking car and help your sister with this fucking boot clamped to the tire," Lil snapped.

Ren looked down at the RV's front driver's side and discovered the aforementioned apparatus. He'd never encountered a piece of rusty yellow metal he hated more. "Shit."

"I can get it off," Isabel pleaded, "but not quickly."

Ren glowered at Lil. "Remind me again why you were so dismayed about Rotreego selling this piece of shit to my father?"

The elf shrugged and the others shifted uncomfortably. None of the obvious options were attractive. There was certainly a chance the other Bant wards would've sent the white Corvette corkscrewing through the air until it landed on its top and crushed Ashley's skull down into her spine, but that was wishful thinking. The thought that she'd blow right past the shopping center without stopping to investigate seemed like a similarly unlikely best-case scenario.

Which left dealing with her right then and there in that parking lot. Sure, there were five of them and one of her, but what chance did they really have against someone who could vomit up enough fire to put the fear of God into a King of the Forest? He was pretty sure whatever extinguisher the RV was packing wouldn't be enough.

Instinct made him glance back to the car. He almost crapped himself when he found Muffintop climbing into the driver's seat.

"Don't worry guys!" the little troll shrieked. "I got this!"

Ren couldn't make himself move. Watching Muffintop drive away with his new Jaguar was like watching some roided out football player abscond with his prom date. All he could do was stare, slack-jawed, as that green slice of heaven peeled out of the parking lot and took a sharp turn back the way they came.

"How can he reach the pedals?" Isabel mused.

"Troll Buddha shit," Ren said stoically.

Half a second later, the white Corvette appeared, squealed into a U-turn, and burned off after Muffintop.

"Well," Lil said, "can't deny his timing."

Knowing he'd never see that car again, Ren dropped to his knees and wailed toward the heavens. An elderly couple pushing a shopping cart past them crossed themselves and hurried onward.

— CHAPTER SEVENTEEN —

I swear I wasn't actually in love with a car," Ren said as he offered Isabel a beer.

"Sure," she said, taking the can, cracking it open, and answering one of Ren's many questions about her, "and my depth perception is *perfect*."

After a six-hour drive down the back roads to avoid detection, they'd stopped at the Friendly Pines campground on the bank of Lake Erie, just outside of Toledo. Consensus had been that approaching Detroit was better done after another check of the numbers station and whatever they could get that mimicked a good night's sleep. There were only two bunks in the RV, so Ren and Isabel would be sharing a tent.

As he sat down on the opposite log, he pointed at the little green hockey puck at her feet. "Anything new on the Tallisker telegraph?"

Isabel scribbled as Talora listed a couple more numbers. "Things are getting weird in Evitankari, and Talvayne's shut off their transport stone."

Dread welled up in Ren's gut. "Shit. My mother was headed that way."

"That was how many days ago? She probably made it before the lockdown."

Ren wanted to believe that. It made sense. Ellen had been ecstatic when he'd handed her Nella's token. He hoped she was down there in Talvayne, sipping on margaritas and showing her new friends how to properly downward dog, or whatever the hell the hot yoga pose was in fairy land.

He pretended to look idly out at the water. They had a good view, at the very least, although the crooked shack that passed as a latrine left a lot to be desired. "What was your orientation like?"

To his surprise, she stashed her pen behind her ear and tossed the notepad down at her feet. "It was the worst experience of my life."

Which, given Brian's attempt to force Ren's, should not have come as a surprise. "All right, then. Forget I asked." He hoped she wouldn't.

Her face scrunched up in thought and she took a drink. For a moment, Ren could've sworn the two of them were in the Works, sitting by the fire in a pair of rickety lawn chairs, combining forces to tackle the deepest mysteries of drunken philosophy while the rest of the crew laughed at Doorknob and Jim Jimeson taking turns kicking each other in the balls. Maybe she would've fit in there after all.

"So...the physical transformations aren't random, you know? Your personality, and the...the things you do to let the evil in, they both contribute."

He'd known that, but he sensed it would be a bad idea to rush her explanation. "Ashley obviously loved swimming."

Isabel snorted happily. "I wanted something more subtle. Ed and I talked about it a lot. 'The obviously dangerous ones get shanked in the back first,' he always told me."

Ren almost gagged on his drink. "Yeah, same here. But I suspect he meant it in a slightly different context."

She chewed on that for a moment. "You're lucky, you know. When I told him what I wanted, he made it happen. There was no discussion. He didn't even try to talk me out of it. You, though…he never would've let you follow in his footsteps."

His insides turned to ice. Her tone hadn't exactly been accusatory, but he couldn't ignore the subtext. His mouth slipped open, but no words came out. What, exactly, was he supposed to say to that?

"Don't worry," she said warmly. "I'm envious, but I'm not angry. I would not have allowed Ed to talk me out of this."

He didn't doubt that. "Thanks."

"And besides, he owed me. I saved his life."

When she didn't continue, Ren blanched. "Okay."

"Ashley came for us—all of us. Ed, the other kids, me. I grabbed a fire extinguisher. She walked right through the torrent of foam, so I hit her in the face with the canister."

The image of a teenaged Isabel Salinas Hernandez swinging a fire extinguisher into a murderous demon's chin somehow made perfect sense. "Is that why you and Ashley are estranged?"

"Part of it, yeah."

When she didn't elaborate, Ren decided to bring the conversation back on track. "Thank you for saving my father."

"You're welcome. He was quite embarrassed by it, and he promised me anything I wanted." She paused and pointed to her ruined eye. "This was it.

"I thought long and hard about what I wanted to become. I kept coming back to my own family, to the way I felt when they abandoned me to a sharp-dressed lawyer in a fancy car. And I realized—very selfishly—that I wanted to be able to make my enemies feel the way I felt in that limousine, knowing I'd never see my father and brother again. I wanted to tear them apart from the inside."

She tapped the side of her face beside her ruined eye. "That's what this does. The power in this socket focuses the victim's mind onto his or her worst fears and darkest moments and amplifies them. Short-term exposure can result in depression, bouts of anxiety, PTSD, and suicidal behavior. A long enough session will physically overload the brain and trigger multiple massive hemorrhagic strokes."

Ren shuddered at the memory of Brian Drew's head bursting like a dropped watermelon.

"I had to work at it," she continued wistfully. "Ruining people from the inside with only conventional tools takes a lot of thought. I screwed up my first attempt. Tallisker intelligence handed me a cheating husband and a depressed wife. I got her a gun and arranged for her to walk in on her husband in the act. I hadn't taken the children into the equation. They wound up reconciling."

Beer almost spewed through Ren's lips. "Hold up. That was *you*?" When she nodded, blushing, he slipped into his best Ed Roberts impersonation. "'So I'm mentoring this baby demon— bright young thing, I think, but maybe not quite ready for the gig—and I shit you not she turned what should've been a murder/suicide into a real Hallmark fuckin' moment!'" He sloshed his beer around for emphasis like it was one of his father's highballs.

A blush warmed Isabel's cheeks. "I can't believe he told you about me."

"I can't believe that was you." He took a drink, thinking. "Hey... you're not also responsible for that elf who got locked in the gas station bathroom outside Peoria, are you?"

Her face bloomed. "I plead the fifth. Rumor has it that guy suffered from an acute phobia of public washrooms."

Ren's chuckle caught in his throat as his conscience wagged its finger. The two of them were laughing and joking about some truly horrible shit. Perhaps the worst part of it all was that Isabel had done it all for purely selfish reasons: to latch herself onto a dark power that would forever hold her in its thrall. It felt tragic in its own way.

But what was Ren supposed to do, shun the sister who'd recently saved his life and pledged herself to his quest to avenge his father? Ed would've found the idea laughable. "Always use what you got, kid," that familiar snarl repeated in his mind. "Good, evil, indifferent—it's all the same. What you should care about are the results. And don't be a dipshit like that Spuddner kid."

"What is it?" Isabel asked, obviously tuned into his musing.

"Just thinking about my father, and what he'd make of all this."

"I think Ed would be proud, but also very surprised you've made it this far."

"Sounds about right."

"Although after what happened between us in that cell, you may want to monitor your skin for rough patches."

Her joke didn't land immediately, but when it did every hair on Ren's arms prickled. "No," he said desperately, "there's no *way* one swipe with a cheese grater would do *that*." As far as he knew, even a minor demonic transformation required an extended period of truly heinous deeds. He hadn't exactly been an angel in the past—most people, he knew, would say he'd been a bit of a twat—but there was no way he'd been horrible enough to be pushed over the edge by one hesitant, self-serving assault...was there?

Isabel, seemingly reading his mind again, pursed her lips and shrugged.

"So...Detroit," Ren said, fumbling for a change of subject. "How exactly do we find this Crim guy?"

Lithe and catlike, Isabel leaned back and stretched her legs out straight. "Tallisker won't have completely abandoned the site of their tower. They'll have agents in the area. If we're lucky, I'll recognize one who knows and likes me. If we're not...we'll toss one in a bag and get what we need however we have to."

Ren considered that. "You got a bag big enough in that RV?"

She nodded. "And bigger."

He didn't like it. Isabel's plan relied on several assumptions they couldn't guarantee. "Too bad we don't have access to the corporate intranet," he mused. "Talora," he said jokingly, "do you have the address for a demon named Crim?"

The little green hockey puck blinked twice, chirped, and then responded. "Would you like the address of his primary residence, his summer home, the mooring of his yacht, the mooring of his larger yacht, or his emergency contact?"

Their eyes met in a shared expression of "what in the fuck?" It couldn't possibly be that easy, could it? "Uh...does he have a Detroit address?" Ren asked.

The Talora unit ran through its blinky-chirpy routine again. "225 Apple Street. Would you like me to call the home phone and let them know you're planning to visit?"

"No!" Ren and Isabel shouted in unison, bursting up out of their seats.

"Acknowledged," Talora said flatly.

Isabel quickly recorded Crim's address in her notebook. "This could be a trap or a trick."

Ren had been thinking the same. "Still sounds better than scouring an unfamiliar city until we get a lucky break. Talora... what else can you tell us about Crim?"

The device's pre-response routine really made it seem like it was thinking. Ren found the effect eerie. "I have access to corporate biographies describing all members of Tallisker's senior leadership team."

"Read Crim's, please."

"Acknowledged." Talora paused as if gathering herself. "Jonathan Lacriminovicwz joined Tallisker as a Sales Agent in the fall of 2003. After shattering his team's monthly conversion records and then constantly breaking his own, Jonathan was promoted into a management role where he introduced his own methodology to the team at large and revolutionized Tallisker's top-of-the-funnel processes across our various acquisitions departments. After proving his dedication and work ethic through a variety of increasingly difficult roles, Crim—as he insists his friends and coworkers call him—was promoted to a role on Tallisker's board as the Junior Executive Director of Special Projects and Transformational Initiatives. In his spare time, Crim enjoys golfing, sailing, and long walks with his corgi, Hyacinth."

After a few moments of silence brought on by the utter uselessness of that description, Ren raised his beer. "I've got it! We kidnap the dog!"

Isabel bounced her head back and forth, skeptical but not dismissive. "I've heard worse ideas."

"Got anything better?"

Her attention drifted skyward as she thought it through. "Not right now, no."

"There. Then it's settled."

She took a drink, sharp and sudden. "What was it like being Ed's biological son?"

Every muscle in Ren's body constricted in what he could only think of as a form of rigor mortis. "It was..." Demanding? Confusing? Awkward? Surprisingly good at preparing him for the outside world? He couldn't find a word to encompass all that, so he took the easy way out. "It was weird."

"How so?"

God damn it. "Well...it was strange learning so much about a situation I was mostly forbidden from engaging with. But now I think about what I've learned about that side of his life in the last few days and I realize how little I actually knew at the time."

She oozed down onto the ground and leaned back against her log. "What do you think Ed expected of you?"

God fucking damn it. He dug a little hole in the dirt with the toe of his shoe as he thought it through. "He very much didn't want me to end up like him."

"That doesn't answer the question."

Well, shit. "No, I suppose not." The mouthful of beer he swallowed didn't heed his silent pleas for assistance. "I think he wanted me to find success on my own, in whatever form felt right."

"And what does that look like?"

Right now it looks like finding a way out of this conversation without my inner monologue escaping through my mouth. "I guess it's being safe, and secure, and immune to all the weird shit in my father's world."

This time Isabel hesitated and seemed to tense up. "But how were you going to achieve that? What sort of career are you pursuing, for instance?"

Fuck me. "I invest a little."

"That's it?"

Fuck a duck. "Well, there's a lot of research involved. And some math."

"You don't feel like you should be doing more to reach your goals? A life of true safety and security does not come without expenditures of time, effort, and energy."

"That's deep."

"So's that hole you're digging yourself," she said with a wink, though her hands trembled.

The next taste of cheap swill teleported him back to the Works, to the endless nights spent debating and bullshitting under the stars and the watchful eye of the old bulldozer. *She asks deeper questions than Felton after a twelve-pack and a hit of gruss. I guess this proves she can hang,* he thought, although he regretted having poked the bear.

"It's okay to say you didn't put the effort in," she said.

"Ouch," he hissed. "That's blunt."

She giggled, a sound that fit her about as well as an infant's clothing would fit a teenager. "We can't all spend our formative years setting up horrible people for comeuppance through their own hubris."

Ren didn't miss the judgment underneath her ironic tone, and it set him to anxiously adjust his butt cheeks on the log. Rolling with the punches and giving back as good as he got had always been instinctual to him. Lacking an immediate snarky comeback was a new and confusing experience. Did he actually care about winning this woman's approval? Had her words legitimately hurt him? No. no, that couldn't be right.

He let the conversation die, and the mismatched pair directed their attention to the twinkling lake just visible between the slender pines surrounding their campsite. The beautiful view was exactly the kind of scene famous for triggering moments of intimate connection between those sharing it.

So why, when Isabel sighed, did Ren feel like it had pushed them further apart?

— CHAPTER EIGHTEEN —

T he Mark Eight Mobile Espionage Unit roared up the highway under Isabel's careful control, the ride surprisingly smooth and silent. Ren found himself grateful for the distance between the cockpit and the dining/sleeping area. He'd curled up into the corner of the bench that doubled as a fold-out cot, beneath the lofted compartment that served as the master bedroom. A small table that could sink down into the floor to allow space for the bed separated him from the little kitchenette on the opposite wall. An awkward evening trying and mostly failing to sleep, tucked into a sleeping bag mere feet from his disapproving sister, had rendered his mood as dark and muddled as his thoughts.

Rotreego lounged comfortably beside him, humming to himself as he repeatedly stacked, unstacked, and restacked the chocolate bars he'd liberated from the campground's vending machine on their way out. The broken elf had been even more anxious than usual without Muffintop's company.

Lil chewed on her fingernail as she watched Rotreego's nervous fiddling. She'd adopted a camouflaged jacket from the RV's storage that hung off her shoulders like a priest's robes. "I'm going to find him," she declared. Neither man so much as grunted, but Ren shifted so he could see her better.

"This is called scrying," she explained as she stoppered the drain in the tiny sink. "It's tricky, but I should be able to use my prior exposure to Muffintop's magic to roughly approximate his direction and distance."

"And you can do that with a sink?" Ren asked incredulously.

"It would be foolish to doubt the people's capacity for performing great deeds in the face of tyranny, oppression, or socialized medicine," Rotreego mumbled.

"I can do it with *this* sink," Lil said. She twisted the spigot around on its arm once and a hidden mechanism clicked into place. The water that streamed down into the basin when she opened the valves glittered bright blue. "This is water from the Origina, a particularly magical body of water in Evitankari. Every Mark Eight ships with a small supply, and I seriously can't fucking believe Rotreego didn't drain the tank before he sold this thing."

"Capitalism doesn't care about your safe spaces."

Ren stood up to get a better look. Sleek shadows flowed beneath the surface of the water like predatory fish on the prowl. "I take it this is not healthy to drink."

"Turns all the frogs into communists," Rotreego said, studying the upside-down nutrition facts on the back of a chocolate and caramel bar.

"One mouthful of this stuff will drive you insane," Lil translated. "Now if you don't mind, I require silence from the peanut gallery."

Ren pantomimed zipping his lips. The former Pintiri dropped his chocolate bar and sat on his hands.

Lil shifted her feet out wider, tensed her back and her buttocks, and extended her palms out over the sink. For almost two whole minutes nothing happened. Ren looked around at the white walls and brown storage cabinets, unsurprised to find Rotreego positively vibrating with the effort it took to keep his hands under his thighs and away from the chocolate bounty beckoning his manic attention. An empathetic smile bloomed on Ren's face; a wise remark had taken up residence on the very tip of his tongue, banging desperately against the inside of his lips and demanding to be released.

Then the water wobbled as if it'd turned into Jell-O. Tiny bubbles reminiscent of carbonation wafted up to the surface to gently burst. Ren stood up straighter, peering over Lil's shoulder. "Muffintop," she whispered through taut lips.

The bubbling abruptly stopped.

"Shit," Lil said as she slouched in defeat and closed her eyes.

"Didn't work?" Ren asked.

"No, it worked." Ren didn't need further explanation.

Wrappers crackled and crunched as Rotreego swept all his candy onto the floor with an angry swipe of his hand. The former Pintiri stormed off to the rear of the RV and slammed the bathroom door shut behind him.

Thanks, little friend, Ren thought sadly, the sentiment trapped inside by the dense lump in his throat. He hoped Muffintop hadn't suffered, but deep down he knew that was unlikely. *Fuck you, Ashley. Show your fucking face again and I'll rip it right off.* The thought that one of his new friends had given his life for Ren's quest was not one he was prepared to face.

Lil stiffened and raised her hands over the sink once more, shaking with emotion. "Ashley," she snarled as if hurling the name headfirst into a woodchipper.

The enchanted water bubbled and fizzed, the effect growing in intensity until the previously peaceful sink resembled a Jacuzzi. Eerie light bloomed beneath the maelstrom, flaring once and then coalescing into a single bright point the size of a penny. Then it shifted, moving down and to the right, toward Lil and the edge of the sink. The water it left behind calmed and flattened, seemingly indifferent to the little sun burning in the corner.

"Ashley's about fifty miles southeast of us—and gaining," Lil said.

Muffintop must've told her their destination. Not wanting to imply their departed friend was in any way at fault, Ren tactfully kept the realization to himself. Lil had likely already figured it out on her own.

Instead, he said something he hoped would make the others feel better. "Then we'll have to make sure there's a very warm welcome waiting for her when she gets there."

— CHAPTER NINETEEN —

C rim's address turned out to be a cute little single-family home, two stories, almost a perfect cube. The white siding, cool blue trim, and gently sloping rooflines gave the structure an almost cake-like quality, as if someone had draped the structure in fondant and then carefully piped on the details. Pine garlands hung from the eaves and window boxes, pinned by big red bows. A minivan or shiny new SUV would've looked right at home in the short black driveway. The perfectly straight cement walkway bisected the fading lawn, warmly welcoming passersby up to the stately front porch. Similar homes filled the rest of the neighborhood, though none were quite as attractive as Crim's.

"Looks like the opening shot of a made-for-TV Christmas movie," Isabel mused. She and Ren sat a polite distance from each other on the curb across the street, beside the nose of the Mark Eight. Lil had put them in charge of surveillance and then stomped toward the rear of the RV to try to drag Rotreego out of the bathroom.

"Do we think this is really the primary home of a high-ranking Tallisker executive overseeing some of the company's most shadowy projects?" Ren asked, pulling his peacoat tighter around his body. Mid-December had decided to assert itself, turning the air frigid and hard underneath a gray sky threatening snow. Their breath floated out in little white puffs as they spoke.

"You'd be surprised how Tallisker's brass spend their time," she said. "Living simply is another way they can cling to their humanity. Marafuji, for instance, is famous for residing in a log cabin with no electricity or running water."

Ren didn't know Ed's exact salary, but he had some idea of how much money their luxurious lifestyle required. It stood to reason that Marafuji—his father's boss—would be pulling in even more. "Must be a hell of a cabin."

"I hear it's drafty and the outhouse is kind of gross."

Wary of the time and place and the awkwardness between them, Ren hesitated to ask his next question. Though there was no telling what, if anything, awaited them inside Crim's idyllic home, whatever they were about to encounter would be best approached with the two of them on the same page. But then Isabel, who'd proven to be crazy in tune with her brother's thinking, gave him a look that let him know it was okay.

"What was Ed's...orphanage...like?"

Her lips quirked up in a nostalgic grin. "Ever seen the *X-Men*? It was like Xavier's mansion, all dark wood and cavernous hallways full of damaged children weighing each other down with their own drama. The gardens were beautiful. I was too afraid to learn to ride the horses, but I enjoyed visiting the stables. And I've never had better food to eat." She paused, clearly weighing her next statement. Ren returned her previous encouraging glance, and then she continued after a few more seconds of evaluation. "Ashley and I were roommates for ten years."

He reached down by his side for a drink but only found the cold, hard asphalt of the curb. "Were you two friends?"

"'Confidantes' sounds like the proper term," she said thoughtfully, her eyes distant. "She had the top bunk—insisted on it, of course, just as angrily as you're picturing. We used to stay up late and tell each other secrets. I told Ash all about my father and my brother, and my tia's dulce de leche, and the first boy I kissed, the spelling tests I cheated on...everything. I couldn't see her, but I swear I could hear her listening. Only rarely would she offer advice, and when she did it was blunt and straightforward." She chuckled. "I lost track of how many people she told me to punch in the face."

Ren quickly glanced past his sister to the Mark Eight. There was still no sign of Lil or Rotreego. He hoped they'd be at least a few more minutes. "What sorts of things did she talk about?"

"She wanted to be a veterinarian. Can you believe it? Ashley loved animals. She brushed each of the horses every day. Named all the barn cats. Even stopped the janitor from killing a squirrel, once. She must've brought home a dozen strays in just that first year I knew her. Unfortunately, that made her vulnerable, too."

The RV's door leapt open, banging loudly against the vehicle's exterior. Rotreego stumbled out into the street like a prizefighter leaving the ring after a bad loss. The cold stopped him in his tracks, and he shivered for a moment before he managed to cinch his bathrobe up tight. Lil emerged behind him, draping a camouflage jacket over his shoulders that matched the one she'd taken from the vehicle's storage.

"Let's get this over with," she said in a way that made it clear she wasn't sure how long the former Pintiri would be able to keep it together. After what had happened to Ren when he'd entered Ed's safehouse, they'd agreed that no one would do anything alone. Leaving Rotreego in the Mark Eight by himself was out of the question, and neither Ren nor Isabel thought it wise to investigate Crim's home without Lil. This job required all four of them.

Ren imagined they looked like something out of an action movie as they crossed the silent street side-by-side-by-side. He wished he'd worn a pair of cool sunglasses to complete the look, or an impressive rifle to prop up onto his shoulder. Isabel clasped her hands together and cracked her knuckles, perhaps swept up in the same moment.

"Eyes up," Lil said softly. "If anyone's home, they've had more than enough time to prepare for us."

A distract-o-gram jostled in Ren's left front pants pocket. On the other side, the Talora was an uncomfortable weight against his thigh. If things went sideways his primary responsibility would be to get the valuable device as far away from the action as possible. He was quite happy with that job.

The lump in his throat expanded with each step forward. Crim's cute little house waited for them like a gallows. One of Ellen's best frenemies from a few towns west of Harksburg was a New Age weirdo who believed that every home had its own unique soul. If that were true, Ren thought, then this one belonged to a cute child hiding a giant knife behind its back.

The front door swung slowly open, though the person responsible remained hidden. Ren found himself wishing Ed had thought to leave some sort of "That's magic!" alarm in the safehouse's supply stash. His eyes darted left and right, searching in vain for potential cover. Unfortunately, this wasn't the type of neighborhood that allowed its hedges to grow to a useful height. If it came to it, running straight back to the RV as quickly as his shaky legs could take him would be his best bet.

"Movement in the neighbor's house to our left," Isabel hissed.

They froze. An old woman in a pink dressing gown jerked her curtains shut. "I know that look," Ren said, flashing back to so many of the late nights with his Harksburg friends. "That woman's about to call the cops."

"Globalist boot licker," Rotreego spat.

"All the more reason to make this quick," Lil said. Something unspoken passed through a quick glance between her and Isabel. The demon continued forward. Ren decided to stick close to his sister and the scary pistol he knew was holstered inside her jacket. The two elves followed a pace behind.

The creak of the front stairs would've been quaint and welcoming under different circumstances. Ren almost leapt out of his skin when Rotreego stepped onto the tread behind him.

Isabel knocked on the storm door just to be polite, then eased it open and stuck her head across the threshold. "Hello!" she called into the house. "Anyone here? We've got a few questions for a man named Crim."

It struck Ren that this frontal assault flew wildly in the face of his father's advice. Storming a Tallisker demon's home certainly didn't fall under the "cautious approaches" category. Then again, Ed hadn't counted on his son having so much competent backup. *Score one for me, Dad.*

Isabel drew her pistol and crossed inside. Ren waited for a few seconds until she motioned him to continue with a flick of her fingers. Unlike the safehouse, this floor plan attached the front door to an open concept living space: a living room with expensive looking furniture, a dining area with a long metal table underneath a chandelier tipped with round bulbs, and then a black and gray kitchen behind a tall island. It reminded Ren of the décor in his family's own home, cold and industrial but not unwelcoming. The big difference—and the thing that made it all unsettling—was the utter lack of personal touches. The walls were bright white and bare, the surfaces clear of framed pictures and knickknacks. There were no bookshelves. There was nothing haphazardly stored under the coffee table or atop the kitchen cabinets. It was as if the home's owner had made the conscious decision not to leave behind any clues about his personality.

Rotreego stomped past them all to examine a charcuterie spread waiting for them on the dining room table. His nose twitched like a dog's as he sniffed at the array of cheese and cured meat. Then his body suddenly went rigid, his lips curled back, and he growled angrily.

"What is it, boy?" Ren asked, unable to help himself.

The front door slammed shut behind them. Lil, the last one through, reached for the knob and then jerked her hand back in pain when a bright spark slapped it away. Isabel raised her gun and stepped in front of Ren.

"Relax," a feminine voice cooed from up the stairwell. Slender legs concealed in a floor-length black dress descended toward them.

An uncomfortable chill shook Ren's bones. Rotreego's growl turned guttural and vicious.

"Welcome to Crim's home," the woman said ominously as she stepped off the stairs. Ren felt the weight of her dark eyes pressing into and through him. Her jet-black hair made her pale skin all the whiter. "My name is Rayn," she continued, brushing a lock of hair behind a pointed elven ear, "and I'll be your hostess for the evening."

"The fucking *Witch*," Rotreego snarled.

As Ren's brain linked that outburst with Driff's last words to Kevin Felton, the former Pintiri—growling, frothing at the mouth, rage boiling in his wide eyes—crossed the room in an instant. Ren couldn't believe the frail Pintiri was moving like that. It was like watching a lioness spring into action to protect her cubs.

The air turned cold a split second before the Witch's spell activated. Invisible hands intercepted the Pintiri just as he was about to claw Rayn's face off. She watched placidly as her magic lifted him away. Though his upper body stood stiff, his legs wind-milled underneath him like those of a cartoon coyote about to plummet off the edge of a cliff.

Rotreego's mouth still worked too. "Nasty, nasty woman! Crooked Rayn and her fucking emails! Drink the blood of any children lately, you devil worshipping interdimensional vampire?"

Rayn cocked her head in curiosity. "Not exactly the eloquent tongue lashing I expected from Evitankari's famously verbose ex-Pintiri."

"Lady, you have no idea," Lil snapped. "If you harm one hair on his head, I swear—"

"I won't. I must say, Rotreego, you've assembled quite the little dream team here! One of Evitankari's most decorated former intelligence officers, with whom you share a tragic past. A mysterious demon who's still sexy as shit, even though she's missing half her face. And a human for that little bit of spice only they can bring to a dish." She looked at Ren the way most women looked at Doorknob. "I guess it's more Guardians of the Galaxy than Avengers for now, but we can fix that in the sequel!"

Indignant stupidity launched Ren's tongue into action. "Listen up, bitch: my name is Ren fucking Roberts and this is *my* crew and *my* epic quest for vengeance, and *you* can piss right off!"

"Seriously?" the three women said in eerie unison. Across the room, Rotreego cackled as Rayn's spell settled him into a recliner and pinned him there.

"Seriously!" Ren shouted, his cheeks hotter than the surface of the sun.

Rayn's hard eyes softened. "Okay then, champ, it's your story, too. But right now the grown-ups need to discuss Rotreego's search for relevance in his brave new post-Pintiri world."

The elf in question vibrated against the spell holding him in place. "I've pledged my red-hot American blood to a higher cause than a filthy socialist like you would ever be capable of comprehending!"

"What is with you? This little act of yours isn't very funny."

"It's not an act," Lil said. She glanced at Rotreego for permission to explain. He responded with the most triumphant shit-eating grin Ren had ever seen. Lil continued. "A…ah…sorcerer…helped him meld the personality of a local talk radio host into his brain as a means of protecting everything he knows from any assholes who might want to exploit it."

Rayn's tongue flicked out through her pink lips, sampling the air like a snake's. "That can't be right," she muttered, and then repeated the test twice more. "Oh. Oh shit."

And then she disappeared.

Squealing hinges drew their attention to the kitchen. The Witch reached into an open cabinet to withdraw a wine glass while a bottle of red levitated out of the rack beside the fridge and floated to her side. With a sharp pop, the cork leapt out of the bottle and embedded itself into the plaster ceiling. Crimson wine arced up out of the open bottle and into Rayn's waiting glass.

In the recliner, Rotreego cackled like a madman. Lil tried to shush him. Antagonizing this powerful woman clearly wasn't the best idea.

Rayn's sigh shook the house. The flow of wine into her glass halted, and the bottle settled gently onto the counter behind her. The slender woman seemed to shrink in on herself as she took a drink.

What the hell? Ren mouthed to Isabel.

No idea, his sister mouthed back. Behind her, Lil tested the lock on the nearest window and received another jolt in return.

The lights flickered after Rayn's next sigh. Ren caught his cowardly bladder just as it was about to let go. When it came to being terrifying, Ashley and Brian had nothing on this woman. Hell, as far as existential dread went, the experience was right up there with that time Billy the reaper had torn his soul out through his nose and imprisoned it in a travel mug. There was no telling what Rayn was about to do, and little doubt that any of them would be able to survive the encounter if she didn't want them to.

Would she snap her fingers and pop their skulls? Maybe enchant that wine and turn it into flesh-melting acid? Was she capable of driving them all irrevocably insane with just a few words or a quick touch? Waiting for the next shoe to drop was torture. Ren almost wished Isabel would take a shot at the Witch just to make something happen.

When Rayn finally spoke, Ren hung on every word. "I've infiltrated secret demonic cabals, toppled kings and heroes, and brokered shady deals with more horrible assholes than I care to count. Every single one of those steps meant walking a razor's edge so narrow that even the slightest breeze could've sent me plummeting." She sipped angrily and jabbed an accusing finger at the former Pintiri. "I can't believe it's all going to fall the fuck apart because the one thing I thought I could absolutely count on—your macho fucking pride—turned tail and fled."

Lil darted over to Rotreego and clamped her hand firmly over his mouth. Though he couldn't speak through her iron grip, victory shone in his manic eyes. This was exactly the sort of situation he'd hoped to thwart when he'd asked Muffintop to throw his personality into a blender. He'd planned ahead, and he'd won.

Which didn't bode well for their chances of escaping with their lives. The Witch had trapped them here because she thought they had something she wanted. There was nothing stopping her from wiping her prisoners out and getting on with her day. Judging by the distress clear on the faces of Lil and Isabel, Ren knew they'd come to the same realization.

"So, what?" Ed's voice asked in his head. "That's it? Come on, kid. Use your head. Find that angle."

"We have a Talora device," Ren said, slipping the little puck out of his pocket. "We think whoever's dropping Tallisker's towers is coordinating their attacks using a numbers station streaming through these things."

Lil and Isabel gaped at him in shock that he'd just given away that kind of information. Rotreego, however, nodded emphatically, clearly urging him on.

Rayn's eyes glittered. "Which brought you here why?"

"We suspect Crim has the cyphers we need to decrypt those messages."

A second glass floated out of the still-open cabinet. Red wine arced up out of the bottle in a delicate stream to fill it.

"Whiskey, please," Ren said, his butt cheeks clenched tightly enough to snap a two-by-four in half.

The Witch shook her head. "Crim was a lightweight. Where'd you get that Talora?"

He'd hoped he'd be able to avoid the personal side of things, but it was too late for that. "In one of my father's safehouses. Ed Roberts was a mid-level Tallisker executive tasked with infiltrating the project by his superior, Marafuji. He knew the end was coming, so he left a message instructing me to steal Crim's cyphers and use them together with the Talora to bargain with Marafuji for protection from the rest of the company."

The flow of wine shut off and the glass floated slowly across the room. "I assume your father was in one of the towers that fell?" Rayn asked.

"Detroit," Ren forced out around the lump in his throat.

"My condolences," she replied warmly. "Once you acquire these cyphers, will you follow your father's instructions?"

That question proved surprisingly difficult to answer, even though Ren hadn't once considered *not* immediately bringing everything to Marafuji. Would immediately trading his only real leverage be the best way to protect himself? Now that he'd been prompted to actually consider it, he wasn't so sure. Once the Talora and the cyphers were out of his hands, he'd effectively be defenseless—not unlike Rotreego without his memories.

"We'll decrypt those communications and make a decision from there," he said a few moments later. Isabel's nod of approval was a huge relief.

The floating wine glass nuzzled his hand like a puppy in search of affection. He took hold of the stem with his fingers. Though he hadn't tasted a drop of wine in years because the stuff always gave him a headache, he knew better than to turn this glass down.

Rayn raised her own beverage in his direction. "I think I'm starting to like you, Ren Roberts," she said with a smirk, and then took a drink.

Ren matched her gesture, though he struggled against the urge to retch—whether because of the unfamiliar alcohol or her ominous statement, he wasn't sure. "Do you know where the cyphers are?" he asked.

"I don't. You're free to search the house, but Crim's the type that would keep such things close to himself at all times."

A drawer in the console table by the door popped open. A legal pad and a pencil floated out.

"Last I heard his car was spotted at this address. It's been there for a couple days," she said as the pencil scribbled away on the yellow paper. The pad and the implement then settled gently atop the console.

"Why are you helping us?" Lil asked, clearly freaked out. Her body stood tensed like a spring, awaiting her brain's decision between fight and flight. She lowered her hand from Rotreego's mouth, and he reached up and squeezed it.

"I need Tallisker distracted and in disarray," the Witch replied, "and I would like to cultivate a mutually beneficial relationship with a team of skilled contractors. I'd been counting on a certain former elven bigwig to help me in both cases. Perhaps he'll still contribute, in his own way."

"The government is going to enslave your children as organ farms for uber-rich elites looking to extend their lives indefinitely," Rotreego snarled.

"We'll see about that!" Rayn said cheerily. "So, one more thing: who here has heard of a group called Rejuv500?"

The former Pintiri raised his hand emphatically.

"Let me rephrase that: who here has heard of a group called Rejuv500 and can describe it to me like a normal fucking person?"

"They're a group within the Tallisker Corporation," Lil said. "Like a secret society or social club."

"They're a cult," Isabel added.

"Correct!" the Witch crowed, smiling between her wine-stained lips. "And who can explain their end goal?"

No one answered. Neither Ed nor any of the other Tallisker demons Ren had met at various functions had ever mentioned Rejuv500. He had no idea where Rayn was going with this, but he was sure it was only going to make his life even more difficult.

Rayn let the suspense linger a few seconds longer before providing an explanation. "They're a doomsday cult dedicated to culling the world's human population down to a much more manageable 500 million people using a spell that can only be triggered through the sacrifice of a former Pintiri."

That revelation landed like a ton of bricks. Every eye in the room swiveled to Rotreego. The elf decided to study his fingernails and pretend he didn't care, though his face flushed red.

"Ashley?" Ren asked Isabel.

"Yes."

"Well, shit."

That explained Brian's interest in Rotreego as well. Evading the pursuit of the walking conflagration would be difficult enough; keeping the elf out of the clutches of a cult of demons intent on wiping out most of humanity sounded downright impossible. Ren had thought they'd been after him the whole time, but the bullseye on the former Pintiri's back had turned out to be so much bigger.

"They must know Rotreego's alive," Isabel said. "They wouldn't have sent Ash otherwise."

"Of course they know," Rayn said haughtily. "I told them. Good luck!"

— CHAPTER TWENTY —

A nxious to put as much distance as possible between themselves and their pursuers, the team decided to forego an in-depth search of Crim's home. The address the Witch had provided wasn't far.

"Chances are it'll still be standing if we need to come back," Lil said as they buckled into the RV, her hands quivering and her eyes furtive. Rayn's revelation about Rotreego and Rejuv500 had left her shaken.

"I know little about the group," Isabel said as she accelerated the Mark away from the curb. Ren settled into the copilot's seat beside her, though he was far too wound up to find any comfort in that welcoming leather.

"They are spoken of in hushed tones when they are spoken of at all," Isabel continued. "I always thought of them like the Masons: a secretive group to be sure, but one that is unlikely to live up to its shadowy reputation. But I also heard from Ed and others that Rejuv500 is not to be messed with."

Lil leaned between the seats, one hand on each headrest. "The scuttlebutt when I was in elven intelligence claimed it's an old elven psy-op originally designed to destabilize Tallisker."

"You think a bunch of evil demons would actually fall for something like that?" Ren asked.

The elf shrugged. "They're still human, deep down." And then she left, walking all the way to the rear of the vehicle to whisper to Rotreego through the door of the bathroom in which he'd once again barricaded himself.

Ren studied the Mark Eight's broad dashboard as Isabel drove. A GPS system by her right hand guided them to their destination with a green arrow and a list of the next three turns. Mixed among the familiar gauges and controls were a variety of meters, levers, and displays he didn't recognize. One looked a bit like a crystal ball filled with roiling fog.

"Magic stuff," Isabel explained, once again seeming to read his mind. "You did really well back there, by the way."

"Thanks. Honestly, I almost pissed myself."

"I almost took a shot at her."

"Not gonna lie: there were a few moments where I hoped you were going to put one right between her eyes."

"I doubt that would've ended well for us."

Ren pictured the pistol kicking in Isabel's grip, the bullet streaking across the room...and Rayn's predatory smile as she stopped the projectile with a wave of her hand and let them all stew for a few moments over where it might be headed next. "Any idea who the fuck that was?"

"No, but she is clearly someone it would not be smart to fuck with." Isabel's grip on the wheel tightened. "Rotreego clearly knows her well."

"Well enough to hate her guts, at least."

Their encounter with the Witch had certainly complicated matters. Had news of Rotreego's survival spread beyond Rejuv500? Just how many people were out there searching for the former Pintiri? The bits and pieces Ren had heard about the elf's life painted the picture of a man who'd probably pissed off a lot of people. Dodging Ashley had already claimed one member of their team. What chance did they have if one of Rotreego's old enemies turned up on every corner? Surely this wasn't a situation Evitankari or its new Pintiri could just ignore.

Isabel lowered her voice. "We don't *have* to take him with us."

Hearing it spoken aloud gave that dark thought the momentum it needed to escape the corner of his mind in which he'd subconsciously tried to bury it. Rotreego had proven helpful, sure, but were the benefits of allying with him worth the danger? And how committed to this venture were the two elves, anyway? Did they really care about Ren's mission, or was he just the most convenient safe harbor they currently had access to? Would it even be possible to get a straight answer out of either of them? Ed had trusted the two elves, but that had been a whole different situation. God, Ren wished he had a way to get the old man's opinion on all this.

He responded to Isabel with a non-committal grunt and swung his feet up onto the dash. This wasn't a problem he was going to solve without much more consideration and perhaps the assistance of a strong beverage.

Still, if either of the elves gave him an immediate reason to cut bait…he knew he wouldn't hesitate.

Tiny snowflakes melted against the windshield as the Mark Eight powered up an on ramp and onto the interstate. Isabel stuck to the right lane. Smaller cars, bigger trucks, and even a few school buses passed them on the left. Ren didn't doubt the RV could've blown past them all, but he agreed with Isabel's choice to avoid drawing attention to the vehicle.

"She's an elf, isn't she?" Ren asked, the thought leaping directly to his tongue. "Rayn, I mean."

"I believe so. I couldn't see her ears underneath all that hair, but she certainly had the proper…bearing."

He studied the moisture left behind by a particularly large flake that had landed on the windshield right above his toes. "Ed always said they're a bunch of bootlicking hypocrites. Do what I say, not what I do, and the like."

Isabel grinned. "'Scrawny fucking sellouts,'" she growled, her impression of Ed's slur after a few highballs dead on. "'They'll sell ya righteousness and then spend the profits on the worst shit imaginable.'"

Lil appeared between them once more, putting an abrupt end to their shared laughter. "Exactly why I left. Probably the reason for whatever Rayn's deal is, too," she said, her face neutral. "We must be getting close."

"Screen says another five," Isabel said.

"All right. I don't think we're going to have Rotreego's help on this one, by the way."

Do we really have his help on any of them? Ren thought. "Is he going to be okay?" he asked instead, his face flushing.

Something dark flashed in Lil's eyes. "Yes. We should be quick about this. Tallisker executives don't typically spend a lot of time at highway truck stops."

Ren bit back several inappropriate jokes Waltman and Jim Jimeson would've loved. "I hadn't considered that."

"Crim could be in trouble of his own," Isabel said.

"Or this place is a secret Tallisker sex den and he's on an extended vacation," Ren suggested, finally letting one of those inappropriate jokes out into the world.

"Either way, let's start with his vehicle and hope we don't have to go any further," Lil said. "Either of you know how to pop a car door?"

"I can do it," Isabel said. "Ed made sure we were all taught a variety of useful real-world skills."

"Then you two are on the car. I'll stay here, behind the wheel."

Ren chose to interpret that as "I want to stick by Rotreego" and not as "I'm going to drive off as soon as you step away from this vehicle."

Ahead, the truck stop's massive sign towered over the bleak Michigan landscape, promising gasoline, cheap hamburgers, and giant Styrofoam cups of burned coffee—all the comforts of the road. Ren realized he had never been to such a place. Ellen had always packed plenty of snacks and insisted everyone empty their bladders prior to any long drives. "Jesus, no," he remembered Ed barking the one time he'd asked if they could stop. "Are you trying to catch an exotic breed of tetanus?" He wondered if that lent credence to his secret Tallisker sex den theory. Either way, it seemed a shame he wouldn't have time to duck in for a burger and a piss just for kicks.

Identifying Crim's car in the mostly empty lot was not difficult, thanks to the license plate number Rayn's enchanted pencil had written down. The blue coupe was parked about a hundred feet from the main building. Several spaces sat empty between the vehicle and its closest neighbors.

"Definitely a trap," Isabel said, guiding the Mark Eight in a slow loop around the lot so they could discuss.

"It's not clear from where, though," Ren thought out loud.

"Gotta be something in the car," Lil said.

"Like a bomb? Or a curse?"

"Maybe not something that dramatic or that lethal, but you're in the right neighborhood."

With an evil grin, Isabel pushed down on the accelerator. "Lucky for us, we've got a Mark Eight."

"Why's that?" Ren asked nervously. "Mark Seven not good enough?"

"This would be slightly more dangerous in an older model, yes," Lil said as she headed for the back. "Isabel, see if you can push Crim's car out of place a bit, just in case someone or something has line of sight on that particular spot."

"Good call."

"Rotreego! Buckle up back there, or at least hold on tight to something! And for Rot's sake, close the toilet lid!" Lil shouted. Ren made sure his own belt was secure and braced himself.

The RV gained even more speed as Isabel whipped it around the parking lot, skimming way too close to a row of parked cars as it made the turn. An old man in a heavy parka and a knit cap dropped his coffee as the Mark Eight whipped past him. Ren wondered if he should worry that Isabel had made little effort to avoid the guy.

"This is going to attract a lot of attention," he said.

"All part of the plan. More chaos means more complications for whoever we're dealing with."

They struck Crim's car flush in its rear bumper. Metal squealed as the parking brake lost its grip against the superior force of the RV. Isabel plowed the car forward a good twenty-five feet before she decided to lay off the gas.

"Let's go!" she ordered as she unlocked her seatbelt and spun to her feet. "Lil, you've got the wheel!"

The elf met them by the exit. "Good luck," she said, "and don't hesitate to get back in here if it gets dangerous."

Ren felt all the blood drain from his face. This couldn't be that dangerous, could it? They were in the middle of a vast, open space offering little cover for anyone watching, and they'd bulldozed Crim's car across the lot without triggering a bomb, a landmine, getting shot at by hidden snipers, or breaking the seal on some magic portal to a hellish alternate dimension full of primordial terrors starving for the taste of mortal flesh. What the heck else could possibly be waiting for them?

He scrambled outside after Isabel, hoping she hadn't noticed his hesitation. She waited for him beside the car's driver side door, holding up her hands to tell him to stop where he was and keep his distance.

"Pay very close attention," she instructed. "I'm only going to show you this once."

Ren nodded for her to proceed, excited to learn and strangely happy that she wanted to teach him. She reached into her jacket, pulled out her pistol, and drove it butt first through the driver side window. Glass shards tumbled down onto the asphalt and into the vehicle. Isabel reached past a jagged chunk, pulled the lock upward, and swung the door open with her other hand.

"Get in there," she ordered. "I'll keep watch."

"Thanks for the lesson, professor," he quipped as he dove past her.

The pristine interior reminded him of his dearly departed Jag—minus the treacherous broken glass—and for a moment the memory threatened to choke him right up. He pushed through, ignoring the cut he'd opened in his knee as he ran his hands under the dash and then the driver's seat, checked the cupholders, and opened the heating vents to peer inside. He wasn't sure what he was looking for, but he knew the Talora unit had a slot for a microSD card. It seemed likely the cyphers would be stored on such a small chip.

His search turned up nothing. He turned to the glove compartment. Surely there was no way a Tallisker demon up to his eyeballs in a global conspiracy would keep his secret codes somewhere that dumb. He popped the latch and flipped the little door open anyway.

Something small and fleshy rolled out and onto the passenger's seat. At first he thought it was a doll, a handsome plastic man with bright blue eyes and a crooked smile. He kind of liked the dragon motif on its gray t-shirt. Ren frowned, confused as to why Crim had left a toy in his car.

"What in the fuck hit me," the doll said, clearly dazed. Its gaze met Ren's. "Oh. Shit."

And then it unfurled a pair of gossamer wings and lifted itself into the air.

The door slammed shut behind Ren, telekinetically yanked from Isabel's grasp. "Shit!" Ren shouted, cringing away from the pixie. "Shit! Shit! Shit!"

He didn't know much about the tiny humanoids, but they had a reputation for being powerful and vicious. One of the little bastards had imprisoned Kevin Felton and Rotreego in his basement and tortured the latter by repeatedly killing and eating him while the local reaper was out of commission. Even Ed had spoken of the pixies warily. Being trapped inside a sportscar with one of the diminutive psychopaths was not a place Ren wanted to be.

The pixie wobbled in the air, clearly still not in complete control of itself.

Seizing the opportunity, Ren grabbed him by his slender legs. The pixie screamed as Ren tossed him violently over his shoulder and out the broken window. He impacted the side of the Mark Eight with a wet thump.

"What in the hell did you just throw at me?" Isabel asked.

"A fucking pixie!"

"A fucking pixie?" She paused, processing. "Oh. Shit!"

Crim's car jerked upward, lifted by an unseen force. Ren immediately recognized that magic was involved—and understood that he was in deep trouble. He slammed all his weight against the door while trying to open the latch, but neither would budge. Jagged glass poking up along the bottom of the window promised to cut him to shreds if he tried to squirm out that way. He looked down toward the ground and realized he was already too high up to escape safely. The car had been lifted a good hundred feet into the sky.

A dozen brightly colored lights surrounded the vehicle, distant enough to obscure the forms of the pixies within. Ren and Isabel had been so focused on watching things along the ground that neither had thought to look skyward.

This, Ren thought, *must be what an alien abduction feels like.*

He looked left and right, desperate for an escape he knew didn't exist. Something on the passenger seat where the pixie had landed after falling out of the glove compartment caught his eye: a little black data card in a clear plastic case. *Fuck.* He shoved it into his pocket, hoping the pixies wouldn't make him regret taking it with him.

Below, Isabel set her weapon on the ground, sank to her knees, and locked her fingers together behind her head.

— CHAPTER TWENTY-ONE —

Ren wrapped the scratchy blanket around himself and tried to melt into the wall at his back. He refused to open his eyes. What little he'd already seen of the horrific room would surely haunt his nightmares for years.

The pixies had telekinetically torn the Mark Eight apart like its armored hull was a cheap sandwich wrapper. Ren and his friends had been zip tied, blindfolded, and tossed into the back of a truck. He found Isabel and they clung together, his fingers wrapped around hers, desperate for some sign that things were going to be all right. Her warm presence almost made him believe it.

"So," he'd asked her at one point, "what do I do if they start pulling my fingernails out?"

"Scream, give them what they want, and hope they believe you," Lil replied darkly from the other side of the vehicle.

And then the short drive came to an end, and they were separated, the women from the men.

Rotreego's sobs echoed in the small space he and Ren shared. He'd been crying uncontrollably since the pixies had plucked him out of the RV's bathroom. The former Pintiri's last encounter with one of the little fuckers had been hellish. Ren felt for him. If these were going to be some of their last moments, it would be best if they spent them together—and doing what he could to help his friend might stop his own mind from worrying about why the pixies had separated them.

But getting to Rotreego safely meant opening his eyes. He really, really didn't want to do that.

Isabel would do it.

That one thought, confidently barging into his attention like it owned the place, was all it took. His eyelids snapped open.

A man's torso hung suspended a few feet from his face, dangling from a hook driven underneath the clavicle. Ice crystals speckled the purple-ish skin like demented glitter. Ragged wounds crusted over with blood marked where the butcher had removed the man's head, limbs, and genitalia. A dozen similar corpses filled the freezer in which Ren and Rotreego had been locked, some men and some women, some thick and some thin. There was no telling if they were elven or human. All were disgusting reminders of the fate that could befall Ren and his friends.

Ren dry heaved, his stomach already empty after he'd vomited in the corner after his first look at their makeshift holding cell. He hoped it would fester and ruin everything in there.

What the hell kind of creatures would do this to people? he wondered. He'd assumed the pixie that had captured and eaten Rotreego was a rare, deviant psychopath. Did all of them enjoy the taste of intelligent flesh? Were there whole dinner parties revolving around the practice? Was there a five Michelin star chef somewhere renowned for his finger sandwiches? Thinking about it was only going to make things worse, so he forced himself to stop.

Ren set his feet flat in front of him and leaned back against the wall to maintain his balance as he stood. The knee he'd scraped leaping into Crim's car burned in protest as he straightened it. *I hope they eat that part first and get an infection,* he thought darkly. He leaned hard on his shoulder blades, creating a pocket of space between the wall and the small of his back for his zip tied hands, and shuffled sideways along the perimeter. Trying to step in between the frozen corpses was out of the question.

Luckily he didn't have to go far. Rotreego lay in a heap just around the next corner. He gave no sign of noticing Ren's approach. Sobs sent tremors through his frail body as if he'd stuck his tongue into an electrical outlet. Ren reached out, then hesitated. There was no way to know how the damaged elf would react to a sudden touch. Would he lash out violently? Would he become even more inconsolable? God, Ren wished Lil was around for this part. He'd never really been the comforting sort.

But he did have a fantastic recent example of how to do the job properly. "Hey," he said, squatting gingerly. "I'm here."

Rotreego sobbed harder. *Fuck it,* Ren thought as he swung his legs around to meet Rotreego's. "Did I ever tell you about the time Billy the reaper pulled my soul out through my nose and shoved it into a coffee cup?"

The elf didn't stop crying or shaking, but at least he didn't kick Ren in the face. That seemed like permission to continue. "I've never felt anything like it. It was like...like there was somewhere I absolutely, desperately needed to be, but I had no way of getting there. And the longer I was stuck, the more it felt like I'd never find my way there." He shivered at the memory. "That's vastly over-simplifying it, of course. It was overwhelming. Like it was all I was made of. My whole universe."

Doubt stayed his tongue. Was this helpful? Was it making things worse? If Rotreego felt strongly either way, he wasn't showing it. Then again...Ren hadn't either, back while Isabel comforted him in Brian's trap. Maybe no news was good news.

"God, that whole experience sucked," he said with a cathartic chuckle. "But you know...even in the face of crushing existential agony, deep down I knew things were going to be all right. I knew the people that cared about me weren't going to leave me like that. And they didn't."

The earthquake that was Rotreego quieted—gradually at first, but then faster as Ren's words sunk in. There were aftershocks, but they were few and far between.

"Lil and Isabel will get us out of here," Ren said confidently. And he believed it. He'd never met a more competent, resourceful pair.

They sat like that, wordless but together, for a long while. At some point Ren fell asleep.

And then the door opened.

— CHAPTER TWENTY-TWO —

A pair of beefy thugs wearing too much denim secured black cloth bags over their heads and led them out of the freezer. The men appeared to be human, but Ren suspected each was controlled by a pixie in a crystal ball embedded in his chest, like Mr. Gregson back in Harksburg.

Deprived of his sight, Ren tried to use his other senses to gather intel as he shuffled along—as he thought Lil and Isabel would. That plan mostly failed. The bag reeked of old, unwashed sweat, masking any aromas that might've provided more information about their location. Their footsteps echoed as if they were walking through a large, open space. Occasionally they passed other people, but there was no telling who they were or what they were doing. The effort felt fruitless, but trying hard to listen for something useful distracted him from the stench.

He supposed he needed some plan for dealing with what he assumed to be an impending interrogation. Their captors had yet to ask the pair any questions. Honesty had worked reasonably well with the Witch, so he hoped it'd do the same with these pixies. He couldn't figure out why the little assholes had been lying in wait in Crim's car to begin with. *Either they're working with Crim,* he thought, *or they* think *we're working with him.* Ed had rarely mentioned any pixies, except to say that Tallisker was smart not to do business with them. Clearly they didn't know what was on that microSD card that had fallen out of the glovebox. Otherwise, why just leave it there?

Ren had not yet dismissed the idea that Rayn had set them up, though he thought it unlikely. He simply couldn't identify anything she stood to gain from the situation—unless, of course, she'd lied about *everything*, which he knew was basically the favorite sport of magic assholes everywhere. Still, the pieces just didn't quite fit.

A door squealed on its hinges not far up ahead. Ren took that as a sign they were close to their destination. Dark dread quickly overwhelmed a temporary moment of relief. His captors had shown him that they were willing to pull out a lot more than just fingernails.

Warmer air suggested they'd reached the next room. One of the thugs grabbed Ren's bicep and escorted him around something. His imagination expected the worst: a butcher block, or perhaps a buffet table.

"Bags off," a feminine voice commanded.

The nasty fabric was yanked away from Ren's head, leaving a warm, lingering stench in its wake. He winced at the bright light assaulting his face and blinked the blurriness away.

"Sit them down."

Heavy hands pushed down on Ren's shoulders. A hard couch caught his butt and thighs. Rotreego crashed down beside him with a yelp.

Ren's vision began to clear. They'd been taken to a cavernous room with a concrete floor and brick walls. To his right, paneled floor-to-ceiling windows overlooked a river streaming through a ravine below and a pine forest on the opposite side. He couldn't tell if the sun's position in the sky meant it was midmorning or midafternoon.

A familiar grunt drew his attention to the left. He locked eyes with Lil and Isabel, similarly bound and seated on another black leather couch. Neither appeared injured, but the fear and desperation on their faces was unmistakable. Unlike the men, the women were gagged with strips of dark fabric tied tightly behind their heads.

"Welcome," the female voice said. In front of them, a tiny woman with a shock of bright white hair sat in a golden throne with red cushions. The pixie from Crim's car rested on an ottoman at her side. The right half of his face was now covered with a purple bruise.

"My name is Minthalusetherenhirn," the pixie in the throne said. "You may call me Hirn. Your friends tell me you've been on quite the journey." Her emotionless inflection sent a chill down Ren's spine.

"Yes, we have," he replied, hoping to cut off any outbursts from Kotreego. Honesty still seemed like his best option. "We were looking for something that belonged to Crim: a data card."

Hirn leaned forward, rubbing her hands over her black jeans and craning her neck through the puffy collar of her blouse. "Did you know Crim?"

"No. My father knew him a little, and left instructions for finding that card I mentioned."

One of the thugs—a heavyset man in a gray track suit, with a face like a bulldog's—stepped in front of Ren, pulled out a measuring tape, and checked the width of his chest.

"Hmm," Hirn mused while her lackey worked. "Is the information on the data card valuable?"

Ren frowned at the thug, confused. "To the right buyer, yes." What was he supposed to say? That they were looking for something completely worthless?

Her attention swung to the bruised pixie like a blizzard bearing down on a coastal town. "You told me there was nothing of value in there."

"I'm sorry, ma'am. I didn't know."

Hirn's wings fluttered in annoyance. "You never do."

Another thug wrapped a blood pressure cuff around Ren's arm and then shoved the business end of a stethoscope underneath. "I'm not sure my insurance covers all this," he muttered. The thug smirked as he pumped up the cuff.

The lead pixie hurled her attention back to Ren. "Are you familiar with a woman named Talora?"

His eyebrows shot up in confusion. "I know of an experimental AI assistant named Talora."

"The green device we found in your pocket."

"Yes."

"And I assume the data card we also found in your pocket works with it somehow?"

"Yes."

Hirn's expression remained neutral, but her silence spoke volumes. Ren was pretty sure the two of them had come to the same conclusion: somehow, there was a connection between this woman and Tallisker's mysterious technology. But what?

The hiss of the blood pressure cuff deflating sliced through the room like a missile. "Any allergies?" the thug asked as he tore the Velcro apart.

Ren's tongue found an ounce of courage. "I break out in hives when faced with inexplicable bullshit."

"The car you broke into was driven to that rest stop by a woman wanted by human law enforcement in connection with the destruction of Tallisker's office building in Detroit," Hirn explained. "One of my associates took her into his custody after recognizing her from a report on the local news. She managed to escape after immolating him. My sources tell me she's now in

Evitankari, where she's using the name Talora and living with the new Pintiri—a human named Roger Brooks."

The dots connected in Ren's head immediately. "So you booby-trapped the vehicle in case she returned for it." Ironically, in a way, she had.

"Instead, we caught you—and an interesting piece of technology that shares a name with our quarry. So. Tell me why I shouldn't send the elves to the butcher, put a bullet in the demon's skull, and install a control sphere in your chest and take you out for a test drive."

Ren's heart skipped a beat, but his mouth didn't. "Because we can make each other rich. That Talora device, combined with the data card we were looking for in the car, can give us access to the Tallisker Corporation's most secret transmissions." He leaned forward. "Imagine the value in knowing what those bastards are going to do before they do it. We also suspect that what happened in Detroit was an inside job, and that the perpetrators are using these things to communicate. That's also worth a lot to the right people. And if I'm not mistaken, the device's name can't be a coincidence. It seems likely it can lead you to vengeance or justice or whatever you're seeking for your fallen comrade."

Hirn considered his proposal for what felt like forever. Ren struggled to maintain his poker face. The only card he hadn't played was revealing Rotreego's identity. He was surprised to realize he hoped he wouldn't have to.

"I like it," the pixie finally said. "Let's work together."

Relief flooded Ren's veins like high end Glenlivet. He'd negotiated that perfectly. If only Ed had been around to see it!

"Prep the human for surgery," Hirn commanded.

Strong hands picked him up by his armpits. Lil and Isabel protested into their gags as he was dragged over the back of the couch. A new thug with a crooked goatee swooped in and lifted his legs. Together, the two men settled him down onto a gurney and then strapped him down.

Oh, a shell-shocked Ren thought as a silver band tightened across his chest. *Oh fuck.*

Rotreego burst to his feet. "Now listen here, you psycho-socialist vampire scum! That right there is one of the finest Americans God has ever placed on his beautiful green Earth! Any red-blooded patriot righteous enough to follow Ren Roberts into battle shall earn a spot in eternal paradise! His enemies, however...ohhhh, you don't want to go there. This, I promise you."

Hirn cocked her head in curiosity as if one of her men had just delivered her an animal long thought extinct. "And just what in the fuck is wrong with you?"

"I am a modern-day George Washington, bitch!"

Ren took that as permission to play that last card he'd been saving. "That's Rotreego, the former Pintiri. He commissioned a mighty sorcerer to overlay that personality on top of his own to keep everything he learned on the job from falling into the wrong hands. If you want to meet Talora, I bet Rotreego could at least get you a phone call with the new Pintiri."

The pixie drummed her fingers on the cushion. "That is the dumbest shit I've ever heard. If it's true, I'll know soon enough. Surgery. Now."

One of Hirn's men silenced Rotreego's next outburst with a punch to the gut that knocked him back onto the sofa. Lil and Isabel struggled against their zip ties and tried to scream through their gags.

Ren writhed against his own restraints, but the seatbelt-like straps held him tight. The gurney rattled as it crossed the threshold into an adjoining hallway. He didn't realize he was screaming until another strap was pulled tight across his mouth.

"It's really not so bad," the bulldog-faced thug walking beside the gurney said, unbuttoning his shirt. "No more stressful decision making, no more worries about maintaining a job and an income…you're just along for the ride." The thug opened his shirt, revealing a glass sphere embedded in his chest. The pixie lounging inside waved mischievously.

Ren screamed so hard he felt the force of it rattling his skull.

When he was spent, he closed his eyes and slammed his head back against the gurney in frustration. *Okay,* he thought, desperate to hold onto this moment of composure, *what do I have left?*

His closest allies were all locked up in a separate room. Kevin Felton's territory felt so far away. It seemed unlikely the pixies would kill him, anyway, so his friendship with the reaper probably wouldn't help here.

Maybe the Witch was still watching? Doubtful. She'd seemed disinterested in Ren and his crew as more than a distraction in a much larger plot. If she'd been paying attention and cared to intervene, the best time and place to do so would've been back in the truck stop parking lot. There was also a possibility that everything happening here was going exactly according to her plans.

He opened his eyes and examined the straps holding him to the gurney. There was no way he could reach or manipulate any of the mechanisms he'd need to free himself.

So he'd have to count on his captors making a mistake.

Ed's bemused snort echoed in his mind as if his father were right behind him. "Fat chance of *that,* kid."

"So what would you do in this situation?"

Mental Ed took a long drag on his cigarette. "Remember when useless ass Sally McMajor got that promotion that should've been mine? What did I do about it?"

Ren couldn't remember his father taking any action that seemed germane to his current horrifying predicament. "Cut the shit and give me a hint."

"Three years later, when Sally was assigned to one of my project teams, I buried her under a pile of impossible tasks, filed multiple formal complaints about her piss poor performance, sabotaged the thermostat in her office so she had to work in a sauna, and paid an intern to harass her children on their walk home from school. Ran her out of the company in a month and a half. Last I heard she's selling mattresses in a shithole in Iowa."

"So I should leave the surgeon that's about to implant a bowling ball in my chest cavity a bad Yelp review?"

"You should persevere. Bide your time. And then when they're not looking, shank everyone responsible right in the jugular."

Which still meant he was completely boned in the short term and justified in screaming one more time.

A sharp left turn brought the gurney into a bright operating room trimmed with metal cabinets. An antiseptic smell assaulted Ren's nostrils; he supposed he should at least be thankful that the room was sterile. The gurney stopped in the center and the thug pushing it turned to slam the door shut behind them. Ren's attention turned to the sharp tools on the counter to his left—and the ominous glass orb beside them.

Bulldog Face, now wearing latex gloves and a surgical mask, leaned over Ren and brandished a syringe filled with clear liquid. "This needle's gonna hurt," he said flatly, "but when you wake up...you'll be a whole new man!"

Ren screamed and thrashed—mostly just to keep up appearances—but Bulldog Face clamped down on his arm with one hand and expertly plunged the tip of the syringe into a vein with the other.

As his consciousness faded, Ren swore he heard the fire alarm.

174 • SCOTT COLBY

— CHAPTER TWENTY-THREE —

L ight.

A faint sensation of motion.

And that was definitely a fire alarm.

"We should just fucking leave him," a familiar voice said above his foggy head. One of Hirn's men—the ugly one that had put him under.

"Wanna keep your wings?" the other thug asked. "Cuz the boss'll pull 'em off real slow if we don't save her new meat puppet. We have to get him outside."

Ren's eyelids fluttered opened. They were back in the hallway. His arm ached where an IV catheter dangled from the muscle. His chest, as far as he could tell, remained intact. The fire alarm continued to blare.

Ashley. Fuck.

It had to be, but how in the hell had she found them—again? Was there magic involved here, something akin to Lil's scrying? Had Ashley bugged Isabel's Mark Eight?

"The fire demon's here!" he tried to shout around the strap in his mouth, only to wind up gagging on his own saliva. Warning Hirn's men and potentially changing the situation seemed like a wise move here. Being burned alive while strapped to a gurney wasn't the way he wanted to go out.

Then again, would that kind of death really be that much worse than spending the rest of his life as a remote-controlled terrarium? He wasn't sure.

The gurney came to a sudden halt. Ren groaned as the strap chafed his upper lip.

"What in the fuck is that thing?" Bulldog Face asked.

"Hi guys! My name is Muffintop! What are your names?"

Ren's heart did a backflip. He couldn't have been more relieved to hear a friendly voice. But how the hell had Muffintop escaped Ashley and tracked them down to Hirn's lair? And what chance did the little guy stand against a pair of meatheads piloted by psychotic fireflies?

The thug who'd been pushing the cart frowned. "I can't lift that thing. Can you?" His voice quivered with fear.

Bulldog Face shook his head. "Nope. I can't lift anything else, either."

Realization filled Ren with hope. His captors—specifically, the two pixies inside Hirn's men—couldn't use their telekinesis. How in the hell had Muffintop managed that?

"Wanna see my scrapbook?" the troll asked.

"If you don't get the fuck out of here, the next thing you're going to see is my foot caving in your skull," Bulldog Face said.

"Awwww. You probably don't want to do that, mister!"

"Oh really?" the big man said, sauntering forward. "And why's that?"

"Your foot would have a better time if we were all friends!"

Bulldog Face laughed menacingly. "We'll see about that."

Ren snarled and thrashed, trying to distract Hirn's neanderthal so he wouldn't turn poor Muffintop into a pulpy red smear. Try as he might, he couldn't sit up far enough to get a look at the action.

Bulldog Face's broad back filled the hallway in front of him like an eclipse.

The man braced himself and kicked his right foot forward. There was a wet, sickening thud, and then a burst of blood spattering against the wall. A horrific scream somehow blocked out the sound of the fire alarm.

As Bulldog Face spun to the floor, Ren got a look at the ragged stump where his right knee had once been.

"Told you so!" Muffintop crowed.

"Shit!" Big Ears shouted. As his partner writhed in agony on the floor, crying and screaming, he fumbled to release the straps holding Ren to the gurney. "You can have him! Please don't hurt me!"

"Thank you!" Muffintop chirped. He hopped up and down so Ren could see him, waving merrily.

Big Ears undid the final restraint with the tips of his fingers and then bolted back down the hallway. Ren capsized the gurney as he swung himself onto his feet. For a moment his legs were jelly, so he reached out to steady himself against the wall.

"Muffintop, I fucking love you!"

"I missed you too, Ren!" He smiled a big, toothy smile. He appeared none the worse for wear. Blood covered the floor around his sneakers and the nearby walls, but somehow none of it had dared to touch the twisted troll. Bulldog Face had pulled himself into the fetal position and pressed himself tight to the wall.

"How did you do that?" Ren asked.

Muffintop shrugged. "I don't like people who try to hurt me."

Ren's brow furrowed. "That effect you had on their magic...is that why Lil couldn't scry your location?"

"Yuppers! I'm set to Do Not Track."

"What about Ashley?" Ren hoped she'd been dumb enough to try to backhand the little guy.

"She made me ride in the trunk, but maybe she's not so bad. There were snacks, at least!"

"Is she here?"

The troll nodded. "Yuppers! She told me to get in here and find you, and then she lit the place on fire! We should leave!"

The sound of the alarm took on a new urgency. "Let's find the others."

— CHAPTER TWENTY-FOUR —

Ren made the strategic decision to make Muffintop enter Hirn's throne room first.

"All clear!"

He carefully scanned the room as he sauntered in, his hands in his pockets, intent on looking as cool as possible in front of the others. Lil and Isabel looked at him hopefully over the back of the sofa they'd been left on. Hirn and all her men were nowhere to be found.

"Don't worry, friends! The cavalry is here!" Muffintop announced as he approached. Then he realized something was missing. "Where's Rotreego?"

The women rolled their eyes and shook their heads, unable to answer through their gags. Ren didn't need them to explain: Hirn had taken him. She'd taken the most valuable hostage and left the others behind to burn.

And it's my fault because I told her his secret.

Lil beckoned Muffintop to her side, then turned and grabbed his wrist with one of her bound hands. He went rigid as she siphoned the power she needed to fuel her magic. The zip tie securing her wrists snapped and fell away. She released her grip on Muffintop and removed her gag.

"Holy shit," she said. "You're like the biggest, strongest battery ever. Why weren't you like that outside the safehouse?"

Muffintop's cheeks flushed purple. "I didn't know if I could trust you. And I had to go number three!"

Isabel offered her own zip tie to Lil, but the elf ignored her and stomped up to Ren instead. He flinched away from her pointing finger, preparing himself for the tirade he was sure the elf was about to unleash.

"Don't do that to yourself," she snapped.

"Uhh...what?"

She crossed her arms and stuck out her hip. "Do not get all bitchy because you think you're responsible for whatever's happening with Rotreego. Do you have any idea who we're dealing with?" After a few moments she took his stunned silence as a no. "Hirn is one of the seven Grand Dames of the House of Razor Wings—the pixie mafia. She's one of the most feared creatures on the *planet*. Hell, look at my jeans."

"You...you pissed yourself."

"Twice. Giving up Rotreego was your only option. Hell, he *encouraged* you to do it, because he recognized what we were up against, too. I love Rotreego, but if *you* hadn't done it, I would've found a way to do it myself. He would've given himself up in a heartbeat to save the rest of us if he'd been capable. So stop feeling sorry for yourself and get your shit together. We need you. Rotreego needs you, too."

Ren blinked a few times, processing. There was no mistaking the sincerity in Lil's eyes. Her speech really had made him feel better. "All right. Let's get our asses in gear and get the fuck out of here before Ashley finds us or Hirn's men come back."

Lil smiled. "Never thought I'd be glad to hear you mansplaining."

He laughed. "Can you pop Isabel's zip tie?"

"I can, but there's something more important we need to deal with first."

She returned to the couch, untied Isabel's gag, and pulled the fabric away. "How does Ashley keep finding us?" the elf demanded.

"Hold up!" Ren said. "What's with the accusatory tone?"

"Don't you think it's a little odd that Ash keeps tracking us down? I know you like your sister, Ren, but something's going on here and it's logical to assume the new girl's involved."

"But—"

"It's all right, Ren," Isabel said firmly. "Ash can see me in her flames. Anyone she's burned, she can find."

"I fucking knew it," Lil snarled. "You really didn't think that was something the rest of us needed to know? What else are you hiding?"

Tendrils of brown smoke wafting in through an adjoining hallway drew Ren's attention away from the stare down. "Ash technically saved our bacon here," he said. "If we manage this right, she's another weapon we can use."

"That is a dumb risk," Lil said immediately, "but maybe just the kind of thing we need. Muffintop, hold my hand!"

"Yay!"

"Thank you," Isabel said to Ren, obviously relieved. There would need to be another conversation about this, of course, but at the moment they had a burning building to escape.

While Lil and Muffintop went to work, Ren investigated the rest of the room. He didn't know what he was looking for—maybe a weapon that could aid their escape, maybe some clue as to what Hirn had planned for Rotreego, maybe something else entirely. Nothing jumped out at him in that bare space. He wrinkled his nose in distaste as he stepped beside Hirn's throne. "Ugh, new money never has good taste," he said with a sigh. Behind him, the zip tie binding Isabel's hands snapped.

He noticed an old trunk on the floor behind the throne. Had it been there during their interrogation? He couldn't remember. And why was it whimpering?

Ren froze. After everything that had befallen them, he fully expected a trap. The kind of people devious enough to lay an ambush on Crim's car surely would have no problem rigging up a battered old box with some terrible surprise. Then again, if it was a trap, why secure it with such an imposing lock? The thought that it might contain someone or something useful was too tempting to ignore.

He gingerly kicked the side of the trunk with his toe.

"Please," a little voice in the trunk cried. "Please! I promise I won't screw up again! Please let me out!"

"One of Hirn's men brought that in here right before the fire alarm went off," Isabel said, appearing at Ren's side.

"There's someone in there," Ren replied. "We should open it."

"Carefully, this time," Lil said, still clinging to Muffintop's hand.

Ren nodded. "I'll drag it out into the center of the floor. Lil, pop the lock and then the lid. Isabel, be ready to give it the eye."

His instructions were met with a round of nods. "'The eye?'" Isabel asked playfully. "Is that what we're calling it?"

"Got a better name for it?" Ren asked as he dragged the trunk across the concrete by one of the leather handles on its sides.

"El Ojo Magnifico de la Diosa Mas Hermosa."

"That's a bit melodramatic, don't you think?"

She shrugged and took hold of her eyepatch. "That's kind of the point."

Lil, her thin fingers entwined in Muffintop's plump digits, knelt down beside the trunk and pressed her hand to the lock. The troll went rigid and giggled like the Pillsbury doughboy as her magic turned the metal to dust. A wave of her hand popped the trunk's lid open.

The smell of blood made Ren recoil. Isabel leaned over the open trunk, ready to obliterate whatever was inside if she needed to.

"It's the pixie that ambushed us at Crim's car," she said, "and he is in *rough* shape."

Ren swallowed a bit of bile and leaned over for a closer look. The pixie lay curled up on the bare floor of the trunk in a pool of his own blood. The gossamer wings on his back had been torn away, leaving a pair of ragged stumps protruding from his back. Ren couldn't help feeling sorry for the guy. Judging by the dark stains on the trunk's interior, this wasn't the first time it had been used for something horrific.

"The House of Razor Wings is famous for this," Lil said sadly. "Without his wings, he can't use his magic."

"Then he can't hurt us," Ren said, an idea forming, "and if he can't fly there's no way he can get out of here on his own. We have to take him. He might be able to help us figure out where Hirn took Rotreego."

"Not the worst idea," Lil said.

He knelt beside the trunk and forced a smile. "My name's Ren," he said. "My friends and I are going to get you out of here and get you patched up. Then we need to have a talk about Hirn and see if we can work together to save our friend."

The pixie shivered and grunted. "Gurk."

Ren cocked his head. "For real, we're going to help you."

"I think that's his name—or a shortened version—not an expression of distrust or dismay," Lil said, her eyes glued to the dark smoke billowing into the room. "Grab him. We don't have much time."

Gritting his teeth, Ren reached down into the filthy box and gently slid his fingers through the sticky blood and underneath Gurk, trying avoid the stumps on his back. The puddle of blood made a gross slurping sound when he lifted the pixie up out of the crimson pool. Ren hesitated, unsure how best to carry the creature.

His pants pockets weren't quite big enough and certainly wouldn't be comfortable against a pair of open wounds. He settled for lifting the hem of his shirt and resting Gurk in what was essentially a makeshift hammock, and then holding the whole bundle tight against his torso.

"Like a kangaroo!" Muffintop said happily.

"We probably shouldn't try to escape through the smoke," Isabel said quickly, cutting off any delaying banter.

Ren swung his attention to the windows. A light snow had begun to fall. "Too bad we can't get across that river."

"Actually, we can," Lil said, "but at least one of you is going to vomit."

Ren shrugged as best he could while gently holding an injured pixie in his shirt. "Worth it."

"Yeah," Isabel added, "probably."

Still hand-in-hand with Muffintop, Lil stepped to one of the glass panes and pressed a single finger to the window. Tiny fissures crackled outward through the glass from underneath her touch.

"If it's any consolation," Ren said to Gurk, "we're about to seriously fuck up your boss's throne room."

Gurk replied with a pathetic attempt at a thumbs up.

The window shattered and fell away in a shower of shards. Cold wind whipped in through the open space, pelting them with snowflakes and making them all shiver. Ren really wished he knew what the Razor Wings had done with his coat.

Lil looked down at the rushing river nervously. It was clear she wasn't sure about whatever she was planning.

"You've got this," Ren said as visions of wet hypothermia danced in his head.

Lil reached toward Isabel with her free hand. "Make a chain. Ren's on the end so he can hold onto Gurk. Normally I'd take something like this slow and easy, but in this case, it'd be best to be quick and try to avoid detection."

Isabel grasped the elf's hand first and then her brother's. Her palm was warm and sweaty, but Ren found himself grateful for the contact. Should he have hugged her after she'd been freed? Maybe. He supposed there'd be time for that later.

He shifted his grip on his shirt to make sure Gurk was secure. "So wha—"

With a ferocious grunt, Lil telekinetically launched them all out through the window.

Holy shit! Ren thought as they tore through the sky, soaring over a rushing river splashing against glacial rock. The wind howled in his ears and raked the skin on his face. Isabel's hand tightened and crushed his own.

Trees!

Their flight jerked to a sudden halt just before they collided with the thick stand of pine trees on the opposite cliff. Ren swore he felt all his organs bounce off the inside of his rib cage. Beside him, Isabel projectile vomited all over the nearest tree as Lil set them down in the snow.

"Sorry," Isabel rasped as she released Ren's hand and stumbled forward, coughing and spitting.

Lil put a reassuring palm on the other woman's spine and held her hair back away from her face as she finished. "My fault."

"Can we do it again?" Muffintop asked happily.

After a quick check on Gurk, Ren glanced back across the gap. Hirn's hideout turned out to be a sprawling old mill. Flames danced across the far end of it. As he watched, a towering smokestack lost its battle against the fire and collapsed.

"Come on," Lil said. "There's a road on the other side of these trees. Hopefully it leads somewhere warm."

— CHAPTER TWENTY-FIVE —

F uck, it's cold," Ren gasped in between chattering teeth.
The narrow road along which they trudged wound its
way through that pine forest as if those who'd built it hadn't
wanted to fell a single tree in the process. There was nothing to
see but snow and trees. It reminded Ren of some of the roads in
Harksburg, which dropped his sprits because none of those led
anywhere particularly useful. They'd chosen a direction entirely
based on quickly putting as much distance between themselves
and Hirn's hideout as possible. Though he couldn't argue with that
logic, the loss of sensation in his fingers and toes, combined with
the lack of anything resembling civilization, made him wonder if
they'd made the wrong choice.

Gurk shivered in Ren's shirt, once again wallowing in his own
blood. His wounded stumps had opened back up. Isabel had
wrapped an arm around Ren's shoulders and pressed her hip
to his in search of warmth. There wasn't much heat to be found
between the two of them, but at least her presence was reassuring.
Lil walked beside them, close but keeping her distance. Muffintop
toddled along to her left, seemingly indifferent to the cold.

"None of you magic people can fart fire or turn snowflakes into
handwarmers, right?" Ren asked.

Lil's sigh manifested as a thick cloud. Muffintop, however, scratched his chin as if searching for an answer. "I once played Go Fish with an elf who could light cigarettes with her toenails!"

"Did you get her number?"

The troll deflated. "No. Sorry."

And so they soldiered on. Intellectually, Ren recognized this as a better fate than the one that would've befallen him on Hirn's operating table—but there, in that frigid, desperate moment, he thought maybe he would've been better off with a fishbowl in his chest.

An idea stopped him in his tracks. "Hold up!" he declared, his eyes darting back and forth to the woods on either side of the road. "We're in a *forest!*"

"If the king of this forest was interested in us, he would've shown himself by now," Lil said. "Very few of them are like Donovan. They typically prefer to keep to themselves unless their domains are threatened."

"I know I'm not supposed to sass the forest, but what if I kicked that tree?"

"Please don't."

"It would at least make me feel better."

"I suggest you stop letting so much of your body heat escape through your flapping gums."

She was right, of course, so Ren shut his trap. Their trudging continued. Ren side-eyed the tree he'd been targeting, just in case it was sensitive enough to take a mean look personally. He didn't doubt Lil's assessment, but he prayed the King of the Forest hadn't shown himself yet not out of disinterest but because he hadn't quite put the finishing touches on his elaborate entrance.

"Get on the shoulder," Lil instructed, suddenly perked up. "There's a car approaching."

Ren's inferior human hearing didn't pick up the roar of the vehicle's engine until a minute later, but when it did—nothing had ever sounded so much like salvation. Surely no driver would leave them on the side of the road in this weather. That vehicle meant warmth. It meant life. It meant a way out. He couldn't believe their luck.

Wait, he thought, *I'd know the sound of that engine anywhere.*

"Muffintop," he said around the lump in his throat, "what's Ash driving these days?"

"Your new Jaguar!"

Lil groaned. "Give me your hand again."

"Don't do anything too aggressive," Isabel said, her voice quivering. "We need that vehicle."

"She'll stop," Ren added. "She wants Rotreego."

"And she's going to be really pissed when she realizes he's not here," Lil said.

"I'm pretty disappointed about that myself!" Muffintop declared as he wrapped his fingers around the elf's.

The green sportscar glided around the bend like a hawk stalking its prey. Ren had never felt so many mixed emotions at the sight of his beloved make and model. On the one hand, it was amazing and uplifting to encounter such a familiar sight after all he'd been through. On the other, he could clearly see Ashley behind the wheel.

And she looked *pissed.*

The car screeched to a halt about ten yards from their position. Ren cringed, his heart going out to those poor, abused brake pads.

Ashley left the engine idling as she shoved the door open and stepped out. A satisfied smirk twisted her gray face. Ren supposed he would've worn a similar shit-eating grin had their roles been reversed, although he knew he never would've been able to pull off the air of barely controlled violence lurking underneath. After several days on the hunt, Ashley finally had her quarry cornered— not in a dark alley or in some back room, but against the edge of hypothermia, with the promise of life saving warmth if they gave up without a fight.

"Where's Rotreego?" she rasped.

Ren saw no harm in directing her rage at the House of Razor Wings. "The pixies have him."

She turned back toward the car. "Then I'm done here."

An invisible force lifted the Jag a few feet off the ground and left it hovering. "Lie down on the ground and put your hands behind your head," Lil growled, "and you don't get hit in the face with a luxury automobile."

Flames danced in the demon's eyes. "I should warn you: I'm a lot tougher than those losers you squashed back in Harksburg."

"Then I'll have to put some actual effort into it this time," Lil replied. Muffintop pumped his fist.

"Ruining this vehicle just to kill me won't stave off the cold." Ash spat on the ground at her feet. Her saliva steamed and sizzled on the pavement. "But I could warm you up a bit if you like."

Lil shook her head. "Last chance—"

The elf gasped in pain as Isabel's boot collided with her forearm and forced her hand away from Muffintop's. As the Jaguar slammed back down to the asphalt, Isabel followed up with a forceful shove that sent Lil sprawling. The elf rolled onto her back and tensed, ready to spring back to her feet, but froze when she found the demon above her, ready to tear her eyepatch away.

"I knew it!" Lil snarled.

"You don't know anything," Isabel replied matter-of-factly. "I am not leaving any of you here. Not in this weather, and not with the House of Razor Wings on the hunt. Ash: get in the trunk."

"What?" Ashley and Ren protested in eerie synchronicity.

"You heard me. We're going to get everybody to safety and then we're going to sort this out."

Ren didn't know what the hell to make of any of this. "I thought you two were estranged."

Ash snorted. "That's news to me."

"We got married in a secret ceremony five months ago," Isabel said, her cheeks flushing. "Ashley is my wife, and I love her very much—even though she tried to kill Ed."

"I forgave you for the fire extinguisher thing," Ash said, "even though it tasted horrible. This getting in the trunk bit, though...I'm going to need a few dozen foot rubs to get over this."

Isabel's words struck Ren like a blow to the gut. He stumbled backward, almost losing his grip on Gurk in the process. Isabel had been lying about Ash all along, just like Lil thought. What else had she been lying about? Did the bond they'd forged as adoptive brother and sister mean *anything*, or had she faked that too?

One thought stood out above the rest: *I really should've fled to Talvayne with my mother.*

"And now that I've proven I trust the three of you, Ash is going to prove she trusts me by getting in the trunk," Isabel commanded.

The walking conflagration scowled and sighed, then reached back into the car to push the release. The trunk popped open with a firm *thunk*. "Remember when you said we could get a puppy?" Ashley rasped as she backed toward the rear of the Jag. "Now we're getting two."

"And you can name them both," Isabel agreed. "Is there a first aid kit back there? Put it on the ground."

There was and she did. Ren didn't start breathing again until Ashley pulled the trunk shut over herself.

Isabel let go of her eyepatch and extended her hand down toward Lil. For several moments the pair stared at each other, their silence speaking volumes. Ren recognized his sister's gesture as yet another offer of trust and vulnerability. Once Lil took the demon's hand, she'd have a life force to power her magic. She'd be free to hurl Isabel into a tree or launch the Jag up over the trees and into the river—with Ashley inside. Isabel was betting the elf wouldn't lash out.

"Lil," Ren said, "let's see this through. I'll strangle the both of them myself if I don't like what they have to say."

"Ha!" she cackled. "That, I'd like to see. Muffintop, what do you think?"

The troll clapped his hands together and stood up straight, clearly proud that she'd thought to ask him for input. "Please don't fight anymore. Let's all be friends!"

"Fine," she said as she grasped Isabel's arm. The other woman pulled her to her feet in one fluid motion. "We'll go somewhere safe and warm, and then we'll see if Ren has to make good on his threat."

— CHAPTER TWENTY-SIX —

And so began the warmest, most awkward drive of Ren's life.

"We'll discuss this once we reach the Friendly Pines campground," Isabel declared as she curled up in the passenger's seat. "All of us."

Ren's protest that Ashley could probably hear them through the trunk fell on deaf ears.

Lil reached forward between the seats and cranked the heat up, then got to work on Gurk's injuries using the first aid kit. Isabel quickly fell asleep. Muffintop watched the scenery roll by, occasionally humming to himself or swinging his feet. Turning on the radio seemed like the wrong move.

Silent introspection while attempting to jostle Ashley by hitting every available pothole it was, then.

So, he thought, *Isabel's married*. That this was the first thing his brain decided to examine and how disappointed that simple fact made him feel left him deeply uncomfortable in a way he didn't want to dwell on.

So Isabel lied about her relationship with Ashley! That one didn't feel much better, but he suspected it'd be a more useful topic to attempt to understand.

Okay! Isabel lied about her relationship to Ashley because...

Because...

Hmm...

Because she wanted to get close to Ren so she could steal the family fortune?

Because she and Ashley were working to recover all of Ed's Talora devices for Tallisker's special projects group?

Because, like most of the other magic assholes he'd met recently, she couldn't resist an opportunity to fuck with Ren Roberts?

The answer that fit best turned out to be the most frightening: that Isabel, like Ashley, was a part of Rejuv500, and leading Ren and his crew along had been a complicated scheme designed to get a hold of a certain former Pintiri. Assuming, of course, that she'd told the truth about any of that crap to begin with.

Maybe I should make up my own secret society with shady motives just to fuck with her. If only Oscar Spuddner were available to help. That would've been right up the former Immortalist's alley.

"Thank you," Gurk croaked as Ken turned off the highway.

"You're welcome," Lil replied, her voice surprisingly gentle.

Friendly Pines was just as they'd left it: empty for the season. Some sixth sense woke Isabel moments before they arrived. Ken stopped in front of the entrance so she could get out to open the gate. For a brief moment he considered popping the Jag into reverse and fleeing the scene as quickly as all that performance engineering could take him. He could ditch Isabel, dump Ashley in the gutter somewhere, and then head off to rescue Rotreego with the trio in the backseat. The temptation almost overwhelmed him—but then guilt set in, and he shifted his foot away from the clutch. Isabel had saved his life back in Ed's safehouse. He owed her a chance to explain herself.

"And besides," their father's voice interjected in his inner narrative, "she might provide you with something you can use."

He tried to act normal when she got back in the car, but he couldn't fight the blush warming his cheeks or his white-knuckle grip on the steering wheel. "It's all right," she said. "I would've thought about abandoning me too."

He didn't know what to say to that, so he popped the car into gear and drove onto the access road.

Without the Mark Eight and its cache of camping supplies, they'd need to take shelter in one of the campground's administrative buildings. The long, flat structure that served as both a cafeteria and an activity space was the only one they knew for sure had working heat and electricity, thanks to Rotreego's previous mission to raid the vending machine. It would do for a night or two. There was also ample room inside for a brawl if that became necessary after their big discussion.

Ren expertly guided the Jaguar down the access road's shallow decline, made slick with a light coating of fresh snow. Their destination awaited them beyond a trio of smaller buildings. For a moment Ren pictured the place on a bright summer day, buzzing with happy visitors and smiling staff in matching polo shirts, flowers blooming brightly in the gardens and window boxes. It seemed pleasant. Hopefully he'd have the opportunity to return under better circumstances and with nicer weather.

He parked behind their target building to hide the car from the access road, then realized with embarrassment that the tire tracks he'd left behind in the crusty snow would give them away. Isabel exited the vehicle as soon as it stopped, clearly anxious to let her wife out of the trunk.

"Muffintop," Lil said sternly, "do not let go of my hand until I tell you to do so."

"Okay! I like holding hands! When you do things, I see fireworks!"

Ren reached into the backseat and took Gurk from Lil's lap. Bandages covered the pixie's bare torso like a white puffer jacket.

His green eyes were unfocused but alert. "This is gonna get weird, isn't it?" he muttered.

"Those two demons are the adopted sisters I didn't know I had until a few days ago. They're also married, which I guess makes both of them my sisters-in-law."

"Dude."

Ren couldn't tell what that was supposed to mean, so he left it alone.

They found Ash free of the trunk and stretching like a cat. Up close, in person, and free of hypothermia's encroaching influence, Ren was struck by just how short the Walking Conflagration actually stood. If she were five feet tall, it wasn't by much— and yet somehow, she filled the space around her like a large appliance.

"Issy says you're Ed's kid," she rasped curiously. "Must've gotten your good looks from Ellen."

Several jokes about Ash getting her own good looks from a toaster died on Ren's tongue. "That's me," he said awkwardly. Gurk's assessment had been right on the mark.

The demon grunted. "It's nice to officially meet you. Just so you know: I didn't burn down Donovan's, like I implied back at that safehouse. That would've taken a lot of time I didn't have. But it sounded pretty terrifying, right?"

Ren and Lil traded a glance. "Top notch work," the elf growled. "Five stars."

"Did you have to torch my car?" Ren asked.

"Yes."

Ash cocked her head and seemed to focus on something off in the distance. As far as Ren could tell, the only thing over in that direction was a snowy pine forest. Maybe that thousand-yard stare was a tic. Isabel ignored it and got to work picking the lock on the door they needed to get through.

"*Tch-tch!*" Ashley snapped out with her tongue. With a crisp flap of its wings, a white barred owl with a hooked beak swooped down out of the forest, startling the rest of the group. The bird landed on Ash's shoulder and looked around, groggy, as if it had just woken up. "I didn't take any joy in incinerating what I had to, but…I know a run-around when I see one." The owl cooed as she scratched its neck.

Ren recalled something Isabel had said about a much younger Ashley's dreams of becoming a veterinarian. He'd been polite for about as long as he could stand. "So what, you're like some kind of cartoon princess that sings songs with all the forest animals?"

Isabel snorted and the door she'd been working on popped open. "She is certainly no princess."

"Love you too, cyclops." Ash winked at the owl, and it launched itself back into the forest.

They entered the cafeteria mostly single file, save for the inseparable pair Lil and Muffintop had become. Ren flashed back to that time he'd been sent to the principal's office back in fifth grade after he got busted for running a highly lucrative dodgeball gambling ring with Waltman and Jim Jimeson. A similar sense of dread hung over their little procession. Confessions would be given, tearful apologies would be offered, and the man in charge would be tasked with weighing it all and issuing the appropriate response. The realization that he'd be the one playing the principal's role this time didn't make Ren feel better.

The first to step inside, Isabel reached to her left and flicked on the light. The empty cafeteria sprawled out before them, its folding tables and plastic chairs neatly organized against the wall to the right of the entrance. A raised stage trimmed with a thick green curtain watched over it all from the opposite end. Bulletin boards bursting with out-of-date schedules and activity flyers covered most of the remaining wall space, save one spot in between a pair of windows dedicated to a smiling woman named Chiyo, the campground's most recent Ranger of the Month. The whiteboard underneath her photo declared that she loved Friendly Pines's visitors almost as much as she loved her two cats.

Ren knew from the brochure he'd skimmed during their first layover that this room was the social center of the entire operation. Every morning began with a continental breakfast—including both organic and gluten-free options—served community style to encourage campers to get to know each other. Hourly nature lectures began at eleven and ran until three. Tuesdays at sunset they had soft serve ice cream and flavored slush. Family movie night with complimentary popcorn happened every Thursday night. And on Saturday, the rangers of Friendly Pines gathered onstage to perform the staff skit. It all sounded exhaustingly wholesome.

Isabel and Ashley got to work setting up chairs in a rough circle. Muffintop moved to help, but Lil jerked him back as if pulling on the leash of a misbehaving dog.

Ren looked down at Gurk, cradled once again in his blood-stained shirt. "How you doin'?"

"Please put me down before you punch anyone."

"Will do. I'm going to need your boss's address, by the way. Dry cleaning bills."

"Gotta be a spare ranger uniform around here," Lil suggested with a smirk.

"Says the woman who's been wearing pissy jeans all day," Ren replied.

"Whoa!" Muffintop said. "I want a ranger uniform too!"

"Of course," the elf replied. "You and Ren can be nature buddies."

"This is what you've been hanging out with?" Ashley asked Isabel.

"They grow on you after a while."

"After a while?" Ren asked incredulously. "Not a long while, right?"

Isabel smiled. "Take a seat, Ranger Ren."

"Yes!" Muffintop cheered. "I love alliteration!"

Where there's banter, Ren decided, *maybe there's also hope.*

Though they'd attempted to arrange the seats in a circle, it wound up looking like the demons were on one side and everybody else was on the other. The uncomfortable chairs creaked and groaned under even the slightest movement. Lil found a spare pair of black jeans in one of the staff lockers and changed into them. Once they'd all claimed a seat, Isabel wasted no time kicking off the discussion.

"As I mentioned, Ash and I got married in a secret ceremony five months ago. Ed served as both officiant and our only guest." She paused to let that detail sink in, and then reached over to take her wife's hand. "We agreed a long time ago to keep our relationship a secret revealed only to those we trust implicitly. Ed Roberts was the only person who ever fit that description. We both learned a long time ago that the world in which we operate views loved ones as targets, leverage, and vulnerabilities, and although we ached to be together, neither of us wanted to be put in a position where we could be used against the other."

"I can appreciate that," Ren said, "and I understand what it means that you chose to tell us your secret. What I don't get is why it took so long. You could've saved us all a ton of trouble if you'd said something at the safehouse."

"I know," Isabel said sadly. Ash squeezed her hand, a gesture that left Ren feeling strangely rattled. "But I didn't know then if I could trust you—any of you—and more importantly I didn't know if you'd be capable of keeping such a secret. Ren, you in particular seemed so lost, so desperate. I wanted to trust you the way I had trusted Ed, but I didn't think you could handle the life you were stepping into. Ash is my whole world, and there are much worse things out there than Brian Drew. Could you stand up to them, or would you sell us out the first time it looked like your best option? I didn't know for sure. But back in the mill, you could've given up

Rotreego first thing. You didn't. Not until he gave the go-ahead. Now I know."

"And for all I knew, you'd taken my wife hostage as part of some fucked up scheme," Ash said. "I don't mess around with people who might be my enemies."

Ren rubbed his temples. "Fine. But what's the goal here? What are you two trying to accomplish?"

"My mission is to recover the former Pintiri so we in Rejuv500 can reset the world into a more equitable, sustainable state," Ash said matter-of-factly.

"Are you one of them, too, Isabel?" he asked.

The plastic chair squealed as she shifted uncomfortably. "Think about my life, Ren. Would I have had to spend my childhood hiding in a garage if there were enough for everyone? Would the government have arrested my whole family just because we weren't supposed to be where we were? Would my father have sold me to a stranger if he hadn't been cornered like an animal?" Her voice cracked. "I'm not positive Rejuv500 can do what they claim, but I have not yet met anyone with a better plan for making sure more little girls don't go through what I did."

"You can't have Rotreego," Lil growled. She squeezed Muffintop's hand so hard the little troll winced.

Ren agreed, but he wasn't ready to let this conversation degenerate into a fight. "So you stuck with us...why? Just to bide your time until you could sneak off with Rotreego?"

Isabel shook her head. "If I'd decided to take Rotreego, none of you would've been able to stop me. I wanted to make sure you were all right, Ren, and to help you find a direction. Ed did so much for us. In you, I saw a chance to finally pay some of that back.

"I knew you'd never willingly give up Rotreego unless something in the group's dynamic changed. I needed *you* to be okay with it, or at least with leaving the others behind so Ash could swoop in. It was not the best plan, but it was the best I had."

"Your plan sucked, Issy," Ash interjected.

"I know. I didn't think we'd escape that car chase. I thought Ash would corner us at the Mark Eight and we'd be forced to turn over Rotreego." She flicked her attention to Muffintop. "I did not expect you to lead her away."

"I'm full of surprises!" he said triumphantly.

Ren tapped his foot on the hardwood floor, letting the puzzle pieces coalesce. "So when Hirn ran off with Rotreego and we were all about to die of hypothermia, you felt good enough about us to open up. And that was your first chance to make contact with Ash and clear things up with her. Fine. But here's the big question: what's next?"

"If I asked you to walk away, would you?" Isabel asked.

"No way," Ren replied immediately, surprising himself. "I have to see this through. I'm sure you'd give me the same answer if I turned the question around. And I am not okay with letting you drag Rotreego away."

She sat up straighter. "Then I think we should work together to rescue our friend from Hirn and then figure out the rest."

"Another shit plan," Ash growled.

"You're not helping."

The cheap plastic chair creaked as Ren leaned back. He studied Isabel's face, searching for some sign of duplicity and finding only warmth and a bit of desperation. The simplest solution to this problem would be to give Lil the go-ahead to launch the two demons into Lake Erie. But he couldn't do that, for the same reason he couldn't give up on Rotreego. He couldn't let this fucked up little family he'd found splinter.

There had to be another way, if only he could find it.

"Ren," Isabel continued, "Rotreego's the only part of this we want. The Talora device and the cyphers are yours to keep. I can arrange a meeting with Marafuji once you've got them. You and I are not enemies, and I don't want us to be. Let me do for you what Ed did for me. Let me give you a new life."

"This is exactly the kind of bullshit Rotreego wanted to avoid when he microwaved his brain," Lil snapped. "He's out of the game, demon, and I will not let you drag him back in." She looked to Ren, her posture and expression softening. "I won't let you do it either," she said softly, clearly hoping she wouldn't have to back up that threat.

"I'm not trading Rotreego for anything," Ren said with calm conviction. "But I also don't like what I think happens if we fight over that, and I don't want to lose my sister, and I don't think you and I can rescue him on our own."

"I'd agree with that assessment," the elf said.

"Is there anywhere else we could go for help?"

She rubbed her face with her clear hand. "Not quickly, and probably not without drawing Evitankari's attention. There's no telling what those bastards would try to pull if they found out their former Pintiri's still alive."

"Hirn took him because she sees him as something of value," Isabel said. "It is likely she sees the most value in a trade with Evitankari."

"That is highly likely," Lil agreed.

"The bitch loves money," Gurk croaked from Ren's lap, "and she's done business with the elves before."

"Okay," Ren said, the seed of an idea germinating in his mind—albeit one he thought it best to guide the conversation toward, rather than blurt right out. "So Rejuv500 thinks a former Pintiri can help them achieve their goals. How?"

The demons traded a look. "We don't know," Isabel admitted.

"You *don't know*? How do you not know?"

She shrugged. "It's a secret. Only the top levels of the organization are given that information."

Ren frowned. "So you joined a cult? How much of your income do you have to contribute before they tell you that hooking Rotreego into the remains of a UFO will grant ultimate enlightenment to all true believers?"

"It's not like that," Isabel said.

"Rejuv500 gave us a place to go when we had nowhere else," Ashley added.

Ren's eyebrows leapt toward the ceiling. "Nowhere? Not even with my father? Not in his mansion full of other adopted children?" Something wasn't adding up.

"You don't want to go there," Isabel said sadly.

He leaned forward, aching for just one sip of his beloved Glenlivet to steel his nerves. His idea would have to wait. "Why did Ed have his own orphanage to begin with?"

Isabel seemed to shrink. "You really don't want to go *there*."

"We're going anyway," Ren insisted. "Right now. Otherwise, I'm walking out of here and I will not hold it against Lil if she launches you to the fucking moon. Start talking."

— CHAPTER TWENTY-SEVEN —

Remember when I told you about Ash's love for animals? One of Ed's rivals saw that as an opportunity. Cute puppy, white van."

"Damn, Iz," Ash interjected in disgust, "do you have to make me sound like a total airhead?"

"You are a total airhead. I'm *trying* to make you sound sympathetic," Isabel said. "Back to the story. Ed's enemies took little Ash and decided the best way to take advantage of their new asset was to turn her against him. So, they told her the truth."

Isabel took a deep breath and fidgeted with her fingers, her gaze on the floor. "Every summer, Ed threw a lavish party on the orphanage's grounds to celebrate those of us who'd just finished high school. Usually this was two or three kids, rarely more, and they all moved out the next day. We all thought it odd that we never heard from those graduates afterward. We were told that they were busy with college or their new jobs, or just with settling into their new lives."

A chill crept up Ren's spine. This, he knew, could not possibly go anywhere good. His flesh grew colder as Isabel continued.

"Remember: the more atrocities a demon commits, the stronger he becomes—and setting up forgotten, abused, disadvantaged children for success and then ripping it away is pretty damn evil. The structure of it all allowed Ed to maintain control and shape himself as he wished.

"The people who took Ash had video evidence of Ed Roberts brutally murdering the prior summer's graduates. There was our beloved patron tearing our older siblings apart with his own two hands, making sure each lived long enough to understand exactly what he'd done to them and what he was taking away. Ash's captors made it clear that this would also be her fate—and mine, and that of all our brothers and sisters—unless she did something about it.

"So they taught her how to light people on fire. After a few months of incinerating living things, she no longer needed the help of matches or a lighter."

Tears streamed from Isabel's good eye. "It would have been the perfect murder: a lost daughter returned to her adoptive father, only to set him ablaze. Luckily for Ed, they made a mistake in giving her a degree of autonomy. They knew she hated him, but they underestimated her love for me. She sent me a message, alerting me to be elsewhere on the day it was all supposed to go down.

"I didn't listen. I made sure I was there, and I stopped her. I saved Ed's life.

"After Ash told the two of us what was going on, your father came clean. He agreed to spare us, to help me find power like Ash's, and to find us roles within the Tallisker organization—but we were banished from the orphanage and forbidden from ever returning. We still saw Ed regularly, of course, and he set us up with a new life and made sure we were well taken care of, but we had literally no one else. So when Rejuv500 came around recruiting...well, it sounded nice to once again be part of a community of people like ourselves."

Ren waited to see if there was more, then he set Gurk in Muffintop's lap and rose to his feet. A vein pulsed wildly in his forehead as if struggling to escape. That cold sensation in his flesh had done an about face and turned into red hot fire. "How do you expect me to believe any of that?" he snarled.

"Because it's true," Lil croaked. "Every August, Ed came into Donovan's alone. The boss would set me up in one of the VIP rooms to serve him drinks. He'd get drunker than I ever saw him, and he'd scream and rant and rave and bawl his eyes out. I never got much detail about what was bothering him, but one time…Rot, I remember one time he collapsed on the bar top and said 'I killed them all' over and over and over again, and I knew for sure he'd done something abominable. I'm sorry, Ren, but it all lines up."

He calmly took one more look around the room, unmoved by all the sympathetic expressions he found, and then he whipped his chair against the wall and stormed out.

— CHAPTER TWENTY-EIGHT —

Every pair of eyes in Big Lou's locked onto Ren and watched him cross the ten paces from the door to the bar. There was no automated defense system on the planet better at tracking potential targets than the regulars at a small-town bar.

For his part, Ren could not have given less of a shit about who thought he belonged there or not. Even though he'd typically been the type to have his friends fight his physical battles for him, he hoped one of the other patrons would give him an excuse to take a swing. The nervous energy vibrating through his body needed a release.

A bartender built like a sasquatch met Ren at the short leg of the L-shaped bar. The towel used to wipe down the bar top looked like a tissue in his huge hand. Ren wondered if one of the thick silver rings in his earlobes was a talisman masking a troll or some other large nonhuman.

"What'll it be?" the bartender rumbled through a long brown beard shot through with streaks of gray.

Ren scanned the bottles lined up along the wall to the bartender's left. His usual was nowhere to be found. He felt surprisingly fine with that. "Shot o' well whiskey and a light beer chaser," he said as he lowered himself onto the stool closest to the wall. Fake brown leather crackled under his weight.

The bartender lumbered away to fulfill his order without a single word of acknowledgment. Ren was fine with that too. He felt the attention of the regulars fade; by choosing to serve him, the bartender had essentially broadcasted the order to stand down. Ren cased the joint anyway out of careful barfly habit. He estimated another two dozen or so seats at the bar, four of which were occupied—two by an older couple in matching fleece pullovers, sharing a basket of fish and chips and sipping daintily at their white wines, and the others by a pair of twins frantically scratching lottery tickets. Most of the tables were vacant save for one by the windows where a trio of men in cold weather gear worked their way through a bucket of cheap bottles. Ren's position also offered a great view into the kitchen at the far end of the building. Sports memorabilia covered every inch of wall that wasn't taken up by a television. Each screen showed a different hockey game.

Not that different from the Burg back home, Ren thought. How many days had it been since he'd last been somewhere he felt so comfortable? He'd lost count, and he didn't want to think about it. He didn't want to think about much of anything, at least for a little while. His attention settled onto a convenient flat screen on the far wall, and he lost himself in the Zen-like back-and-forth of professional ice hockey.

Though his consciousness disengaged, his bar senses monitored the vicinity. The older couple nibbled at their meal and occasionally leaned their heads together in whispered conversation. In the kitchen, a chef in stained whites leaned around the corner to scan the crowd and then disappeared once more. One of the twins got up to use the bathroom. On Ren's chosen screen, a defenseman recovered the puck behind his own goal line and rifled it up the boards to his winger.

Life went on, simple and carefree.

The bartender returned with Ren's drinks and a plastic bowl of the yellow popcorn popped in a dinged-up box beside the register. "Menu?"

"Nah."

Jealous thoughts barged into Ren's inner peace as he watched the bartender's broad back move away once more. Greet the guests, pour the drinks, send orders to the kitchen, deliver the food, wipe the bar, bus the dishes, occasionally pop some corn, drop off the bill, pick up the payment—the simplicity of the man's life was alluring. That bartender knew exactly what he had to do and when. Ren, meanwhile, had no clue what to do about anything. What move could he possibly make that wouldn't lead to more heartbreak and a greater chance of a gruesome death? Why bother avenging a man who'd turned out to be such a monster? What the hell had anything he'd done since leaving home even accomplished?

He banished the thought with a shot of fiery whiskey and slammed the door behind it with a mouthful of watery beer. Mind cleansed, he returned his attention to the hockey game, occasionally picking at the popcorn. It was a little burned underneath all that butter powder, but it hit the spot.

The twin who'd gotten up to use the bathroom stopped at the lottery machine and bought a fresh pile of scratch tickets before returning to his stool. The home team's goaltender desperately wormed his way across the crease to flick away a puck surrounded by sticks and skates. Though they hadn't finished their entree, the older couple ordered coffee and dessert. The bartender brought the dudes by the window a fresh bucket of beer. The cook wiped down his prep area.

At some point, Ren's own beer disappeared. He'd intended to only have one and then get back to business, but he hadn't quite had his fill of this blessed normalcy. He examined a set of framed baseball cards on the wall as he awaited his next round, finding he recognized most of the names but very few of the faces.

A blast of arctic air announced a new arrival. Ren was not surprised to find the newcomer settling into the stool beside him.

"Rum and cola," Lil said as the bartender approached, "with a straw, please, if you've got one." The man turned and got to work.

"I was expecting Isabel," Ren said after a moment.

"Don't worry, Muffintop's babysitting." She'd put on a knit cap from the campground's gift shop to conceal the tips of her ears. The green wool matched the color of her eyes. "Ashley's petrified of the little guy. She says he can't be burned."

"I believe it. One of Hirn's goons tried to kick him. Dude's leg exploded."

"No shit. Maybe Donovan was right about that reincarnated prophet thing," Lil mused.

"You walk?"

"Borrowed a truck from the garage. The clutch sticks and there's some sticky shit in the cupholder, but it runs. You all right?"

"Been better." He paused when the bartender arrived with Lil's beverage and a fresh bowl of popcorn, and then continued when the man was far enough away again. "Mostly I feel stuck, like none of the paths I could take will lead anywhere worthwhile, and like the journey that got me to this point was a waste of effort in the first place."

"Been there," she said.

"When?" he interjected before she could unload whatever impersonal advice was brewing on her tongue.

Lil stirred her drink with the straw, went to take a sip, and then thought better of it. "You heard enough tragic backstories for one week or can you handle another one?"

"I'm all ears."

"All right. Rotreego and I…were married." She paused to let that revelation sink in. Ren wasn't particularly surprised. He'd noticed that extra something between them plenty of times. "I suppose technically we still might be. Not really clear on that part of elven law. Our sixty-second anniversary would be this August."

That stunned Ren. "You both look amazing for your ages."

"Superior elven genes. We also married young, right out of school. We grew up next to each other and our families go way back. Each of us is descended from a member of the original Gadukah, the commando squad that aided the first Pintiri in slaying the demon lord, Axzar, if any of that means anything to you."

It didn't, and Lil could tell, so she continued her tale. "It took us thirty-eight years to conceive. Not for lack of trying, mind you, but just because our people's physiology sucks in that regard." Her voice turned wistful. "Rori was our world. We named him using pieces of our Gadukah ancestors' names, hoping he'd grow up to do great things too. That was dumb, but the sentiment still makes me smile.

"Elven children have until their twelfth birthdays to prove they have magical ability. Those who can't are declared shala'ni, dusted, and exiled to the island of Poa for the supposed good of Evitankari. Not even the Pintiri's son is above that law.

"Rotreego was out on assignment when they came for Rori. Aldern—the guy who's mostly in charge—promised that nothing would happen until Rotreego returned, but Aldern is full of shit and always has been." She steeled herself with a drink. "I managed to break Rori out and we evaded the authorities for the next two weeks. I'd hoped to stall for time until Rotreego could return, thinking we could figure out a solution together. We got caught an hour before he arrived. I killed three men that day. Shame I couldn't get them all. I was sentenced to death.

"Now, guess who's supposed to oversee the exile of all shala'ni? That's right: the Pintiri. Rotreego was expected to wipe his son's memory and teleport him across the globe using a special transpoint. He agreed to do it in exchange for my life, and he got me to Ed...and that was the last I'd seen of my family for over a decade, until he came sauntering into my bar the other day."

Ren studied his beer for a moment, giving her story room to breathe. "I'm sorry to hear all of that," he said gently. "Thank you for letting me in."

"I can't prove it," she said around another sip, "but I will go to my grave believing we were set up. I'd taken an interest in our families' history and done a lot of research. Lots of pieces and parts of the Gadukah story are missing or don't add up. Someone realized I was getting close to something important and decided a simple dusting wasn't good enough."

Ren thought she sounded like Rotreego, but he bit his tongue. And besides: hadn't he seen enough evidence to prove that all these magic weirdos were up to their eyeballs in each other's horrific schemes?

The elderly couple at the bar asked for their check. The husband kissed his wife on the forehead, slipped on his coat, and headed outside presumably to warm up the car while his wife transferred their leftovers into a takeout box. Ren and Lil traded nods with the old man as he shuffled past.

"I know you think you've got it bad, but look at who you've been spending your time with," Lil said. "You don't see any of us giving up."

He sighed. "You're right, but that doesn't necessarily make it easier."

"Say what you want about your father," Lil said, "he did his best to keep you and me and to an extent Isabel and Ashley out of the shit."

"Yeah, but it wasn't enough. You and I stumbled into it anyway, and my sisters joined a damn cult."

"Pardon me," a soft, friendly voice said from their left. The pair had been so engaged in their conversation that neither had noticed the old woman rise from her seat. Though her shoulders could barely support her wool coat and her hands shook as they held the takeout container, her bright eyes and warm smile glittered vibrantly. "I get a bit silly after half a glass of wine these days, but I just wanted to say: fuck Tallisker, fuck Evitankari, fuck Talvayne, fuck the House of Razor Wings and the Knights of Sanit and the Impalore monks and all the rest. Don't worry about any of them. Take what you do well and use it to build a path for yourselves and anyone else who wants to join you. The biggest mistake we've *all* made is in rejecting one way without building a viable alternative. Now I will bid you both a polite farewell, as I'm sure my husband is wondering what set of polite strangers I'm drunkenly harassing this time."

"G-g-good night," Ren stammered as she departed.

"I thought I smelled another elf," Lil muttered.

"You know what I smell? An idea."

— CHAPTER TWENTY-NINE —

"...and if this doesn't work, all I ask is that you give Rotreego a week's head start," Ren declared from the stage, his arms spread wide like a televangelist who knew his flock was going to buy him another yacht.

Halfway across the cafeteria, Isabel and Ashley sat in their plastic chairs in stunned silence. Beside them, Muffintop and Gurk lounged in a flamingo-shaped pool floatie they'd found in a storage closet. Lil leaned against the far wall, her judging eyes watching the others. She'd already heard and approved of Ren's pitch back in Big Lou's and had agreed to let him deliver it here on his own.

"I know it's a lot to take in," he said confidently, but not without empathy. He took three steps forward and then sat down at the edge of the stage, letting his legs dangle. "And I do regret my lack of appropriate visual aids and detailed revenue projections. I would be happy to answer any questions you have to the best of my ability."

To the surprise of everyone in the room, Ash spoke first. "Just to make damn sure: after we've recovered Rotreego, the Talora device, and the cyphers, we go straight to Ed's orphanage."

That hadn't quite been the idea—he'd assumed a few days of logistics would be involved—but if it meant making the sale, he could agree to it. "We will go straight to the orphanage, yes."

The demon narrowed her gaze and leaned back in her chair, seeming to smolder, but thoughtfully. Ren knew he had her. He almost couldn't believe it. He thought she'd be the toughest sell.

"Any other questions?"

Muffintop raised his hand enthusiastically. Ren shot him an approving point of his finger.

"What's the maximum retirement contribution eligible for employer match? At what date do my options vest? Do you have EPS statistics for similar ventures?"

Ren drummed his fingers on the edge of the stage. "I don't know. Want to be Chief Financial Officer and deal with all that?"

The troll's gnarled face lit up. "Boy, do I ever!"

"Awesome. You're hired! Welcome aboard!"

"Count me in," Gurk said from within a little cloud of weed smoke, his eyes glassy. He'd found a ranger's stash underneath one of the vending machines and used it to roll the tiniest blunt Ren had ever seen. "Wingless pixies don't have a ton of job prospects."

"Glad to have you!"

He took a long drag on his tiny joint. "Rad."

That left just one person—arguably the most important, both to Ren and his scheme on the whole. She studied him in a way that made him feel like he was a complex mathematical equation hanging out on a chalkboard. He'd hoped the connection they'd forged—whatever was left of it—would come into play here. The longer her silence dragged out, the more he worried her objectivity might win out.

Isabel was a survivor. If she didn't see this as the best way to move forward safely, she wouldn't agree to go along with it.

Finally, she spoke. "Evitankari and Talvayne do not take competition lightly. Neither will all the smaller interests operating in their shadow."

Ren smiled. He and Lil had discussed how to address this very problem back in Big Lou's. "They've all got much bigger things to worry about than one little startup company," he said confidently. "Think about everything we know. *Someone* went out of their way to create a living former Pintiri. Talvayne's cut itself off from the transpoint network. Tallisker's offices are under attack. The elves will get drawn into all of this while dealing with their new Pintiri, who, oh by the way, is in cahoots with a woman conspicuously named after a top-secret AI assistant built by their biggest rival. This is a mess." He paused for dramatic effect. "Someone's trying to bring it all down. Our new venture can fly under the radar while picking up the pieces."

"That woman in Crim's house," Lil said thoughtfully, right on cue. Ren could've kissed her.

"There's a reason Rotreego wanted to tear her apart," he added. "He knows more about her than he can effectively communicate."

Isabel frowned. "You think Rejuv500 is being manipulated?"

He hadn't quite put that string of words together in his own head, but they fit well. "I do."

"But why should we care as long as it helps us reach our goal?"

He raised an eyebrow at her. "You're not worried that someone with an agenda has gone so far overboard to stir up a group that wants to murder a huge chunk of humanity?"

"Of course I'm worried about it, but former Pintiris don't exactly grow on trees. Are we really supposed to pass up an opportunity that may never present itself again?"

"I could make the same point about what I'm offering you." He slid down off the stage and sauntered forward. "The difference is that I'm asking you to be an important part of something instead of just another nameless lackey that doesn't have the full story about how she's being used."

"Careful," she said darkly.

"Whatever," Ren replied with a shake of his head. "You can help me fix things, for me and your wife and the rest of our extended family, or you can betray your friends in this room and go be a bigger monster than my father ever dreamed of being."

Lil had been very skeptical of this approach, but Ren knew that if there was one thing these demons valued above all else, it was their tenuous grip on what remained of their humanity. That was where they were most vulnerable, the weak spot they all aimed for in their internecine battles with their rivals. He had to believe Isabel's to be a particularly huge bullseye, dreams of global genocide be damned.

She didn't respond. Ren continued his approach. Her good eye began blinking more rapidly, like the processing light on a computer tower. Something was happening in there.

He stopped right in front of her and waited. His heart beat up into his throat. He didn't think she'd hurt him, but there was no way he'd be able to stop her if she decided to put an emphatic end to the discussion. His insistence that Lil keep her distance from everyone else began to feel like a mistake.

"Fine," he said, unable to take it anymore. He reached out toward Ashley and offered her the back of his hand. "Burn me."

Isabel gasped. "What?"

"This way you'll always know where to find me," he said, struggling to keep the fear out of his voice. "I won't be able to run off with Rotreego. If I fuck you over or do anything other than what I've promised, you'll be able to collect whatever debt I owe at your leisure. And you'll be able to sell me out to save your own skin if it comes to that. You proved yourselves to me by making yourselves vulnerable. I'm returning the favor."

Before Isabel could reply, Ashley pounced. She took Ren's hand in both of her own, stuck out her tongue, and licked a line of hot, searing pain along the back of his middle finger. Ren hissed and flinched but didn't pull away. The stench of burning flesh made his eyes water.

"Yo," Gurk drawled, "that chick kisses her wife with that mouth?"

Her task complete, Ash shoved Ren's hand away. "You're ours now, rich boy," she said, and wiped her mouth with the back of her wrist.

Ren paid her no mind. His attention had locked onto Isabel.

"All right," she said after another moment of consideration. "We're in business."

— CHAPTER THIRTY —

I 've known some of the boys in Hirn's crew for decades," Gurk explained. "Since long before the House of Razor Wings took over the local scene. But after what she did to me, I'm dead to all of them."

Ren frowned. "So we're stuck?"

"I didn't say that," the pixie replied after a quick puff of his tiny joint. "We just gotta do a little end-around if we want to score."

Gurk's trick play involved calling an old associate from Ashley's cell. She dialed the number he dictated—after a few canna-bis-addled false starts, one of which resulted in a very confusing conversation with a pizza place—and then she set the phone down beside the pixie and activated the speaker phone so they could all listen in.

"Yo, Moss, it's Gurk."

"Gurk! Long time. How's ya ma?"

"She's great, thanks. Just got a new bread maker. Hey look, I've been burned."

"Fuck me with a chainsaw, Gurk, I'm sorry to hear that. You tell her yet?"

"No, ma doesn't know, and I'd thank you not to spoil the surprise. Any chance you could get me a meeting with the old man?"

"Fuckin' right I will, dude."

None of this inspired much confidence.

Ren became too distracted to follow the remainder of the conversation. He nudged Ashley with his elbow. "I never expected you to have a sparkly pink phone case," he whispered.

She wrinkled her nose. "Can't put flames on everything, idiot."

He knew a few guys back in Harksburg who would've disagreed with that statement. "I'm just saying, it ruins your whole vibe."

"Like how you seem like an intelligent, reasonable human being until you open your mouth?"

Before Ren could respond with a witty retort, Isabel interjected. "He does that when he's nervous. Eventually it becomes endearing."

Lil snorted.

"Thanks, man. We'll be there," Gurk said smoothly. He tapped the screen to end the call. "We're on for tomorrow. Lustreya Park, noon sharp."

"That was too easy," Ren said.

The pixie shrugged and sat down on the edge of Ashley's phone. "If I had to guess, the old man knows *something* happened at the mill and he wants to know what. He and Hirn ain't exactly drinkin' buddies."

"So who is this guy exactly?" Lil asked.

"If he wants you to know, he'll tell you. He hates when other people spread his business around. Best we all show him the respect he's lookin' for." He lit another tiny joint using an even smaller match and waved it at Lil. "Ya know, lady, I know a cop when I smell one."

"I'm ex-intelligence," she said flatly. "There's no love lost between me and Evitankari. And make no mistake: I know a career criminal when I see one."

The pixie took a long drag, let the smoke marinate in his lungs, and then exhaled a perfect ring. "As long as you and me stay on the same page, we're gonna make a hell of a team."

"Yay!" Muffintop cheered. "Teamwork makes the dream work!"

"I like this kid," Gurk said. "Just trust me when I say the old man's got about as much reason to hate Hirn's guts as I do, but he's still plugged into the Razor Wings just well enough to know what she's got going on. If anyone can point us in the right direction, it's this dude."

The expressions surrounding Ren made it clear no one—save Muffintop—felt super comfortable with this plan, but none of them voiced an objection or an alternative. "What should we expect, then?" Ren asked.

Gurk leaned back, his face stoner thoughtful. "Expect...an asshole who fucks with you for a bit before he finally gives you something close to what you want for secret reasons of his own."

"Oh, good. We know the type."

"I don't doubt it, dude."

— CHAPTER THIRTY-ONE —

Ren parked the Jag right in the middle of the big, empty lot and cut the engine. "We made it!" he said with mock jubilation as he leaned around the seat to look at Isabel, Ashley, and Muffintop in the back. It had been a very long drive, past where they'd been held by Hirn's crew and then even farther north into metro Detroit. "Now you three be good and don't touch anything!"

"Sure thing, Pops," Ash deadpanned.

He stepped out into a bright, crisp day. It was warmer than it had been, but it would be months more before the snow melted. He unzipped the top of his new peacoat to let some air in. That morning's diversion to a nearby department store had been productive, if not particularly fashionable. He felt good knowing Rejuv500 was covering their new threads via Ashley's credit card.

Gurk stuck his head out from the big pocket by Ren's hip. "Smooth ride, bro."

Ren recoiled from the scent of smoky funk that followed the pixie's words. "Please don't catch my new jacket on fire."

"No prob, Bob," the pixie replied happily. "Through the gate, up and over the hill. Look for a big bastard chillin' with some birds."

Lil slammed the passenger door shut. "Wish our backup had better line of sight."

"I'm sure that hill's a big reason why the old man chose this meeting spot," Ren said. The path up the rise was paved, shoveled, and sprinkled with sand, but it still looked treacherous.

"Come on," the elf said, shoving her hands in the pockets of her bright orange parka. "If this guy's what I think he is, he won't appreciate it if we're late."

They crossed the parking lot side-by-side, each alert for any sign of a threat. There were only three other cars, none of which stood out in an interesting way. Ren wondered where the old man's lookouts were hiding. Were there pixies watching from high in the sky, their lights obscured by the sunshine? Was the homeless woman digging through the garbage near the gate more than she seemed? What about the guy out for a jog in bright green tights? Did the giant pile of brown snow that had been plowed to the side of the lot conceal an elite strike team of vicious gnomes? Could there be a curse or hex attached to the iron arch above the park's entrance, waiting to alert the old man to anyone who entered? Anything was possible.

Ren kicked those thoughts out of his mind before they made him hyperventilate. He hadn't been thrilled when Gurk had insisted they leave the more obviously threatening members of their team behind as backup, but he acquiesced when Lil voiced her approval. They were headed in unarmed except for their wits and Lil's magic. Though Ren recognized the wisdom in this approach, the logic of it all wasn't enough to make him feel any braver about this.

Worse still: Lil had insisted that he do all the talking.

"You're the one with the epic tale of loss and revenge," she'd said mockingly. "Hit him with that and be honest about everything. All of these fuckers have a sob story. They'll be able to relate to yours—like we all did."

"Your history won't work?" he'd asked, mostly to be contrary.

"No one's going to rush to help out the former Pintiri's old lady. You're the star here. Get used to it, Mr. CEO."

And so, Ren strode toward Lustreya Park with as much confidence as he could muster, his asshole clenching a little tighter with every step. If things went well, this would be the first of many such presentations, given his long-term vision for the group. He made a mental note to take a few classes or hire a consultant who could help shoulder some of that load.

They crossed underneath the metal arch without triggering any traps or obvious alarms. The park inside appeared to be relatively new. The grounds were sparsely planted with short, slender trees, skeletal without their leaves. They poked up out of the surrounding snow like fingers sticking out of ruined gloves. Given the bulbous shape of the hill ahead, Ren suspected they'd stepped onto a reclaimed landfill or some such.

The pair found themselves breathing heavily less than halfway up the steep slope. That paved path would've been downright dangerous if it hadn't been so well cleaned. Even the benches had been cleared of snow. Though Lustreya Park was a bit off the beaten path in an underdeveloped neighborhood, there was no doubt that someone was taking very good care of it. Ren suspected they were about to meet the man responsible. He considered the implications. Their contact, it seemed, had at least some sway with the city government. After days spent among nonhumans who explicitly and carefully kept themselves separate from humanity, the idea that one of them might work hand-in-hand with the locals on such a project seemed near impossible.

The top of the hill provided an amazing panoramic view of downtown Detroit a few miles to the east. Ren paused and examined the empty spaces in between the skyscrapers, wondering which patch of blue sky had once been home to Tallisker's headquarters. Lil, always the empath, waited beside him in silence.

"Might be the closest I get to my father again," he said a minute later. "If the body's still there."

"For now, let's pretend we know right where it is."

So he did. He lost track of time as he gazed out across Detroit, searching for a connection to whatever was left of his old man. Profound thoughts and meaningful gestures eluded his thoughts like leaves fluttering past on the breeze, forever just out of reach.

Thanks, I guess, but I really wish you hadn't fucked up all those kids, Ren thought. *I guess...I hope it wasn't painful? If the reaper around here was mean to you, tell me so I can complain to Felton?*

He rocked back on his heels, frustrated. This felt like an important moment, and like he'd let Ed down if he failed to seize it. But what, really, was there to say or do? His old man had left behind a complicated legacy that he couldn't figure out how to compress into a simple sentence or action.

"You know," Lil said thoughtfully, "Ed would tell you the best way to honor him is to get your ass in gear and go talk to that troll."

Ren laughed, feeling lighter. "You're not wrong, but...what troll?"

"On that bench." She pointed down the hill and off to Ren's left. "The big bastard chillin' with some birds."

"Holy shit. That is easily the biggest troll I've ever seen."

The elf raised one suspicious eyebrow. "How many trolls have you met that aren't named Muffintop?"

"Just the bouncer at Donovan's," he admitted as he started forward again, "but let's keep that to ourselves."

A dozen pigeons mingled around and between the old man's tree trunk legs, cooing happily as they pecked at the seed he sprinkled onto the asphalt path. He was shirtless—a bold move given the weather—but he wore a thick pair of jeans secured to his massive frame by a set of bright yellow suspenders. Scars and wrinkles twisted his green skin into something otherworldly.

Long strands of wispy gray hair billowed out from the top of his head and down the backs of his muscular arms.

His nipples are the size of pizzas. Don't stare. Don't stare. Don't stare.

Ren stopped short about ten feet away when the birds became anxious, and then he and Lil waited patiently as the old man dispersed the remainder of the seed he gently cupped in his palm. Given Gurk's description of the guy, it seemed best to show some respect.

"I appreciate your concern for my feathered friends," the troll said slowly as he rubbed his palms together to scrape away the clinging bits of seed.

"They seemed to be enjoying their lunch and your company. My name is Ren Roberts. This is my associate, Lil." The elf nodded, her eyes active and alert.

"Ah, my twelve o'clock. Right on time." The troll turned his upper body to face them, draping his arm over the back of the bench on which he sat. "Welcome to Lustreya Park. My name is Lustreya. Please take Gurk out of your pocket so I can see what that pixie bitch did to my friend."

Gurk stuck his head out of the pocket as Ren reached down "Yo, Lustreya! Good to see ya, dude. Appreciate you takin' the time."

"It is my pleasure, old friend."

Ren took hold of Gurk's legs with his right hand and carefully braced his shoulder with his left as he lifted the pixie out of his pocket. The last thing he wanted to do was hurt Gurk's injuries in front of the old man. His cargo free, Ren knelt on one knee and released the pixie onto the pavement.

"All this walking and standing's gonna take some getting used to," Gurk quipped as he did a little turn to show his wingless back.

Lustreya clicked his tongue. "Oh, Gurk, I am truly sorry Hirn took your wings."

"Thanks, man."

The troll flicked his attention up to Gurk's taller companions. "I used to run Detroit, a long time ago, before the House of Razor Wings moved in and took it from me. Some—like Gurk here—remained as loyal as they could. I am forever grateful for their support, as without it I would be dead. Hirn knows she'd have a civil war on her hands if she put an end to me. I am old, and that arrangement has suited me, but I cannot abide such…butchery. I'm told you've come seeking information?"

"Yes, sir," Ren replied confidently. "Hirn's taken another of our friends: an elf named Rotreego."

Lustreya's eyes narrowed. "The man himself or his corpse?" Clearly he'd heard news of Evitankari's new Pintiri.

"Rotreego is alive."

"Most curious. It is not supposed to work that way." He turned his head to look over his city. "First Tallisker's tower, now this."

"My father died in that attack," Ren said. "He and Rotreego were friends. We've been searching for those responsible."

"Have you found them?"

"Not yet. Hirn also took our best lead."

"If you find them, what will you do?"

The question struck Ren as if he'd been asked to explain the standard model of particle physics. His lips opened briefly, doing their part, but his tongue didn't move. Vengeance, he realized right then and there, was a nebulous concept. It could be achieved just as fully via damage to the target's property, family, or livelihood as it could through the pull of a trigger. Which would he choose if he cornered those responsible for Ed's death? How much did he need to take from them to balance the scales?

He swore he could feel hot steam streaming out through his ears. He'd expected this meeting to be a challenge, but not quite in this way.

Lustreya leaned forward, curiosity dancing merrily in his eyes. "Only one thing matters when it comes to vengeance: its meaning to the individual exacting it."

So. What would finding my father's killer mean to me?

Ren watched a pigeon strut past as his mind churned. He knew better than to fake an answer or otherwise deflect the question. Though Lustreya's tone was friendly, there was no mistaking the anticipation in his tensed muscles. Gurk had warned him to treat the old man with the utmost respect. He could see why.

What would it mean?

Beside him, Lil seemed about to burst. Her old elven intelligence instincts had kicked into high gear—although there was no telling whether they were holding her back or whether she was barely restraining them from causing a scene. Either way, she clearly knew she needed to let this play out. She needed an answer to see an answer.

Shit. So do I.

"I'd ask them why," he said, his gaze meeting the troll's, "and then I'd make the best decision I could to protect myself and what's left of my family."

Lustreya considered this in silence, perhaps allowing time for elaboration. Ren let the moment pass. He'd said his piece and he believed it. His father's death had fucking *hurt*; the unknowns, made worse by the complexities of the world in which Ed operated, had made it hurt exponentially more. He needed to know why.

The troll clasped his hands together. "You, Mr. Roberts, are terrible at vengeance." A yellow smile stretched from ear to ear and his hearty laughter echoed out over Detroit.

Ren joined him, and then Lil and Gurk did the same. The pigeons fussed around each other, unsure whether this strange activity constituted a threat.

"Yeah, I suck at this. I've been captured, what, three or four times?" Ren asked Lil.

"If you count the Witch and the standoff with Ashley, yes. Four times."

Lustreya wiped a tear from his eye. "The Witch too? There is something going on here, Mr. Roberts, and it is much bigger than your father. I hope you know that."

"We came to the same conclusion."

"Good. Although I stand by my assessment, I like your answer. It pleases me to hear that you are not the type to clip someone's wings without learning the full story, and that you're not following the same dark path as the pair you left in your car." He stood up, scattering a few birds. "I lack the manpower to physically assist you, but I will tell you what I have learned about Hirn's intentions for your friend."

Relief warmed Ren's chest. "Thank you, sir. We'll do you proud."

"Let's not set the bar too high, shall we? I know where Hirn and Rotreego will be tomorrow night. My contacts tell me she's made a deal to sell him to Evitankari."

Lil gasped and then hyperventilated. That pleasant warmth in Ren's chest was obliterated by an oppressive chill. There was no telling what the elven government would do with Rotreego, but he knew that once Evitankari had its claws sunk into its former Pintiri, it would never let go.

And if Hirn sold Crim's cyphers, too…

He wrapped a reassuring arm around Lil's shoulders. Surprisingly, she leaned right in, shivering.

"That's far from ideal," he said, not bothering to hide the fear in his voice, "but we'll make do."

— CHAPTER THIRTY-TWO —

Hirn will expect you to show up," Gurk had said in between tokes. "I mean, she'll think you ran away and gave up, but she'll be ready for the possibility you didn't. Thinkin' that way is what got her where she's at. But we know that she knows that we're coming, so we can make her think she knows that we know what she knows and use what we know about what she knows to our advantage."

The others had responded with a wide variety of confused expressions.

"Pay attention, kids. She's going to expect you to do something dumb. Like, mega dumb. Like so freakin' stupid you'll probably end up killing yourself in the process. So instead, you do something really smart but make it *look* like it's ultra boneheaded so you can catch her by surprise."

And that was how Ren wound up on a dark country road behind the wheel of his beloved Jaguar once more, a death grip on the steering wheel, the pedal pressed almost to the floor, and a loaded pistol on the seat beside him. He sure felt like he was barreling toward a stupid, easily avoidable death—which, to be fair, was a realistic possibility if any of the steps in their convoluted plan to rescue Rotreego didn't go perfectly.

What if Gurk gets too high and screws up the Bant wards?

What if Evitankari's reps don't take the main road?

What if Lil and Muffintop get caught before I get there?

What if Isabel can't get out of the trunk?

What if I blow a tire or hit a deer or get pulled over or missed a turn a couple miles ago or the airbags don't deploy or I somehow miss when I try to ram the house or the house is magic and jumps over me or I have a stroke or...

"Fucking stop it," he told himself and turned up the radio. Early aughts nu metal had never been his thing but felt apropos. Several of his friends from the Works would've approved.

According to Lustreya, Hirn's meeting with Evitankari would be happening in fifteen minutes at a secluded cabin forty-ish miles northwest of Detroit. Ren had turned the Jag onto the private access road just moments prior. Though life in Harksburg had made Ren more than comfortable driving too fast through the middle of nowhere, that road somehow felt sinister—like it had been waiting for him, like it now had him firmly in its clutches, and like it was conspiring with the surrounding forest to swallow him whole and never let him escape.

"You can't have me," he said to the road. It ignored him.

The gun in the copilot's seat wasn't making him feel any better. He'd fired a few rifles in his time, but that big, black pistol hadn't been designed for shooting bottles in a friend's backyard. Somehow it scared him worse than his father's Uzi—perhaps because the odds he'd have to use it were much higher.

The thick Michigan forest whipped past as he powered along. The road, thankfully, had been well plowed and thoroughly salted. The three-room log cabin a few more miles ahead had been one of Lustreya's favorite vacation homes—a nearby refuge from city life—before the House of Razor Wings had taken it.

"But don't worry about that," the troll had explained. "I'd burn the place to the ground myself if I knew Hirn was trapped inside."

Gurk had visited the place a couple of times himself and knew the layout well. He and Lustreya had agreed that Hirn would likely keep Rotreego under guard in the bedroom in the rear of the home.

Which made the front of the house fair game.

A pair of bright red taillights pierced the darkness up ahead. Ren's heart leapt when he realized they were arranged vertically instead of horizontally. He gave the Jag even more gas and blasted past the overturned van. Gurk had done his job with the Bant wards.

"Last I heard, Hirn has a direct line to Evitankari's Council of Economics," Lustreya had explained.

"Good," Lil had said. "Granger's a greedy pig and he'll want to bring Rotreego in himself. He'll send his own people. This'll be a lot easier if we don't have to deal with War, Intelligence, or the new Pintiri and his Gadukah."

So far, so good. Ren hadn't actually spotted any elves, but given the time and location that had to have been their van. There was no reason for anyone else to be on that road—or so he hoped. The plan was in big trouble if some unfortunate delivery driver had tripped all the Bant wards ahead of Granger's team.

The pavement turned to gravel. Ren eased up a bit on the accelerator. He'd already left their competition in his dust. Best to be safe for the time being.

He risked a glance up at the night sky, just visible in between the trees on either side of the road. The clouds of the last few days had finally cleared—fortunately, since it meant the glow of any pixie air support would be easy to spot. Gurk suggested there'd be one or two lurking in the forest around the cabin instead. That'd keep the little bastards hidden, but it would also limit their own ability to keep an eye on things. Lil had been confident she could lead Muffintop and Ash up close to the cabin without alerting any sentries. Ren hoped she was right.

The car rounded a gentle bend and his destination finally rolled into view. The single-story cabin awaited him at the far end of a little clearing ringed by old pines. A red SUV was parked off to the right. In the warm glow of a single lamp mounted beside the front door, the place radiated tranquility and comfort. Ren could easily picture Lustreya relaxing on the rocking chair on the front porch, feeding the sparrows and forgetting all about his life running Detroit's magic criminal underground.

It really was a shame what was about to happen to it.

"The exterior walls are reinforced with some enchanted stone I can't remember the name of," Lustreya had told them, "and the windows are bulletproof glass."

Ren slammed the accelerator to the floor.

This is so stupid, he thought, bracing himself. *So stupid it's perfect.* He patted the dash. "I'm sorry, baby."

The little front porch was no match for that mass of speeding metal. Shattered floorboards ricocheted off the windshield. The car slammed into the magically reinforced wall a moment later, striking the cabin right below one of its windows. Ren barely registered the shocked face of a man inside before the airbag deployed. Inertia flung him forward against the seatbelt. The hot airbag caught his face. The thing was a lot harder than it looked.

That fucking sucked.

He leaned back in the seat and shook his head a few times to clear away the stars in his eyes and give his heart a few seconds to get caught up. All his pieces and parts seemed intact, though he tasted blood where he'd bit his tongue. The airbags blocked his view into the cabin, but that also meant no one inside could see him. Someone in there was yelling very unhappily.

He reached down and popped the trunk. Hopefully they'd wrapped Isabel in enough blankets to cushion the impact. His seatbelt, however, wouldn't budge. The button was stuck fast. He didn't have time to fight with it. The next task was more important.

He pulled the distract-o-gram from his coat pocket and gave it a quick wind. The ruined decking pressed up against the side of the vehicle kept him from opening the door—*shit*—so he lowered the window instead. He shoved the quivering distract-o-gram out through the gap as soon as it was big enough. The toy car bounced as it landed, then its wheels found purchase on the decking and sent it careening toward the far end of the porch, projecting an image of Ren, panicked and fleeing, as it streaked away.

The man he'd seen in the window opened the front door just as the distract-o-gram passed. He turned and chased the hologram.

Ren knew Hirn's thug wouldn't be distracted forever. He reached over to the passenger seat—*Shit*—searching for the gun.

It wasn't there.

A confused shout drew Ren's attention back to his left. He caught sight of the distract-o-gram just as it tumbled off the side of the porch, taking the hologram with it. The man turned back toward the Jaguar.

Shit, shit, shit!

And then Isabel was on top of the man, pressing her knees to his pelvis and driving his skull into the deck with one hand. Ren looked away as she reached up with her free hand to pull the patch away from her eye.

Gotta find the gun, he thought, throwing himself as far across the center console as the seatbelt allowed. *God, why did I think leaving it on the seat was a good idea?*

A loud *whumpf* signaled Ashley's arrival. Ren glanced up at the rearview mirror and found the section of forest beside the access road burning brightly. A moment later, a pair of tiny blue lights were telekinetically yanked through the night and into those roaring flames.

"Everybody else is holding up their end of the plan," Ed's voice snarled in Ren's head. "Get your shit in gear, kid."

"I'm doing my best!" Ren snapped as he groped along the floor in front of and under the passenger seat.

Outside, Hirn's thug screamed as Isabel's magic ripped his psyche apart. "Blasting a skin's brains does the same to its pixie pilot," she'd insisted during their planning session. "It's something about how the connection works. Trust me—I've done it before."

Ren's fingers found the gun's barrel and traced the metal down to the grip.

The man's head exploded. Crimson gore spattered the car, the cabin, and Isabel. She covered the dangerous side of her face with one hand and drew her own pistol with the other. A brief moment passed between her and Ren as their eyes locked, and then she darted through the front door.

The car's window took forever to lower the rest of the way. Isabel's weapon fired once, twice, and then a third time. Another pixie screamed as it met what must've been an excruciating demise in Ashley's inferno, sucked into the blaze by Lil's Muffintop-powered telekinesis. Ren finally managed to free himself from the seatbelt by pressing the mechanism against his thigh and jamming his elbow into the button.

Ren leaned through the open window, struggling to move forward on the bloody decking. He twisted himself around a jagged shard of Jaguar-wrecked wood and somehow wound up on his back. *Fuck.* He pistoned his legs against the vehicle's interior—an act a small voice in the back of his mind found completely abhorrent—but he couldn't quite find the launching point he needed.

If he got caught there, he'd be a sitting duck.

Isabel's weapon cracked through the night once more. Ren couldn't decide to worry more that she'd be injured if he didn't make it there in time or that she'd lord it over him forever if she rescued Rotreego on her own while he squirmed in a gross pool of blood.

An unseen force suddenly dragged Ren along through the ichor and out of the vehicle. He ignored the mess clinging to his coat and mouthed a silent thank you toward the woods where Lil, Muffintop, and Ashley were hidden.

A pair of distant headlights bloomed to life far down the access road. Granger's team had righted their vehicle.

"Stop gawking and get in there!" Lil ordered, emerging from the trees opposite the empty section of forest he'd just thanked. "We'll deal with the elves!" Ashley sauntered out of her inferno, blood lust dancing on her face.

Inside the cabin, Isabel screamed. Ren didn't have to be told again.

A corpse greeted him just inside the door. Judging by the hole in the man's shirt, Isabel had put a couple rounds right through the glass orb in his chest.

"Drop your weapon or I end your friend," Hirn instructed. She hovered by the kitchenette in the back corner, a ball of angry red light surrounded by a trio of levitating knives. Isabel was telekinetically pinned to the opposite wall, her hands trapped at her sides. White hot energy roiled out of her ruined eye. Her weapon lay on the ground between her feet, out of reach.

"You pull that fucking trigger as soon as you get the chance," she'd told him just before getting in the trunk. "It's us or them."

And so he fired, emptying the cartridge. His first two rounds missed. Hirn dodged into the third. She unleashed an unearthly scream and plummeted to the floor. The knives clattered down around her. Isabel fell forward but caught herself with her hands.

Ren rushed forward, vaulting the couch with a slick move he couldn't wait to tell Kevin Felton about. He found Hirn writhing in pain on the kitchenette's linoleum floor, her right wing shredded.

"This is for Gurk," Ren snarled as he plucked the pixie up. "Isabel!"

His throw was swift and true. Isabel caught Hirn and pressed the tiny crime lord to her eye. "Go to Rotreego!"

Ren nodded, relieved he'd get to skip the next skull popping, and hurried to the back room. *This really is a cute little cabin,* he thought as he rounded a dining table atop a bear skin rug. *When this is over, I'm paying Lustreya for damages and asking for a weekend here.*

He kicked the bedroom's door open, awash in the afterglow of feeling like a bad ass. The room was empty except for a double bed and an antique writing desk. Another of Hirn's crew lay dead on the carpet. A metallic claw of some kind attached to his chest sparked and fizzled. A cold breeze wafting in through the open window rustled the heavy curtains.

Someone else had gotten to Rotreego first.

But that same someone, to Ren's relief, had neglected the Talora device on the desk. The tiny USB nub attached to its side had to be Crim's cyphers. Outside, two pairs of footprints in the snow disappeared into the dark woods.

He took the Talora and returned to Isabel. "Someone else swooped in and stole Rotreego," he said as he crossed the room. Lingering adrenaline turned his voice into an authoritative bark.

Isabel, covered in a fresh coat of blood, secured the patch back over her eye. Hirn's headless body lay in a crimson pool at her feet. She sat up straighter as Ren approached, pressing her back against the log wall to prop herself up. "Hirn broke my left leg when she slammed me into the wall," she said through gritted teeth.

"The others will be here after they run off the elves coming up the road," he said as he knelt beside her. He did not want to consider the possibility that they might fail. He pulled the USB nub out of the side of the Talora and pressed it into his sister's palm. "Keep this safe."

He heard her protest, but the words didn't register. The new path he'd promised the team would never work if he gave up on Rotreego without a fight. Cutting their losses and leaving with the

Talora and the cyphers would be the smart thing—but it would also be exactly the kind of heartless shit Tallisker or Evitankari would try to pull.

"Put up or shut up," Ed's voice said in his mind.

— CHAPTER THIRTY-THREE —

Sliding out through the bedroom window was a lot easier than escaping the Jaguar. Moving through the dense snow was another matter, even with two sets of prints to walk in. His boots and pantlegs were soaked by the time he reached the trees.

The elves must've sent a second team around the back. That van had just been a feint. They wanted what the House of Razor Wings was selling, but there was no way they were going to pay for it.

Typical.

Ren assessed his situation as he stumbled forward through the dark woods. He had no bullets, no magic, no help, and no idea what he was up against. It seemed highly unlikely he'd be able to catch his quarry, and even if he did, what was he going to do? Pelt Rotreego's captor with snowballs?

Then again, he had a clear trail to follow. Whomever he was chasing probably didn't know they were being pursued. And he had the Talora, which had to be good for something. He still wasn't sure what had compelled him to take the thing, but in the moment, it had seemed best to separate the device from the cyphers that would unlock its secrets. Ed had said there were two more Taloras in his safehouses, after all. Crim's cyphers were the real prize.

I need to make something happen. Panting, he stopped to lean against a mighty fir and took a few moments to catch his breath. Then he shouted as loudly as he could. "Rotreego!"

His voice echoed through the night. For a moment, all was silent and still. Could they even hear him? Had they somehow already left the area? He gathered himself for another try.

"Let me go!" Rotreego shrieked from up ahead. "Scum sucking satanist toe fungus!"

Ren had never thought he'd be so happy to hear his friend's gibberish. Rotreego wasn't far, he thought. A fresh burst of adrenaline pushed him onward through the cloying snow.

"Rotreego!" he hollered again.

"Buy my all-natural male enhancement pills or you're a socialist!"

"Definitely can't have that," Ren muttered as he soldiered on. It amused him to think about how thoroughly confused his friend's escort must've been. He hoped it was some young, fresh-faced elf who thought he was king shit because he'd been tasked with recovering the former Pintiri except—*whoops!*—he'd found a rambling conspiracy theorist instead.

Traversing those woods in the dark freaked Ren out. Though his eyes adjusted, he couldn't really tell where he was going until he got there. As far as his senses were concerned, that forest extended forever in all directions. Surely all the hubbub had attracted the local king's attention by now. If this Pym were the inquisitive type, Ren hoped he'd be more interested in the fire Ashley had started by the cabin. The last thing he needed was another unpredictable variable.

Of course, he still hadn't solved the problem of what he would do if he caught up to them. His prior shouts had certainly killed any chance of surprising his opponent. Losing that advantage had to be better than never reaching his target. In that dense snow, it wouldn't be hard for Rotreego to slow his captor down. That the elves seemed to want their former Pintiri alive seemed to make them vulnerable.

Bright red light burst through the black ahead, blinding Ren and causing him to stumble. He raised an arm to shield his eyes and waited for his vision to adjust. The color combined with the wild flickering suggested a likely source: a road flare.

"Ren Roberts is a brilliant patriot who will never fall for your anti-American evil!"

So it was a trap, then—which changed what, exactly? Ren had no choice but to continue trudging forward, armed only with an empty pistol, a demonic personal assistant device, and his winning personality. He'd hoped to force a confrontation by calling out to Rotreego, and his wish had been granted.

He hesitated, glancing back the way he came. There was no sign of the others. Whatever was going on back there, he hoped they were all okay.

Destiny awaited in a small clearing a few dozen yards later. The road flare hissed bright red sparks from the crater it had melted in the crusty snow. Rotreego, his hands tied behind his back, knelt nearby. A lone figure in a dark trench coat loomed above the former Pintiri, holding him in place with the business end of a long silver revolver.

Ren stopped just inside the clearing, his weapon aimed at Evitankari's Council of Intelligence with a shaky hand. "Motherfucker," he and Driff said in unison as their eyes locked.

Rotreego shook his head and sighed.

"I was told that Hirn's contact in Evitankari is a man named Granger," Ren said slowly. His memory of the Council of Intelligence shooting Kevin Felton in the head just to prove Death was on vacation set his knees to quivering. Even though he'd worked with this elf in the past, he knew he needed to tread carefully here.

"Granger is the Council of Economics," Driff said coolly. "Got all his lines of communication tapped. You should know...Granger's not himself these days. He's been replaced by a shapeshifter—and he likely sent a few just like him to raid that cabin."

That seemed like more information than the stoic elf would normally reveal. Driff wanted Ren to freak out and rush back to help his friends, but Ren wasn't falling for it. "I left plenty of firepower back there."

"Bullets won't get the job done. The only way I've found to reliably take them down is to light them on fire."

Ren grinned. "Have you met my friend, the Walking Conflagration? Those shapeshifters are toast. We met your Witch, by the way."

The elf pushed his spectacles up on his nose. "How is she?"

"Very unhappy with Rotreego's current state."

"I'm not surprised." The light of the flare danced ominously across Driff's face. "You're a bit out of Felton's range, you know."

"I'm looking for a man who dropped a Tallisker tower on my father."

"My condolences. Did you find him?"

An odd thought struck Ren. "I don't know. Have I?" he asked, his voice shaking.

"You have got to be shitting me."

"I had to ask. In that case, I could use your opinion on something." He fished the personal assistant out of his pocket, carefully keeping his attention and his useless gun on the Council of Intelligence. "Ever seen a Talora device?"

Was that a flinch? That had to have been a flinch. Driff actually *flinched*, probably for the first time in his life. "Can't say that I have." The curiosity in his voice was unmistakable.

"Talora," Ren said, "where's the nearest transpoint?"

"One-point-two miles south-southeast," the electronic woman replied calmly. "I would offer to call you a ride share, but you seem to be in the middle of nowhere."

This time Driff gasped. "Where did you get that?"

"It was Dad's," Ren replied. Driff didn't need to know about the safehouses. "It's part of some secret Tallisker project, tied to a magical network."

Driff considered this for a moment and then tested it for himself. "Talora, where did you first meet Roger Brooks?"

"Mrs. Waterston's first grade class. He was eating paste."

The elf's tone and bearing turned sinister. "I want it."

Ren swung his gun down to point it at the Talora. "I want Rotreego."

"Unless that thing's a lot tougher than it looks, the bullet will pass right through and blow your fingers off."

"Worth it."

"When did you grow a spine?"

"A couple days ago. It hurt like a bastard."

Driff lowered his weapon and stowed it in his coat. "All right. Give it here."

"Who's Roger Brooks?" Hirn had explained this earlier, but Ren wanted confirmation—and if the question served to make Driff think he was less informed than he actually was, all the better.

"The new Pintiri. Nice guy, but he's in over his head. Definitely a paste eater. Talora is his wife's name, and that toy you've got there speaks with her voice."

"The globalist conspiracy knows no bounds," Rotreego mused.

"One more thing, just to make sure you don't shoot me in the back after we make this trade," Ren said, putting some steel in his words. "I'm building a new organization that will function independently of Evitankari, Tallisker, and Talvayne. We're going to continue investigating the Talora project, the attacks on Tallisker's towers, and Ed's death. I'd be happy to share everything we learn—off the books, of course."

"And you think you'll somehow be more effective than elven intelligence?"

"No, but I suspect you've got more than enough to deal with right now."

"Commies are everywhere," Rotreego added.

Driff nodded his agreement. "My people will be in touch."

Ren wasn't completely sure he'd protected himself, but he had to take a chance. He stopped breathing as he flipped the Talora across the clearing to Driff. The elf caught it and slipped it into his coat in one fluid motion.

"A pleasure doing business with you," Driff said, adjusting his glasses once more. "A word of advice: you'll be on the shifters' shit list now. Watch your ass."

And then he triggered his magic and turned invisible. Footprints appeared in the snow as Driff departed, heading deeper into the wilderness on that same straight path he'd been following previously.

Ren exhaled heavily as the adrenaline finally dispersed and let him come back down to earth. Had he really just faced down the Council of Intelligence and *won*? He couldn't believe it. Neither could his wobbly knees.

He smiled at Rotreego. "Hey. Want to see something neat?"

The elf nodded. Ren pointed his gun at the ground and pulled the trigger. Click.

Rotreego's eyes bulged out of his skull, and he burst out laughing. "You, Ren Roberts," he said, tears of joy and disbelief streaming down his face, "are a real American hero."

— EPILOGUE —

The video conferencing software shut itself down, and Ren Roberts melted into the big leather desk chair that had once belonged to his father. He paused for a few moments, staring once again at Ed's desktop background: a picture of the whole Roberts family having fun at the beach when Ren was three, tiny, and very, very happy. He still didn't know how to feel about that.

The last week had been a whirlwind of introductions, meetings, problems, and successes—and Ren was officially spent. If his phone rang, he doubted he'd have the energy to lift the receiver from its base.

He wouldn't have changed a second of it.

Upon returning to Lustreya's cabin, Ren and Rotreego had found the others examining a puddle of silver goo that had been presenting as an angry elf before Ashley had lit it on fire. The other shifters had immediately fled the scene.

"Can I taste it?" Muffintop had asked hungrily.

"Absolutely not," Lil had snapped.

They'd scooped some up using a spoon from the kitchenette and stashed it in a plastic bag. It was safely locked up in a freezer in the basement, awaiting analysis—or, more accurately, waiting for someone on Ren's staff to figure out what type of expert they needed to contact to make an analysis even possible. Ren was super tempted to give Muffintop a lick just to see if that got them anywhere.

Ashley had insisted they travel to the orphanage right away as Ren had promised. She'd driven straight through the night with Isabel in the copilot's seat as the others snored away in the back of the spacious van they'd borrowed from the campground. They arrived around lunchtime, with Muffintop once again complaining about needing to go number three.

The skeletal old woman who met them at the sprawling estate's front gate looked like she walked out of a Victorian horror novel. Ren half expected her to whip a magic staff out of a hidden pocket in her prim, proper dress and use it to summon ferocious beasts from an eldritch dimension. Instead, she'd briefly frowned at Isabel and Ashley and then welcomed Ren with a smile that melted her harsh countenance and turned her into a doting grandmother.

"If you're here with these two, something is wrong," she said carefully. "Tell me: why isn't Ed returning my calls?"

The news broke the old woman's heart. Her hesitation toward the two demons disappeared and the three wound up crying in each other's arms.

When they finally separated, the old woman embraced Ren. "I haven't seen you since you were a baby. My name is Eugenia. I've been headmistress of the Roberts Home for Wayward Children for forty years. I know Ed never wanted you to see this place, but...I'm glad you're here."

Introductions with the residents were similarly emotional. Eugenia summoned all the kids to the dining hall. They were a diverse, attentive bunch, each sporting his or her own spin on the orphanage's black and flannel uniforms. The youngest looked to be seven or eight, the oldest close to graduating high school. Several of the teenagers greeted Isabel and Ashley warmly.

Ren told them the truth. As their excited expressions turned dark, he lost control and started to cry. Isabel's fingers took hold of his own, steeling his resolve and straightening his spine. When he finished, he couldn't believe he'd gotten through it all.

Most of the kids decided to stay. Some left immediately. Others agreed to wait for the assistance Ren promised in setting them up with new lives elsewhere. Lil and Rotreego had to intercept one particularly angry teenage boy intent on murdering Ren with a lamp. Strangely enough, that one decided to stick around after a conversation with Muffintop.

"I am so glad I don't have to hide that anymore," Eugenia said, suddenly looking ten years younger.

That night, Ren visited each of his team individually to make sure they knew how much he appreciated their support and that he never would've made it this far without them. Each responded with some version of "Yeah, I know, but thanks." There were no signs of the rifts that had grown between them. Each seemed content with their new roles and lives, and with the people they got to share all of that with. Ren really hoped it would stick.

They got to work the next day.

Ren sent the elves to retrieve the Talora devices from Ed's other safehouses. They returned with only one. Using Crim's cyphers, Ren and Isabel identified the next two towers on the hit list and passed them along to Ed's boss, Marafuji. The LA headquarters fell the next day, just as they'd said. Marafuji promised as much protection as he could offer in exchange for ongoing intel.

All the residents were put on a dose of nariidisone and filled in on the state of things. Under the direction of Isabel and Ashley, a group of student volunteers went out into the community with the mandate that they get the lay of the land. Ren wanted to know who else was in the neighborhood. They identified a small troll enclave posing as a religious community, a family of elven ex-pats, and a low-level Tallisker accountant. Not that different from Harksburg, to Ren's relief.

Through Gurk and Lustreya, Ren arranged an introductory call with the boss of the local chapter of the House of Razor Wings—who, thankfully, was overjoyed to meet the crew that took down Hirn and promised to send a case of champagne.

With Kevin Felton's help, he had tea with the local reaper and her seventeen cats.

And he got in touch with his mother in Talvayne. Ellen had made it to the fairy capital safe and sound and struck up a fast friendship with the new queen. She had nothing nice to say about the lazy, loutish king, however. "He belongs out there in the Works, drinking his stupid face off with Oscar and Doorknob," she said. Ren wanted to meet the guy.

When he wasn't busy with all that, Ren spent most of his time meeting the kids and learning how the Roberts Home for Wayward Children functioned. Eugenia was his constant shadow and an enormous help.

Yet, with all he'd accomplished, he still hadn't identified the man or group responsible for his father's death. Marafuji claimed not to know who'd ordered Ed to the Detroit headquarters, and whoever was behind the coded messages coming out of the Talora hadn't identified themselves. Still, there was no denying that Ren had found the purpose he'd been looking for when he'd struck out for vengeance days ago. Keeping it all safe and secure would be a huge task, but he felt up to the challenge.

He could live with putting vengeance on hold. For now. He pictured Lustreya laughing merrily at that outcome.

A buzzing sound broke Ren free of his reverie. Gurk darted into the office on the little white drone he'd adopted as his main mode of transportation. One of the more technically inclined kids had rigged a set of controls to the top of the thing. Ren suspected the kid had been paid in weed. "A delegation from Evitankari is here," the pixie drawled.

Driff. Ren was tempted to send the elf away and take a nap, but it would be better to get this over with. "Thank you, Gurk. Please send them in."

Ren adjusted his collar and sat up straighter. He reached under the desk and tapped the pistol holstered to the wood, just to make sure it was still there. What threats had Ed envisioned when he'd installed such a thing? It hurt to think that it was probably there as a defense against the orphanage's residents.

"Gettin' a distinct X-mansion vibe here, Professor," a red-haired elven woman said as she escorted a little human boy into the office. He clung tightly to her hand as if he might float away if he let go.

Ren chuckled, taking a moment to read the silver lettering on her pink tank top: *Mondays, am I right?* "If only I had the academic credentials and psychic powers to match. I'm Ren Roberts. It's a pleasure to make your acquaintance, Miss..."

"Hyperion Battlemage First Class Ivree of the Gadukah, representing Pintiri Roger Brooks." She paused. "And Driff too, I guess. He said we'd be welcome here."

Ren barely understood any of that, but he recognized enough of the keywords to know that this was a big deal. "And what can I help you with today?"

"I've been sent to seek asylum at your fine facility with my young charge here. Ricky, can you say hello to Mr. Roberts?"

— ACKNOWLEDGEMENTS —

Thank you for reading my work yet again! I still kind of can't believe how this one turned out. I sat down to write a complex corporate espionage thriller with a whole new main character, but what came out was a road trip featuring some of my favorites from *A Date with Death*. Thanks, pandemic!

Major thanks to Alana Joli Abbott for her excellent (and very fun) editorial guidance. Anne Marie Cochran's cover art continues to blow me away. And thanks also to Lorraine Savage and Shannon Page for their excellent proofreading!

So much gratitude goes to Jeremy Mohler and the rest of the crew at Outland Entertainment. I've had such a good experience working with them on this book and on all of our other projects.

Til the next one!

— ABOUT THE AUTHOR —

Frustrated with the generic, paint-by-numbers state of modern fantasy writing, Scott Colby is working hard to give the genre the kick in the pants it so desperately needs. Shouldn't stories about people and creatures with the power to magically change the world around them be creative, funny, and kind of weird? Scott thinks so.

Check out deviantmagic.com for more from Scott Colby.